25 STORIES HIGH

Fighting Words is a creative writing centre, established by Roddy Doyle and Seán Love. It opened in January 2009 and aims to help students of all ages to develop their writing skills and to explore their love of writing. www.fightingwords.ie

Pobalscoil Neasáin is a co-educational second-level school in Baldoyle, Dublin 13. www.psn.ie

25 STORIES HIGH

Fourth-Year Students,
Pobalscoil Neasáin
Baldoyle, Dublin 13

Introduction by Cecelia Ahern

FIGHTING WORDS
THE WRITE TO RIGHT

A Fighting Words Book
25 Stories High is published in May 2016 by Fighting Words
© Individual authors, 2016
Editors: Clara Phelan and Aoife Walsh
Typesetting: Sam Tranum
Cover Design: Persuasion Republic
Printed by: Naas Printing Ltd, Kildare

Fighting Words
Behan Square
Russell Street
Dublin 1
www.fightingwords.ie
ISBN: 978-0-9935827-0-7

Fighting Words gratefully acknowledges
funding support for its publications from:

CONTENTS

FOREWORD

I was fourteen years old when I was a transition year student in Pobalscoil Neasáin. After beginning school at three years old and only allowed to attend on Monday, Wednesdays, and Fridays till noon until my fourth birthday, it meant that I was always the youngest. The youngest in the class, the youngest of my friends. I was always trying to keep up, always asking questions in my head – never aloud. I felt that I should always know what was going on, but rarely did, and so never asked questions. I'm not sure if this was because I was shy, or because I was embarrassed or because sometimes when you're confused, you don't even know the right questions to ask. So for various reasons, I was a thinker. And a busy thinking head meant that the only way I could clear it was to write things down. I wrote privately, secretly. I wrote diaries every day. I wrote more about how I felt than what was happening, a task that I believe trained me for the stories I write now. At fourteen it wasn't so much about the story ideas, it was about how the character – me – was feeling.

I was shy in English class, embarrassed to put my hand up to answer a question. Reading out loud was my absolute worst fear. Yet at home, I could write anything I wanted, I could say whatever I wanted to say. Everybody in my class, teacher included, was surprised when I received an A in my Junior Cert English exam, but I know how this happened. For someone who contributed very little in class, I was allowed to be free in my exam. I wouldn't have to read aloud what I wrote. I would never know who was reading or correcting my exam. When one of the essay title options was 'My Diary', I didn't have to look any further. I wrote about the importance of my keeping a diary. I told my invisible reader how it was therapeutic, how it helped me to sort things out in my head, how it drained me of my worries, how it made me feel less alone and less weird and less of an outsider because even though I wasn't showing it to anybody, in a way, I was sharing. That's what writing can do for the writer. That's what reading can do for the reader.

Spurred on by this vote of confidence from my invisible reader, my unknown examiner, I started to write more. This time it changed from my reality, to fiction. For English class homework, when told to write, 'An Experience that Changed My Life', I created a character, older than me, who discovered she had AIDS. I put a lot into that story. I remember feeling it was the best thing I'd ever written. My teacher gave me a C+ and told me to write about reality. Embarrassed by the note, I listened as a student who'd received the highest mark read out a story she'd written about her grandmother's funeral. But I wanted more. I didn't want to write about me anymore. I wanted to place a kind of version of me somewhere else, use myself but escape at the same time. Not just to look in and look back, but to look in and look forward, look all around, to ask 'what if?' I taught myself how to type at home on a Mavis Beacon typing course. Then I started writing my first novel which was called 'Beans on Toast (and a Bottle of Beer)'. I even drew the picture for the front cover. This story was about a sixteen-year-old girl named Kelly, and her journey through the summer holidays, the boy she fancied, the parents who bothered her, the freedom she craved, the confusion and concern of what tomorrow would bring. It was an extension of myself. Again there was no big idea, no central premise, no clever hook, but it was all about feelings, her emotional journey. I did not want to share this story with anyone else. Writing was a secret, it wasn't to be showed, it was to help me. Writing had magical effects on my soul.

So it was with great surprise and delight that when I read the stories by the Transition Year students in Pobalscoil Neasáin that I was met with story after story, one wonderful premise after another that showed not just feeling but clever thought, big imaginations. The concepts, the worlds, the otherworldliness to these stories are inspired. Imaginations have come a long way since I was a fourteen-year-old student in Pobalscoil Neasáin; big worlds in small heads that push the boundaries on every side.

Adam Corr has created a hilarious horror with fantastic witty dialogue between three students and two skeletons. Shane Lyons 'God's Game' is an incredibly descriptive story that feels cinematic, where creatures take over, attacking characters in one crazy action sequence after another. Paul Herron's futuristic adventure shows his huge imagination and strength in writing dialogue when a military must battle a mysterious evil of creatures, insects and monsters. In Dara O'Cléirigh's story an atmospheric futuristic story in a maximum security prison is centred around an inmate's desire for coffee.

Caoilainn Hogan Boyle's 'Black and White' is a clever fantastical idea. I felt it was a nod to the great Irish legends, particularly Tír na nÓg. It's touching, with a moving ending, an original story about life and death. Sinéad Farley's 'How Sugar Ruined My Life' is a superb take on the fairytale character, the Big Bad Wolf, retelling the story from his perspective. This is unique, clever and funny.

Christopher Yeate's 'Mistrust' is a James Bond/Indiana Jones style high-energy adventure that travels through Mount Everest, Kathmandu, Dublin, Cairo, Timbuktu. There are explosions, chases, flying missiles all to find the Holy Lance and leaves you wanting to read more of the hero's adventures.

David Farrelly's 'The Unbelievable Truth' has a strong moral message and centres on a journalist interviewing someone who defied all odds to achieve something extraordinary. He has created a character who has great inner strength in the face of adversity. It's a survival story, a story of hope. Niamh Thornberry's 'A Change of Heart' is a moving story of how a friendship between a young boy and a grieving old man can help them both.

Elizabeth Ogundipe's 'The Lie' is a story about shoplifting, about feeling trapped in a situation you want to get out of and the importance of knowing right from wrong, the pivotal moments in our lives that we learn these big lessons.

Dean Ryan's 'Polaroid' is an enjoyable, clever, high concept idea, one that I could imagine watching on the big screen. Not only is it a fantastic premise, but it also has a mature sensibility. Bronagh Furlong's 'Brace Yourself' is a story about two people who become 'bonded' through their braces being stuck together. This is an original premise with fantastic dialogue, a very funny central character who is a rather egotistical male bully and a surprising ending.

Both Stephen Kellett Murray and Emma Keogh created unique ghost stories. Emma Keogh's 'The Milk Man' has a chiller feel and a clever twist. Stephen Kellett Murray's story is a moving story about friendship, about one lost soul who finds solace in an unexpected friend.

Jake Lantry's 'School Time Crime' is classic storytelling; a clever noir about a crime that occurs in a school. Great ensemble of characters as the detective must try to read deeper into the suspects who all have a different interpretation of what happened.

Jamie Hannon's 'The Life Of An Alcoholic Bodybuilder' is a moral led story about the dangers of gym and exercise-related protein drinks with a surprising ending and Jamie's own knowledge of this topic shines through.

Jay Kehoe Hanlon's 'Breaking Pattern' is a unique, original story about two unlikely people who happen upon one another. In Aaron Gorman's story, two students swapping lives and putting themselves in each other's shoes takes a dark twist. Cian Doyle's 'Set In Stone' is a dark story about how a girl who defends herself wanders down a dangerous road. Luke Murray's 'A Night of Survival' is about a boy's relationship and loyalty to his mother, how they can protect each other from the dangers of the world.

The theme of friendship is particularly strong: Rebecca Ormonde's 'My Last Adventure,' a girl risks her life to save her friend, believing it is worth it to have one more day with her. Killian Farrelly's 'The

Drop' is an adventure story about two friends who go cycling together, have an accident and must help one another. Jasmin Humphrey's 'The One' is a true, sweet love story between two friends with a passion for music in common. Scott Redmond's 'What Else Are You Gonna Do On A Saturday?' is about the power of friendship and how one friend stops another from making a huge mistake, which would affect the rest of his life. Sam Callan's story, 'Broken Sticks', delves into the importance of talking about your problems, a positive and mature message that should be shared.

All of these writers should be proud that their imaginations are well and truly alive, that dreaming 'what if' has taken them far from their own lives and deep into their heads and hearts. Story telling is not about 'writing what you know' – that's never enough – you need to write about what you feel.

—Cecelia Ahern

BROKEN STICKS
Sam Callan

It all began with two crazy kids running around with sticks, otherwise called hurls. That sums up me and Tom. After a few weeks of
playing together we were best mates, and ten years later the two
loopers with sticks are still going strong.

I find after ten years that friendship is a peculiar thing, even
though Tom is my best friend, he is my biggest enemy. When we train
we kill each other, smacks of the hurl on the sly. We always push each
other so much; even when it comes to games if we make a balls of
something we go mental at each other. That's friends for you.

It was a cold winter morning. We had a semi-final in the cup; a
big game. The game was just about to start and there was no sign of
Tom. I was disgusted. The game started without him. I couldn't get my
head in the game; I was just thinking 'where is he?' The half-time whistle
blew and it's a draw and here comes Tom, walking so slowly as if he'd
done nothing. The coach was not at all happy but he knew he needed
him so he was subbed on at half-time. I knew by looking at him he was
not ready. The game restarts and this half was a different story.

As the second half whistle blew the players were instantly getting
smashed from both sides. If the ball was in the air and you were
thinking of catching it, there was a good chance your hand would
get smashed with the ball. Every player was pushing their limits. The
hot steam was pouring out of our helmets into the cold air and the

team was going strong. In the last ten minutes I was running towards goal and a player smacked his hurl off my chest. I will always remember that crack. At the time I did not know whether it was my bones or the other player's hurl. It sounded like a crack of a whip against my skin and bones.

The team knew I took a hit for the team and we were given a free that put us back in the game. They were going to take me off but I refused. I felt the game was too important. The man was ahead of him and Tom decided to trip him up, giving the other team a free; it was the worst free to give away. All of the team's hard work could be gone in one hit. Over the ball went, and then Tom did something awful. He let his hurl fall on the ground and he walked off, leaving his hurl on the pitch. My coach tried to talk him out of it but there was no stopping him. It was at this point I knew I'd lost my best friend.

I had never felt anything like this before. Tom was my best friend and as I watched the hurl fall to the ground I knew this could be the end of our friendship. I could not process this feeling as on top of this, the team was crushed after losing in the worst possible way. I knew, as Tom's best friend, I would have to talk to him about what he had done. And I didn't know how to get into his head

A few days had passed and I was hoping to hear from Tom, but nothing. I knew I would have to confront Tom and that could go either way.

The day had come when I knew I would have to knock on Tom's door. It was a horrible misty night and I had to travel on the bus. The whole way I was planning what I was going to say to Tom. Something that always felt so normal, knocking on Tom's door, had changed to make me feel so nervous.

I knocked on Tom's door and his dad, Phil, opened it.

'Ah Andy, how's it going?' enquired Phil

'Good yeah, is Tom around?' I replied.

Phil looked down at his crocs, which he could hardly see with his mountain of a belly. He gave off a worried look.

'Em, I am surprised you don't know but me and Elaine have split up, Tom and her have been gone at least a month,' said Phil.

It was at this moment I realised that I had messed up our friendship. I had lost my best friend and it was all my fault. How could I not have noticed that something this big was happening to my best friend? It must have crushed him. What had happened at the match simply didn't matter anymore; I knew I had to get my best friend back no matter what the cost. He was in pieces and he needed me to put him back together. Never before had I felt this feeling of rage within myself. How could I not have known what was going on at home? I thought Tom was taking a turn for the worse and I decided to turn my back on him when he needed me most.

I got his new address from the coach and tried to get in contact with him. I wanted to see him, but nothing. No message, no phone call, nothing. As the days crept up on me I could feel our friendship slowly slipping away.

I was in town with my school one day on a trip and afterwards I decided I would get some food with a few of my friends. As we were walking down the road I looked up and there was Tom walking towards us. I said to the lads 'I'm off'.

I started to walk over to Tom but he was acting like he didn't know who I was and started speeding up. As if he was trying to walk past me.

I walked over to him and tapped him on the shoulder. Tom turned.

'Oh hey, what's up?' he mumbled as if he hadn't already seen me.

'Nothing, just in town with the school.'

'Why were you trying to walk past me as if you didn't see me? I have been trying to get in contact with you for weeks,' I said.

'That's nice.'

'I went over to the house, Tom; I know what was going on, why would you not tell me?'

'That's not something I have to tell you. Sure you're never around anyway.'

'No, Tom, you are wrong – that is something you have to tell me. We have been best friends since we were small so don't act like it's nothing. You have been on a down for months, now I know why.'

Tom shrugged his shoulders and looked to the ground knowing I had a point.

'You let all this stuff build up and it's affecting you big time, you need talk to someone!'

Tom actually said okay, and for the next few hours we just talked and he let it all out. I started to blame myself for not seeing the problem. But I knew we just had to look forward now. I had one question to ask Tom before we went home.

'Will you come back to team?'

'I have been waiting for you to ask that!'

I couldn't be happier. A few weeks passed and everything felt kind of normal again. Tom joined back with the team. Finally I had my friend back.

THE SECRET SKELETAL SOCIETY
Adam Corr

Hello, dear reader. I hope you are ready for the scariest tale you have ever read!

Well . . . perhaps not the scariest, but it is spooky. So turn your lights all the way up and prepare for my horrific story. But remember, reader, you can't hope for a horror story with a happy ending. Now our story begins outside a perfectly normal high school with a few, not so normal students. The Date? Friday the 13th. The day before Halloween. Oh wait, that's not right. It was the 30th of October, the day before Halloween and the birthday of a very special girl . . .

'I am so sick of Halloween. And it is not even Halloween yet!' said Jason.

Now reader you must understand, Jason was not an easily enraged boy. Jason was a tall, strong and cheerful boy. Born in Peru and raised in Ireland, Jason had such an intense mix of cultural influences while growing up, life had always been a puzzle for him. He never lost his smile and had a positive outlook on life.

This was, in many ways, thanks to his best friend, Daniel. Daniel was another tall boy. Although when it came to the strength department he was severely lacking. But what he lacked in strength he made up for it one hundred times in kindness. Daniel was never one to turn his back on a friend and was always willing to help out his friends – even when it didn't exactly suit him too. Yes, reader he truly was a miracle, a diamond in the rough, one in a million! He was . . . well you get the idea.

'What's up with the sudden hatred towards old hallows eve?' Daniel said in a jokingly but also caring tone.

'It is just ridiculous, I mean just look at all of these stupid Halloween decorations,' he erupted. 'All of these stupid jack-o-lanterns littering our streets. I nearly fell over one on my way out of school, I could have broken my neck!'

'Now, now I'm sure everything would have been fine.' Daniel said in a reassuring voice. 'But I do agree with you, there is way too many bats, spiders and other cheesy spooky stuff—'

Before he had the chance to continue his rant a nearby girl interrupted.

'Hey fuccbois!' said Emily, the birthday girl herself.

'I wish you would stop calling us that,' Jason said, 'What does it even mean?'

'Well, it means . . . um . . . ' Emily laughed, 'I don't know what it means actually. But it is fun to say'

'It is fun to call us fuck boys?' Daniel said a bit confused

'No no no no. It's fun to call you fuccbois. There is a difference. I don't know what it is, but it's there . . . I think'.

Before you ask, reader, not even I know the meaning of the word. But if you do, feel free to shout it out loud for all to hear. Or don't – maybe you are reading this in a library and that would be considered rude. Anyway back to the story!

'Well whatever it is, it's insulting,' Jason said with a fed up expression on his face.

After a few moments of silence Daniel's face lit up. 'Oh I almost forgot, Happy Birthday Emily!'

'Why thank you, Daniel,' Emily said with a smile on her face as she turned towards Jason prompting him to say the same.

'Yeah Happy Birthday, Emily,' the still annoyed Jason said reluctantly. Jason did a loud clap and proclaimed, 'Anyways what are the p;ans for tonight, oh humble Birthday girl?'

'Yeah whatever, *legal* and *reasonable* thing you want to do and we will make it happen!' Daniel stated.

I find it a bit ridiculous that this is something Daniel had to state, but in this case it was a necessity.

'Hmmm,' Emily thought aloud, 'I want to do . . . Nothing!'

'Huh?' Jason and Daniel said in unison. 'You have got to want to do something,' Daniel said puzzled.

'You would think that, wouldn't you. But alas there is no activity I wish to partake in,' she said in a regal tone of voice.

'Enough acting, what is it and how much will it cost us?' Jason said in a direct tone of voice.

'Oh you know me so well,' Emily said mockingly.

That they did, reader, for Emily's true intentions were about to become so clear. For you see, Emily was a girl with a love for the finer things in life, such as graveyards and corpses. You know, like all girls.

'Come on you are going to tell us eventually, so why not now?'

'Well if you insist I, the birthday girl, wish to go to the local graveyard. Tomorrow. At midnight.' She said with a gleam in her eye. I told you reader, graveyards and corpses are a girl's best friend.

'You mean on Halloween? Sounds pretty scary. I don't think this is a good idea you guys . . . ' Daniel said trembling at the idea of visiting a graveyard.

'You said it only had to be legal and reasonable. Last I checked, ain't no law about visiting a graveyard,' Emily stated with a smug expression on her face.

'Legal or not, why on earth would you want to visit a graveyard on Halloween night!'

'Jason,' Emily started speaking calmly, 'are we really going to waste time here?'

Jason saved himself the trouble of arguing with her. He knew it was no use. Although Daniel had no desire to go along, he felt he had to.

'So it's agreed, you fuccbois will be at my house at 11:30pm. Then it's off to spook town, population you two biotches'

'You do realise you will be there too Emily . . . '

'You didn't let me finish you fuccboi!' She clears her throat even though it was painfully obvious that it wasn't necessary, 'the population, as previously stated is you two biotches and the queen of screams, the master of disaster, the one, the only, Me!' Emily proclaimed as she struck her best attempt at a super hero pose. 'Also, no costumes! I will sort all of that out,' The devious girl said with a grin on her face as she started walking home.

'I don't trust her man, she is probably gonna dress us up as carrots and feed us to her rabbit!' a frightened Jason whispered into Daniel's ear.

'Will you stop! I'm sure she just wants us to go as a group costume or something.'

'To a cemetery?'

'Gotta look good for those zombies,' a frightened Daniel nervously chuckled trying to ease the situation. Jason shrugged Daniel's comment off, wanting nothing more than to go home and not think about tomorrow night's activity.

After a rather uneventful day of worrying and thinking about pretending to be sick in order to escape his friends, Daniel was on his way to meet up at Emily's house. After waves of little children banging on Daniel's door in cheaply made costumes begging for food to satisfy their sugary cravings, he had had enough. The idea of visiting a cemetery had almost become a source of solace to him. Nothing in a cemetery could be as scary as the hordes of Minions and Elsas he had encountered that night. Daniel arrived at Emily's home and was greeted by Jason dressed in what seemed like a four-year-old's skeleton costume.

Daniel, resisting the urge to laugh, eventually spoke up. 'Well aren't you festive?'

Jason gave Daniel a look that he would never forget. It could only be described as pure unadulterated hatred and soul crushing embarrassment. Jason said nothing and just handed Daniel a plastic bag. Already having a good idea of its contents the look of smugness fell from his face as one of despair took over. It was his own costume, a perfect copy of Jason's.

'Hey fuccboi.'

As if out of no where Emily appeared 'Welcome to my home, yada yada yada, get your costume on we're late.'

Daniel kept his disgust and discomfort with the situation to himself and proceeded to get changed into his costume. After the trio donned their costumes they set off to the cemetery. The trio of not-so-scary skeletons were on their way to the cemetery and thankfully were not spotted by too many hecklers. Although it wasn't cold out the eeriness of the cemetery made Daniel shiver in fright.

When they arrived Emily finally said why she wanted the two boys to join her on this 'adventure'. 'Now I don't want you to be alarmed. But, now brace yourself, I did have an ulterior motive to wanting to come here'.

A non-surprised Daniel said, 'Just tell us. The sooner we can get out of here the better.'

'Well if you insist. I heard a story about this place. That at midnight on Halloween night in the dead centre of here an entrance to a city appears. Not just any city. But the city of the dead! Home to hundreds of skeletons.'

Although he attempted to hide his fear Daniel was terrified of this and it showed.

'And you actually believe it?' Jason said as if he was talking down to Emily for believing such a tale.

'Hey we don't know until we see for ourselves now do we?'

'I suppose. But why the skeleton costumes?'

'Simple, we will need to blend in with our skeleton brethren. Now hurry up it's almost time.'

'Time for disappointment,' Jason said under his breath. Wanting this all to be over as fast as possible Daniel began to hurry everyone up

'Come on if I'm gonna die to a bunch of skeletons I'm at least gonna be there on time.'

'That's the spirit!' Emily practically squealed with excitement as the trio began to run towards the centre. At 11:58 they arrived. In between his pants and gasps for breath Jason managed to say 'Well, we are here. Now what?'

'Simple. We wait.'

'Guys. What if it exists?' The group went quiet. 'What do we do then?'

Daniel continued rambling on until he was stopped by Emily

'Daniel, listen to me.' On the verge of breaking down Daniel looks into Emily's eyes. 'I promise if you die, and I don't. I will go to your funeral. Heck maybe I will even mourn you.'

Before Daniel could respond the ground begun to shake, not enough to cause any panic but enough for the group to take notice. Simultaneously, the group realised what was going on around them as a large circle in the ground started to glow enclosing them inside. The cold dead air went silent. Not even the insects crawling throughout the cemetery were making a sound.

'You've done did it now, fuccboi,' a disembodied voice crackled.

'Okay, Emily you can stop messing around. It was a little bit believable until you made the voice say fuccboi,' Jason said as he sighed a sigh of relief.

'That wasn't me you, fuccboi. You can't just assume things like that.'

'Oh yeah! Well what other sane person says fuccboi!'

'I don't know, fuccboi but clearly someone does.'

'*Silence!*' a voice boomed in the darkness.

That, my dear reader, is exactly what followed. For a moment everything was silent, not a sound to be heard. The three friends turned to the source of the voice in silent horror. Accompanied by the sounds of bones grinding against each other, a figure stepped out from the darkness. At first glance he could have been mistaken for a malnourished old man. But a closer look would identify him for what he truly was. A skeleton!

Daniel blurted out 'What the frick frack diddily dack patty wack snick snack crack pack slack mack quarterback crackerjack biofeed-back backtrack thumbtack sidetrack tic-tac is that!'

'I don't know but we better run. I ain't taking no chances' Jason said as he began to run back towards the entrance of the cemetery.

As he reached the border of the newly formed circle he found himself unable to move forward. Something was blocking him. Emily and Jason now adopting the same facial expression as Daniel began to scream for help. It didn't take long for them to notice that the barrier was soundproof.

'Are you done screaming yet?' The skeleton asked calmly.

'Almost,' Daniel said before letting out one big final scream. 'Okay go on'.

The skeleton walked towards the three frightened children. 'Why are you here? Is it for an autograph? I knew my fans would arrive. Even though you are 300 years late. But I will forgive you. And to dress up just like me. You must really love me!' The skeleton at this point is overjoyed.

Daniel being the kind of guy that he was, was about to play along when Emily began to converse with the egotistical skeleton.

'Sorry but that's not why we are here. In fact we don't even know who you are,' Emily said now adopting a leadership role within the group.

'You don't know who I am?! I am the great human hunter Wingdings!'

'H-Human hunter?' Jason said while rejoining the group after his failed escape. 'You hunt humans . . ?'

'Well I try, Every year I lure helpless humans like yourself into the cemetery and attempt to take their skulls and sacrifice them to the great Lord Arial. Even though I have never successfully killed a human I remain optimistic.'

'Well good for you, 'cause being positive is the best thing you can do,' Daniel patted the skeleton on the back.

It seems that even with the undead Daniel couldn't help but be supportive.

'But enough about your motives let me ask the real question! How in the world do you know the word fuccboi! And more importantly do you know the meaning?'

Although still terrified the trio leaned in, in hope that they would learn the origin of the word.

'Well, I could tell you. But it would require me to go into great detail about my past and my herit—'

'*Bored!*' Emily shouted. 'Sorry, I didn't mean to interrupt you but if you would just tell us how we can get out of this circle of death and despair, we will be on our way'

The skeleton informed his three new victims that there is no way out. It seems they were doomed. In that moment the trio felt despair kick in. They needed to know more information if they wanted a chance of survival.

'So you are gonna try and murder us then?'

'That's the plan, yes.'

'Oh.'

'Yeah. Sorry about. I hope it doesn't affect any of your plans.'

'Being dead? Surprisingly it won't affect my social life. But I would prefer if I wasn't dead.'

After what seemed like forever, and an incredibly annoying back and forth between Wingdings and Emily, Jason noticed something. In the circle there seemed to be an opening. He wasn't one hundred percent sure but it seemed like their only way out. He informed Daniel of his pseudo discovery. Without hesitation Jason went towards the possible opening. Daniel would have offered to help distract Wingdings but it seemed unnecessary due to Emily's ramblings.

When Jason arrived at the opening he took note of it, he made sure to note his surroundings for any oddities. All he could see were strange childlike drawings on the ground, presumably by Wingdings. *Enough time wasting*, he said to himself and sucked in his gut and began to squeeze through the two invisible walls and to his surprise popped out on the other side. After signalling to Daniel for him to follow him, Daniel grabbed Emily and began to run for the exit. Both Emily and Wingdings caught on to what was happening rather quickly.

'No please, come back. We can make cookies together!'

Although tempting, Daniel kept running and he and Emily ran through the gap escaping the 'evil' Wingdings clutches. A frustrated Wingdings began to chase after the trio and left the circle himself. Not wanting to bring a skeleton to either of their homes or anywhere else, where innocent civilians lurked they decided to run in a single direction and hope for the best. It didn't take long for the three friends to reach a familiar crossroads.

'Two ways, huh?' a now exhausted Daniel said, 'which way should we go? The abandoned factory where all those people were murdered or the park where nothing bad has happened in the last twenty years and has active security?'

'Well, now hear me out on this one, I'm thinking factory. Because that skeleton will assume we went to the park and go that way *and* we don't want anyone to get hurt,' Emily said as she started lugging her tired body in the direction of the factory. After not hearing any steps behind her she turned to see what was going on. She was greeted by Wingdings and the two boys unconscious lying on the ground.

'OH MY GOD!' Emily felt like falling to the ground on her knees and crying but knew she had to run.

As she turned to run she was grabbed by the cold bony hand of Wingdings. 'Don't worry. They aren't dead. What would be the point of killing them here?' Wingdings knocked Emily out and began to bring the bodies back to the cemetery. In an uneasy state the trio began to regain consciousness.

'Ah you are all awake. I'm glad. You nearly missed the best part,' the cheerful skeleton was nearly dancing with joy. 'You see I get to *kill* you *guys* all at *once.*'

He emphasised his words by pointing one of his bony fingers at one of the teenagers. First Jason, then Emily and finally Daniel. Let me be as bold as to ask you, reader, have you ever been pointed at by a skeleton? If not I recommend staying as far away from the experience as possible, it's not as enjoyable as it may seem. Now where was I? Ah yes, the graveyard.

Wingdings had tied our three protagonists up and thrown their bodies to the ground. Alas Wingdings, as perfect as he thought he was, had apparently failed at tying the bindings wrapped around the trio very well. They all escaped with ease.

'What the what!' Wingdings said.

Realising he was severely out classed by the sheer cunning of these three specimens he once called his prey. Wingdings thought on his feet and struck up an offer.

'I have an idea, how about you guys help me! We could be the best of teams! You guys go out and get humans for me and I will chop their heads off and drain the blood from their bodies!'

A concerned Daniel asked, 'Will you let us go?'

'Of course!'

'Well then of course we will!'

Daniel said obviously just trying to escape Wingding's grasp.

'Sweet, we get to murder people!' Jason said before Daniel informed him of his plan. The trio began to leave the cemetery, hopefully for good.

':3' Wingdings said. The trio turned back towards the skeleton

'Umm . . . what was that?' Jason asked.

'He said :3 you dumbass,' Emily said.

'How did you do that!'

'That's for me to not fully understand and for you to pull your hair out trying to comprehend it.'

'XD,' Wingdings replied.

'XD,' Emily added.

'Would you please stop that!' Jason said.

As he prepared to walk away and forget all the events that transpired that night the ground began to shake. This time the grounds shaking was much stronger. Enough to knock the friends right off their feet and behind a conveniently large tombstone. Wingdings was too busy focusing on the current events surrounding him to notice the trio were out of his sight. He assumed they had left to complete their job. A large structure began to rise from the ground. Mossy stones stuck themselves on one another.

'It's like a door frame . . . ' a now thoroughly spooked Daniel said.

The smell of decaying wood filled the air as a door began constructing itself. The thrashing of wood crashing against each other in such fast succession began to match that of the horrified Daniel's heartbeat. They all went silent, a newly constructed door stood in the middle of the circle. Time began to stand still, or at least that's what it felt like. After what seemed like forever, while in reality, was only a few seconds. The doorknob began to turn. As the door opened a loud creak echoed through out the graveyard. Another shadowy figure appeared, this time the sound of bones hitting off each other was accompanied by the sound of heavy armour clanking.

'Wingdings!' Said the armour-clad skeleton. 'Full report. Humans? Dead? Come on, you buffoon I need answers!'

'W-Well you see General TN Roman, the humans t-they escaped my grasp. They were really clever so I decided to get their help! They are off searching for human sacrifices right now!'

'Escape? How in tarnation did they do that!'

'Well you know how we are supposed to draw a circle around the entrance to Acno City . . . '

'Private, I swear to whatever celestial deity is listening right now!'

' I forgot to finish it'

'Son of a b—' before he could finish his statement filled with profanity another skeleton arrived.

'Hello!' A slightly more annoying voice than Wingdings called out. Yet another skeleton appeared dressed in the same clothing as Wingdings. As to say he was naked.

'I don't mean to be rude General, but it's about to rain.'

'And how would you know, private?'

Trying to hide his smile the new mysterious skeleton said, 'Because, sir . . . I can feel it in my bones!'

That joke was accompanied by a moment of silence and a new facial expression on TN's face. One of anger, pain and hatred.

'Private, when we get back I am going to throw your skull into a fuc—' the General was once again interrupted. This time by the feeling of rain dropping on his skull. Baffled Wingdings stared into the sky, curious about this new skeleton but even more confused by the skeleton's prediction.

'Oh my sweet baby Lucifer. The skeleton can see the future!' Said an astonished Emily

'NON- BELIEVER!' Daniel and Emily said in unison. 'Praise the skeleton God!'.

Jason quickly shut the two up as he didn't want to drag any unwanted attention towards him or his friends,

'Well I guess he can . . . '

'Emily I swear to God!'

'Feel it *on* his bones!'

Daniel and Emily tried hard to contain their laughter and did successfully but it seemed at this rate Jason was going to murder them before the skeletons. Jason began to get annoyed, more than he was already, and told Daniel and Emily to shut up before they were caught. This started a back and forth between the friends.

While the trio were bickering, the skeletons had calmed down and General TN Roman began to explain the situation,

'Wingdings! Meet Skelepun. Neither of you two has ever gotten a single human sacrifice in your 3000 years of service. And thus, the army has decided that this is your last chance. You two will get human sacrifices by 2am! You have one hour if you two couldn't understand that! And if you fail you will both face judgement from the grim reaper himself, Manny!'

'WAIT WHAT THE WHAT?!' Wingdings said

'You heard me. Now don't mess this up – or do, I don't care'.

Before they could plead for forgiveness the General informed him that he could smell pesky humans in the graveyard and that they best hurry if they wanted to catch them. General TN Roman entered the doorway and gave no more help than that. A strange green aura surrounded the door. It clearly represented the doors locking mechanism. Well maybe not clearly since Wingdings still tried to open the door with all his might.

'Well we're boned,' Skelepun said, 'But don't worry new buddy. Just stay calm. Don't let it get under your skin.'

This ignited the rage that boiled inside Wingdings. He started insulting Skelepun and unleashed a plethora of bad insults his way. Skelepun was used to this, however; he was never one to take things harshly . . . usually anyway. Amidst the chaos that is one skeleton screaming at another the friends stopped their infernal bickering and started talking sense.

'So we should leave right?' Daniel asked

'Yes, you fuccboi of course we should!'

Before they could evacuate the premises Wingdings turned his attention to the trio. He wasn't letting them escape so easily this time. He remembered that their skills were impressive but with the help of his new 'friend' he could stand a chance. Even if he didn't, what choice would he have?

'Are these the guys we have a bone to pick with!' said you know who.

'Will you please stop with those!'

'Sure no problem. Once I run out of them that is. But that won't happen. I have a—'

'Don't you dare!'

'Skele-ton!'

Now, reader. Let me ask you this, have you ever seen a skeleton want to throw its own skull into the nearest lava pool? Well if you have then congratulations, you know the exact reaction of Wingdings to that 'joke'.

'I asked you to please stop.'

'Geez man. I would offer to play you some relaxing church music but I don't have any organs.'

'I *said* stop! Your jokes aren't even funny!'

'Oh you don't think they are humerus?'

'YOU ARE REALLY GETTING UNDER MY SKIN!'

'I didn't even know that was possible.'

You could imagine but this back and forth just kept happening. Skelepun would make an aggravating skeleton pun and Wingdings would ask him to stop. Meanwhile, the three friends just stood idly by, I mean wouldn't you, reader? If given the opportunity would you leave the arguing skeletons? If you answered yes . . . Then I am surprised you made it this far into the story. But nonetheless you are here and are probably somewhat interested in the ending, I hope. While the two skeletons are arguing Daniel says 'So we should leav—'

'YES YOU IDIOT!'

And with Jason's comment the three friends began to run out of the cemetery. Knowing they only needed to survive for one hour they decided to split up and regroup back there in one hour. While tensions were high and the threat of death near they could not falter now. Worrying never helped anyone, reader. Now, reader I shall tell you what happened to our three scared little children, but let's do it one by one, shall we?

Let's start with Daniel, the scared one of the group. Surely if he were alone with the two bloodthirsty skeletons he wouldn't put up much of a fight now would he? Well that is exactly what he did . . . kind of. You see, reader, Daniel after a few minutes of running found himself at a familiar sight, the school! While the school was obviously locked and inaccessible without setting off the alarm, he could enter the school premises through a hole in the schoolyard trees. Typically used as a way of ditching school by the students, he now used it to enter the area.

'Oh man, why did I come here. Stupid legs.'

Daniel pulled out his phone and used it as a flashlight. He thought about calling someone but who would believe him? Certainly not his parents and what cop in their right mind would? It looks as if he is alone for tonight.

'It could be worse,' he thought to himself, 'I could be getting chased by the school teachers.'

As he chuckled to himself he decided to visit his favourite place in the schoolyard. It was a group of trees which all seemed to point to this one smaller tree. Early on in his school days, Daniel would go there to think about things, mind you his problems back then were trivial things like; what was he gonna do when he got home? How and when would he nap? And how was he gonna get away with not doing his homework? You know. Typical kid's stuff.

'How on earth does this happen? A few hours ago I was handing out candy to children, now . . . Well I have two skeletons with the combined IQ of a walnut chasing after me.'

He let out a big sigh before having a bright light shone in his eye, A million thoughts ran through his mind, could it have been the skeletons? Should he run away now? Should he just give up? Deciding that life is too good to just give up on he leapt forward and threw a punch as hard as he could. Which let's be honest, reader, is never ever the smart thing to do. But he did it. As he expected to hit bone he instead hit flesh. Thankfully due to his lack of strength he could pass it off as a joke. He looked up and saw a security guard.

'Now Son, you mind telling me what in the hell you are doing here? And while you are at it why don't you go ahead and tell me where all your little pals are too?'

Daniel stood up and brushed off the dirt on his knees and began to speak.

'Well, Sir, to answer your first question I am hiding from skeletons. You see they must catch either me or one of my three friends with in the next 25 minutes or else they will be banished from their skeletal society, so me and my friends decided to split up in order to survive, which I believe you will find answers your second question.'

'What do you take me for, an idiot! Every year for the last ten years I have been working this job. And every year without fail some young group of kids come in here and vandalise the school. But you are without a doubt, the worst liar I have ever heard working this job. No, I take that back. You are the worst liar I have ever heard in my life.'

A large smash of glass was heard followed by laughter of numerous teens. The security guard let out numerous profanities and informed Daniel that he better not move from where he was. The guard went running after the teenagers, but Daniel had no intention of sticking around to see what happened and made a mad dash for the hole he had used to enter the school. When he got out he thought to himself *only 20 minutes before I have to meet back up with the others. I guess I better start heading back. I just hope for they are okay!*

Daniel started his slow return to cemetery, as much faith as he had in his friends, he couldn't help but wonder the very same question he asked himself on a daily basis. What if something went wrong?

Now on to our next hero, Jason. Or rather should I say Jason and Emily. For you see, reader while Jason and Emily had every bit of faith in their friend Daniel, they still didn't want to take any chances. So while splitting up Jason took note of which direction Emily was running in. He knew of an alleyway that would allow him to cut Emily off. He caught up with her rather easily, catching her off guard. Emily, thinking it was the skeleton duo, swung a punch as hard as she could. Which, unlike Daniel's, actually had a bit of force behind it.

'Ow what the hell!' Jason said breathing heavily attempting to catch his breath after his dash for Emily, although now he was starting to regret coming to meet the girl.

'What the hell fuccboi! Why did you scare me like that!'

'I-I . . . nevermind.' Jason seemed to have taken a more serious tone of voice. 'We can't leave Daniel alone. I would go myself but honestly I don't trust you to not go back there in an attempt to fight them things by yourself.'

'Things? They have names you know! But I understand what you mean. No doubt if the skeletons catch Daniel he is doomed.'

'That's exactly what we want. See if they corner him we can surprise them from behind and get the jump on them.'

'And we didn't tell Daniel about this why?'

'Simple. He is afraid. Putting pressure on him isn't smart. He will constantly worry about our safety and ignore his own.'

Emily had to agree. As I said before reader, Daniel will always put his friends first even when it doesn't exactly suit himself. So Emily and Jason took Jason's shortcut back to his original route. They then started to run after Daniel. It didn't take them long to realise where he had gone. After reaching the school it was clear that the shortcut had been used to enter the school. Emily and Jason followed inside. As soon as they entered they noticed a big white light. Along with the sound of Daniel's voice.

'Does he seriously expect him to believe this? I know I wouldn't.'

'I dunno. Seems kind of convincing to me,' Emily said shrugging her shoulders. 'Besides, we need to make sure.'

Emily picked up a rather large stone off the ground and had an almost evil smirk on her face.

'And nothing says distraction more than a broken window.'

Jason nodded in agreement. No matter the case, a distraction would help. If the man did believe Daniel, then Daniel would simply wait. If he didn't, he could use it to escape. Jason picked up a rock of roughly the same size. All that mattered was that it would break a window without a doubt. They ran over to the school and prepared themselves. They both agreed they had to stay out of the security guards *and* Daniel's line of sight. If Daniel saw them he might slow down and risk getting caught and if the security guard caught them they would be, as Skelepun would say, *boned*. They took a deep breath and counted to three. When the moment came they both hurled their stones and without missing a beat a large crash was heard. Although they tried hard not to they both burst into laughter. Luckily they were far enough away from Daniel to be recognised. However, they could clearly hear the security guard running as fast as he could towards them. They decided to split up once again to run around the yard 'skillfully' dodging the man. Noticing that Daniel had left they both made a mad dash for the exit. Luckily neither of them were caught.

'So. Should we tell him?' Jason pondered.

'Nah he doesn't need to know who his fallen guardian angels were.'

The two smirked and began to walk back to the cemetery. They looped around a few buildings and arrived back at the cemetery to see Daniel awaiting their return. Daniel's face lit up as bright as General TN Roman's rage. Jason checked to see how long they had left.

'It's 1:58am. I'm glad to see you are still alive,' Jason said to Daniel.

'I would hope so.' All the friends began to laugh at Daniel's comment. As silence began to fill the air again Daniel asked the question no one wanted to ask.

'Where are the skeletons?'

Before anyone could answer a large sigh was heard, from within the graveyard. The three walked into the graveyard.

'OH MY GOD!'

All three friends shouted at the same time. The two skeletons were still arguing! They had spent their entire time arguing. And with no time left the two were doomed.

The same door that let TN Roman in had just reopened and let him re-enter the world of the living.

'Well you two? Humans? Dead? Come on you know the song and dance by now!'

'Wait, what? No way it's already 2am!' Wingdings said.

TN sighed. 'I guess that's a no. Well let's see how Manny decides your fate. I have to admit I'm interested to see what he makes of you two, follow me.'

The two skeletons didn't move at first. Who would? They were essentially being sent to their doom. TN Roman was not interested in humoring the idea of their survival. He clicked his fingers and the same green aura that appeared before to signify the doors locking had now appeared again. This time the aura leapt off the door and towards Wingdings and Skelepun and engulfed them within itself. Slowly it dragged them into the door. TN Roman entered behind them. As the door shut the screams of the two could be heard. The structure descended back down into the ground without a trace.

'Well then. Let's leave, I guess,' Jason said.

'So should we tell anyone about this? You know about the secret skeletal society that's living under our city.'

The trio looked at each other in silence. They all nodded in agreement and said in unison, 'Nah!' They all laughed and started making their way home.

SET IN STONE
Cian Doyle

I sat there, in the corner of the room, a few feet away from the man I had just killed. The corpse was spewing blood from the stomach. He was one of my favourite teachers, what had I done? 'There's no way I can fix this,' I thought. There was too much blood and it had already gotten onto the carpet, there were shards of glass around the room. 'Why did you let this happen?' I kept asking myself in disbelief. The rain was loud against the glass, hopefully that had masked the noise of what just happened from the neighbours. I got up and was about to make an attempt at cleaning up this mess when everything went silent.

'Hello?' A calm, collected voice came from the other side of the room, scaring me. I had thought I was alone. A shadowy figure stood at the other end of the room, and judging by their voice, I assumed they were a woman.

'Who are you?!' I shouted, and began to quickly walk towards them, ready for an encounter; I couldn't have any witnesses.

'Stop!' she commanded, raising her arm powerfully. I could no longer move, my body felt stiff and I had no control over it, no matter how hard I tried to move I couldn't.

'I am a friend,' she said, walking towards me, pulling down the hood of her black robes to reveal snowy white hair, and a light, greyish complexion.

'What do you want, and who are you?!' I exclaimed, trying to follow her with my eyes, yet not being able to move my head, she was just out of my vision, walking around me as she talked.

'My name is Dalia, I want to help you. You seem to have gotten yourself into some situation here, haven't you?'

'Yes.' I spoke plainly, there was nothing I could really do here but listen.

'Luckily for you I am here to offer some help; after all, you didn't want to kill him, isn't that right, Beth?'

'How do you know my name?' I asked, with concern.

'I know a lot of things, now do you want my help or not?' She said, dismissing my question. I didn't have anything to lose here.

'Yes, but why do you want to help me?'

'I like you, Beth. We are friends after all, and this friend wants something you have!' She winked at me and gave me a grin.

'What could I possibly have that you would want?'

'Oh don't worry just something small. Your soul actually, you're not using it, are you?' she said, oddly casually.

'My soul!? What do you mean my soul?!' I shouted.

'Well, your soul is what brings you to Heaven or Hell, and by taking a quick look around the room, I think I might have some idea where you'll be going. However, you could sell your soul to me, don't worry, I'll take good care of it. It's a small price to pay to get you out of this mess, don't you think?' She was so convincing, I didn't want to go to Hell. And she was right, by the looks of things that's where I was headed unless I let her take my soul instead.

'Fine, you can have my soul, but how do you plan on helping me?' I answered reluctantly; it seemed like the only option available.

'You'll see.' She began walking towards me, stopping in front of me, her eyes turned from a deep blue to a bright glowing purple. She put her hands onto my face and threw her head back. I began to feel weak and blacked out.

I woke up in my bed, my alarm ringing. I rolled over to turn it off. I thought that was just a dream, but when I checked my phone, it said it was Tuesday, which I had just been through. I didn't remember much from the night before, nothing from before Dalia had arrived at least. How did she do that, and who is she? Unanswered questions aside, I got up and got ready for school, like I had already done, this day had to be different though, I just had to make sure I didn't make whatever mistakes I'd made before. I got ready quickly, and began to make my way downstairs when the doorbell rang. It was my friend Samara, she came to my house every morning before school so we could walk together. I don't know how Samara manages to get ready and walk to my house before school, she must get up very early.

'Hey, come in' I said, walking into the kitchen.

'Hey Beth, are you ready to go?' Samara asked, following me quickly into the kitchen.

'Yeah, I'm just getting my lunch.'

'Come on, we're already later than usual.' Samara hated being late.

'I know, I know, I'm ready now, let's go!'

'Do you have tutoring tonight with Mr Morrison, or will you be out after school?' She asked as we left the house. That night was when it happened, when I killed him, the reason I'm living through this day again.

'Yeah, I'm supposed to have tutoring tonight, but I don't think I'm going,' I replied, I had to cancel tutoring tonight; I couldn't let the same thing happen, not after I'd been given another chance.

'Oh okay good, we should do something later, do you want to come over to my house, we could watch a movie?'

'Yeah, sure, that'd be cool,' I said happily. I was glad to have made plans later, I could not go to Mr Morrison's house tonight, he won't die and I won't be a murderer.

Samara and I made our way into the school. As we got in the bell rang, we had made it just in time, but we had no time to go to our lockers. We went to Mr Morrison's class. It was so weird to see him alive again; the last time I saw him, he was spilling blood all over the ground.

'Hey, Sir, I won't be able to come to tutoring tonight, Is that okay?' I asked nervously, I knew he wouldn't be happy.

'Oh, how come?' He replied, slightly angrily.

'Well, I have a doctor's appointment tonight.' I was a really bad liar, I was hoping he didn't see through it.

'Why didn't you tell me about this earlier, surely you didn't make the appointment this morning. Look, Beth, if you just don't want to come I can't force you, but I'll be disappointed if I find out you're lying to me; there are a lot of people who wanted the help you're getting.'

He was not thrilled with me at all, I had nothing else to say, I just sat down beside Samara and took out my books. I had never really seen him get like this in class; he was pretty much always a nice teacher. I guess the tutoring was important to him.

'Beth, why did you tell him you've a doctor's appointment, I don't mind you not coming to my house later if you wanted to go to tutoring?' Samara asked in surprise.

'No that's not it, I just don't wanna go tonight.' I didn't know what to tell her, I had no reason not to go tonight except not wanting to repeat what happened yesterday, but I couldn't tell her that.

'Okay, but I want you to go next week, I know maths isn't a good subject for you and I want you to do well.' She said with concern.

'Okay, thanks *Mom*' I joked. Samara was always so concerned with how I was doing in school, sometimes more than I was. The rest of the school day was pretty uneventful, I didn't talk much in Mr Morrison's class. I knew he was angry at me, but at least he wasn't dead.

We made our way to my house when school ended so I could change out of my uniform before going around to Samara's. I struggled to get the key into the door, my hands were full of books that I couldn't fit in my bag. Luckily my dad heard the struggle and opened the door for me. It looked as if it was about to rain, dark clouds were nearing.

'Hey Dad,' I greeted him as I walked into the house and shut the door behind me. My dad stopped me and Samara in the hall.

'Beth, what's Samara doing here, you have tutoring in a while, you have to get changed and ready for that, you know you can't go out on Tuesdays?' He said stubbornly.

'Oh, Beth is feeling sick so she's going to come around to my house and watch a movie. She's not really feeling up for tutoring today,' Samara interrupted.

'Well that doesn't matter, I put a lot of money into these tutoring sessions, and that's not going to waste. She won't die,' My dad argued.

'But, Dad please I really don't—'

'I don't care, Beth, you're going. Now say goodbye to Samara,' he said, opening the door. It was raining lightly outside.

'See you tomorrow, Beth,' Samara said sadly, walking out the door. She seemed like she was really looking forward to watching that movie with me. My dad shut the door behind her, that was rude of him, and I was really embarrassed.

'Dad, you don't understand, I really can't go to tutoring tonight,' I pleaded.

'Beth, I already said you're going.' He began to walk away.

'I told Mr Morrison I had an appointment.' That caught his attention again.

'Well, I'm just going to have to call him and tell him the truth.' He walked into the kitchen.

My dad was on the phone to Mr Morrison, likely telling him that I had made up having an appointment, while I went upstairs to text Samara to say sorry for her being kicked out of my house.

'Beth!' My dad shouted from downstairs. 'I'm dropping you to tutoring tonight.' I had no idea how I would get out of this, I just had to make sure I didn't do whatever I did wrong that got Mr Morrison killed. I don't want to kill him, so why did I before? It was time to get ready. I changed out of my uniform and into a pair of black jeans and a white shirt; I packed my bag with my maths books and a copy, along with my leather jacket in case the rain gets worse. I styled my hair, it was short and didn't take long to do. I didn't know how to prepare myself to not kill someone, I was nervous. Usually

I'd have left by now to be early, but I wanted to spend as little time there as possible so I waited a few minutes , if I could I planned on faking sick so I could leave half way through. I put my bag on my back and went downstairs into the sitting room, where my dad was waiting to drive me to Mr Morrison's house.

'Come on then,' I sighed. He stood up, put on a jumper and took out his keys.

'What took you so long, you're going to be late,' He asked angrily.

'Relax, I'll be on time if we go now, so come on.' I opened the front door, it was still raining so I ran towards the car, it was locked. 'Unlock the car!' I shouted to my dad, who was walking very slowly towards the car, which was at the end of the driveway, leaving me to get drenched in the rain, he didn't hear me. By the time he made it to the car and unlocked it, I was soaked.

We sat in silence the entire way to Mr Morrison's house, the radio was broken and we had nothing to say to each other, I was still mad about earlier, the only sound to be heard was the rain spitting against the car windows, and the squeaky window wipers trying to fight it off.

'We're here' I said quietly. He parked the car on the side of the road, I opened the door.

'I'll see you later,' he said coldly, we were both still bitter from earlier.

I walked up Mr Morrison's driveway. My dad was still parked at the end, making sure I was going in. I knocked on the door; it took a while for him to answer: I stood there with my jacket over my head, keeping most of the rain off. As soon as the door opened my dad began driving away.

'Come on in!' Mr Morrison said cheerfully. I stepped in and went into his office where we usually worked, he went into the kitchen. I put my bag onto his desk and started to take out my things. I noticed a large open bottle of vodka, and a glass that was almost empty beside it. Has he been drinking? Suddenly I felt two hands on my sides, I jumped and turned quickly. It was Mr Morrison, he was so close to me, I could smell the alcohol on his breath.

'What are you doing?' I asked with a shaky voice. I was scared. He didn't answer. He pressed me up against the desk, I tried to push him off but he was too strong, I reached back onto the desk looking for anything that could help me. I grabbed a glass bottle and smashed it against his head, broken glass flew across the room.

'STOP!' I shouted as I pushed him away, but he came towards me again. I plunged the remains of the sharp, broken bottle into his stomach; he collapsed onto the ground, his mouth filling with blood. I began to tear up, I had let it happen again, even after I was given that second chance. I sat on the ground and cried to myself for a while, how did I let this happen again? I finally got up and was about to leave. Everything went quiet.

'Hello?'

HOW SUGAR RUINED MY LIFE

Sinéad Farley

'Hi, my name is Walter, also known as "The Big Bad Wolf".'

'Hi Walter,' replied the support group for troubled animals in the Farmville County Prison.

The support group was held in a spare room in the prison, in the west wing beside the arts and crafts room. It was a dull room, big with grey walls and lots of chairs in a circle. The support group ran everyday from five o'clock until dinnertime, which was six o'clock.

The counsellor's name was Doc. He was a very small dwarf-like man. He looked like a pig and wore a little suit. He was really nice. He always listened to us and helped us, but enough of that; I really wanted to tell everyone why I'm here.

'So I'm here today because I want to tell my side of the story of how I became "The Big Bad Wolf". I got my name because of my past, but I'm not a bad wolf at all. You see, it was my grandmother's birthday and I wanted to bake her a cake. She was turning 70! I had always been very close with my grandmother.'

'Why were you always close with your grandmother?' asked Doc.

'I was close with my grandmother since I was a little wolf. We lived in a small cute cottage with net curtains and a red door. It was a lovely cottage but the only bad thing about living in my grandmother's cottage was that it was on the same street as the Porkies. I don't like the Porkies and my parents never got along with them.

'If you don't mind telling us, what happened to your parents?' said Doc.

'Well, as I said, they never got along with the Porkies. I'm not sure why, I was never told. All I know is that some nasty things were said and they never got over it. It's very childish, but anyway my parents were at the supermarket and they had seen the Porkies. Mr Porkie shouted over at my mother calling her fat, and my mother got very upset and angry. She ran over and hit Mr Porkie and just as quick, Mrs Porkie hit my mother! My mother stormed out of the shop and my father followed, they got into the car and drove home. They were halfway down the road when BANG! The Porkies crashed into my parents' car. My mother and father went straight through the windscreen and fell on to the road. Before they could even get up, Mrs Porkie ran over my parents squishing them both.'

'Oh, I'm sorry to hear that,' Doc said in a sad voice. 'Would you like to explain why you're here?'

'Yes, well as I said, it was my grandmother's birthday and I had no sugar to finish baking her cake and I had no money to buy more, so I decided to ask my neighbours. This was a little bit of a problem, as they were Porkies.

'I walked down the road to my nearest neighbour Sausage. He was a pig. He had two older brothers but it seemed that he wasn't the sharpest pitchfork in the barn because he had made his house out of straw. Like who even does that?

'Anyway I knocked three times asking nicely "Little Pig, Little Pig may I have some sugar please?"

'The little pig waddled to the window and looked out. He had shaving cream smeared all over his chin and said "No, I'm shaving the hairs on my chinny chin chin!"

'He slammed his window shut and waddled away. Out of nowhere a cat fell down from the roof with the fright of the window slamming. I'm allergic to cats so I sneezed. Because Sausage's house was made from straw it blew down!

'Sausage was standing in the middle of the ruins. I hadn't had any breakfast and he looked really tasty so I ate him all up.

'I didn't know what to do but what I did know was that I still had no sugar and my grandmother was home from bingo soon, so I had to get some sugar quick to finish the cake before she arrived. I started making my way to the next house, which was Sausage's brother Rasher. He wasn't much smarter than Sausage because he had built his house out of sticks!

'How and ever I knocked on the door and said "Little Pig, Little Pig may I have some sugar please?"

'He yelled back rudely "No! I'm watching TV go away!"

'I was annoyed but I was going to leave it and walk away, but I suddenly sneezed again and it was too late, I had blown Rasher's house down as well. I was feeling puckish at that stage, so I ate him too.

'I still had no sugar. I was very annoyed by that point because I had spent so much time looking for a bit of sugar. So I walked to the next house. The oldest brother lived there; his name was Porkchop. He was the smartest one out of them all because he built his house out of bricks.

'I knocked on the big blue door and said "Little Pig, Little Pig may I have some sugar please?"

'He opened the kitchen window and yelled "No! Ha ha ha! Who do you think I am? I don't give away sugar to wolves like you."

'At this point I was furious, all I wanted was a bit of sugar. I shouted back "I knew I never liked you Porkies, why can't I have a bit of sugar? It's for my grandmother's birthday cake."

'He replied, "Because I don't like you Walter, you're a Wolf, you well and truly know our parents didn't get along and we don't either and you've the neck to come to my door and ask for my sugar? I don't care about you grandmother's cake; for all I care she could fall and break her leg and I would laugh at her!"

'Well anyone who knows me knows how protective I am of my family, especially my grandmother, because she's all I have left, so I went mad. I couldn't help myself I was just so angry. I bashed on his door, I left my fist prints in it! I smashed his kitchen window and as I was just about to leap through and kill him when the police came and dragged me into the back of the van and shoved me into a cell.

'The next day I was questioned in court and found guilty for the murder of the two pigs, even though their parents had killed mine. So that's how I'm here and that's my story to prove to you all that I'm not "The Big Bad Wolf".'

Everyone in the room was quiet, they all just sat there. They all probably thought I was psycho, they all looked terrified. A few moments later the bell rang for dinner so we all went to the canteen. It felt so good to have that off my chest.

The next morning I woke up to see my cousin Winnie Wolf lying on the bed opposite mine. I wondered what he was doing here. He looked over and saw that I was awake.

'Ah Walter, long time no see!'

I looked at him for a few seconds while I woke up properly and replied, 'Winnie? What are you doing here?'

'Well, do you remember that little mean girl in our class? Little Red Riding Hood, the one who always wore a red cape?'

'You didn't eat her, did you?' I asked.

'No, I ate her grandmother and pretended to be her grandmother when she came to visit, but she realised who I was and called the guards on me, so here I am. Happy to see me?'

'Yes of course I am! But I'm going to the gym now and then to my support group, you coming?'

'Nah, Walter. I'll stay here and have a nap. I got here late last night and couldn't sleep 'cause of your snoring!'

'Ha ha, okay see ya later then,' I replied, walking down the hall.

At 5pm I went to the support group; I wanted to tell Doc about my dream.

'You alright, Walter?' asked Doc.

'I'm fine, I just had a dream about the Porkies last night.'

'Would you like to share it with us?'

'Em yeah. So I remember being younger and playing with Sausage, Rasher and Porkchop and we were grand, no fighting or anything. Then out of nowhere they all turned on me and BAM! Porkchop hit me knocking me to the ground. They all joined in and kept hitting me, leaving me for the dead. I remember seeing my soulless body on the ground surrounded by blood. I felt a hand touch my shoulder. Creeped out, I looked around to see my mother and father standing beside me!

'I screamed, "Mam? Dad? How are you two here? I thought you two were dead?"

'We are dead, Walter.' Said my mother in her soft comforting voice, 'But so are you, you need to never talk to those evil pigs again, they'll hurt you.'

'Then I woke up. I've had this dream before, but when I had it my parents weren't dead. I never talked to the Porkies again, and then their parents killed mine.'

'It's alright, Walter, you're safe here.'

'Thanks Doc.'

The bell rang for dinner and we all went to the canteen. Winnie met me at one of the tables. I know he's only been here a few hours but he's starting to annoy me already. He keeps telling all my friends that I used to get beaten by three little pigs. I told him after dinner when we were going to bed.

I said firmly 'Winnie I'm not happy with you telling my friends I used to get beaten by three little pigs, you know there's way more to the story!'

'Sorry, Walter, I was just tryin'ta have a bit of a laugh. I won't do it again.'

'Okay good. Night, see you in the morning.'

'Night, Walter.'

The next morning we got up and cleaned ourselves up before breakfast. We got our cereal and sat down. Everyone at the table was quiet. It was awkward, so to break the silence I asked Goldie Locks to pass me the sugar. She smiled at me with her cheeky little smile and said, 'No, you're too far away.'

Everyone gasped. I heard a spoon fall, my jaw dropped and everyone went quiet. I was shocked; I knew she was cheeky, but not that cheeky.

'Do you know why I'm here?' I asked.

'Yes I do,' she replied laughing.

'You won't be laughing for long! I killed two pigs for the same reason I'm about to kill you. Now pass me the sugar, please!' I shouted.

Everyone looked terrified, and was staring at Goldie as if they were trying to tell her to pass me the sugar. But she didn't take the hint.

'Do you think you're lethal, Walter?'

'No I don't.'

'Ah but you do, Walter. You think you're great because you're locked up for murdering two pigs! Ha ha.'

'Well you think you're lethal for not giving me the sugar, so give it to me now or else!'

'O-or else what?' she asked with big worried eyes.

'Or else it's time to say goodbye to your friends because I'll eat you like I ate those pigs.'

'No you won't, you're a mouth!'

'Yes I will!' I said in my deepest darkest scariest voice.

Goldie jumped and ran down to my end of the table with the sugar and said, 'Sorry, Walter, please don't hurt me!'

I just looked at her and growled. She ran back to her seat nearly crying. I ate my cornflakes, got up and walked out of the canteen. I could hear people whispering about what had just happened. I heard someone say I was a psychopath, so I ran back into the canteen to see who it was.

I growled, 'Who said that? All of youse shut up talking about me behind my back, say it to my face!'

But no-one answered, they all just looked down and ate their breakfast, I rolled my eyes and walked away. One day I'll end up killing someone else!

Never mess with 'The Big Bad Wolf!'

THE UNBELIEVABLE TRUTH

David Farrelly

'One more person to go! I don't get paid enough for this job,' I thought to myself as I walked into my office to find a man sitting in a wheelchair facing my desk. The man was wearing bandages on his hands and on the stumps that were once his legs, which were missing from the knee down. I introduced myself.

'Hello Mr Growers, my name is Joseph Hamlyn. I'm with *The Times* and here to talk to you about the email you sent us regarding your visit to the Himalayan mountain range.'

I shook his hand and sat down at my desk.

Mr Growers then said 'Please call me Robert.'

'From what I could gather from the email you sent me, you want to get an article published about your trip to Mount Everest, is that true?' I asked in a puzzled tone. As I asked him this question I thought to myself that there's no way this guy actually climbed Everest, he's in a wheelchair for God's sake!

'Robert, if you don't mind can I take down some notes on your experience?' I said.

Robert replied with a simple 'yes' to both of my questions.

'Can you tell me a little about your background, I need to know to know as much information as possible for the article.'

'I am 27 years old and I am paralysed from the waist down.' I took down notes furiously as he spoke.

'So, what exactly were you doing on Everest? Were you helping the mountaineers?' I asked him curiously. Robert began to show a look of frustration and disappointment on his face, his eyes looked to the ground and then back up at me.

Then he said 'Throughout my life I have lived in a wheelchair and when people talk to me they normally talk to me differently, they talk to me as if I have a mental problem, which I don't. This is because of my wheelchair. People also talk to me as if I am incapable of doing anything. This has been the way through my life and for someone to ask a question like that makes it worthless to have climbed Everest, spent all of my money, time and lost the use of my right arm doing so!'

I felt a sense of shame come over me and I said 'I didn't mean to be so blunt, I am sorry I wasn't aware of the situation.'

Robert sighed and said 'it's OK . . . just go ahead with the questions.'

'Can you tell me a little bit more about your life before you climbed Everest? This background information will add to the article.'

Robert then told me the arduous tale that was his life before he supposedly climbed Mount Everest.

'When I was young my own parents used to not allow me to do anything on my own, or to do many things that other people would do while they were growing up. My parents would also constantly belittle everything I did by saying things like "if you were normal you wouldn't be such a disappointment"; I would endure constant remarks like that. So the moment that I turned 18 I left my parents' house and rented my own apartment. Even though I have my own house and independent life I have not escaped the ridicule. For example, when I wheel my chair down the street the local children call me "special", "retarded" and many other insulting things.'

Robert's sad existence prior to his trip to Everest allowed me to sympathise with him more easily, as I myself had had polio as a child and I knew what it was like to be treated differently. I took down Robert's story as I was sure I wanted to include Robert's background in my article. I asked if he could tell me in depth about his life-changing journey, of a person of his physical capability, completing such a challenge that only a rare few can do.

Robert began his story while I carefully listened.

'Last May I made the decision to prove everyone wrong, I decided that I would be the first paralysed person to climb Mount Everest. On the 2nd of May I sold all of my belongings and spent all of the money that I had received from the government as social welfare for my disability on all the essential climbing equipment such as rope, insulating clothes and dried out food. I improved my wheelchair so it would survive the harsh conditions on Everest and carry me up the mountain. I did this by making it so that the front wheels could detach and skis could be put on instead. I also improved my wheels by putting studs on them so they would gain traction on the rocky and icy terrain. I had created the ski chair that would take me to the top of Everest. With the money I had left I bought a one way plane ticket to Nepal, which is located in the Himalayan mountain range near Everest.

'One week later I arrived and upon arrival I had to endure an eight-hour drive in a car that was on its last legs, I knew this because of the smell of the exhaust coming inside the car through the air conditioning. Eventually I arrived at the foot hills of Everest. Here there were areas where people could hire Sherpas to help them get up Everest. I decided that I did not want to employ a Sherpa for two reasons; one being I wanted to climb Everest 100 percent on my own to prove my independence from everyone else and the other reason being that I was afraid they would insult me while climbing the mountain. The eight hour drive ended when the enormous mountain known as Mount Everest came into view. The wide bottom of Everest stretched as far as my eyes could see, to the left and right and the top of Everest soared far up into the sky through the clouds.

'On the next day I began my assault on Everest. I got into my ski chair and fitted the studded wheels and removed the skis, as I knew the first part of Everest had no snow or ice on it. I rolled over large boulders and inched my way up the scree slopes slowly. The landscape at this point of Everest was beautiful, yet rugged and harsh. I wheeled my way towards the spot where climbers normally set up base camp to acclimatise to the altitude. I didn't have to worry about adjusting to the altitude as I had would have time to acclimatise because I would be travelling a lot slower than most people up the mountain.

'There were several base camps set up by other climbers in this area; I stayed clear of the other climbers as I knew there would be negativity held towards a person in a wheelchair climbing Everest. I pitched my tent as far away from the other climbers without being too far, in this case being around 300 metres away from the nearest tent. There were four other tents clustered around each other in the base camp area. This indicated to me that about six other climbers were attempting to climb Everest at the same time as me. The tents that belonged to the other climbers were top mountaineering tents; I had come across those tents before while I was buying my climbing equipment. The tents the other climbers had were top brand tents that cost about €5,000 each. From their tents I had concluded that the other must be really experienced professional climbers. That evening I had a feeling that my presence wouldn't go unnoticed. The next morning I awoke to the sound of six voices talking to each other, the voices spoke to each other in a mixture of tones; some with defensive tones, some with aggressive tones and some with a friendly tone. Four of the climbers were arguing among each other and others were talking to each other. The four climbers were arguing about what course they would take up the mountain. The other two climbers who were not arguing were talking to each other about the fact there was another tent in the base camp area. The two climbers were both female, I can recall one of them saying "what do yea think that other climber over there is doing up on Everest with climbing gear like that!?" "I dunno . . . Maybe trying to get them self killed," the other said. "I know, must be some religious fools trying to do it for charity or something," the two of them chuckled egotistically together.

'I decided that I would attempt to pack up my camp swiftly and unnoticed by the other climbers. I had my tent packed away in under a minute and I was on my way, but I had underestimated the speed at which my chair travelled at. It crawled along, as it bumped over the small gravelly stones and bounced over the larger boulders. It was too late, the other climbers had spotted me and they raced over towards me. The other climbing group consisted of two females and four males. I ignored them until one of them said something. A tall man with a ginger beard said "hey, look here, that fella in that tent yonder is one of those retards." I didn't care about what that ignorant fool had just said so I continued up the mountain and ignored him. The rest of his group caught up with him and some of them started shouting abuse after me such as; "They shouldn't let people like you set foot on this mountain! You should give up now because if you continue, you're gonna' die and you are making the rest of us who are at the peak of our climbing career look bad!" "You are never going to make it to the top!" they shouted after me.

'The fact that those ignorant fools thought I was incapable, or people like me were inferior to ordinary people who can use their legs made me more determined to reach the summit. I continued on my way, more determined than ever.

'I decided that I would not take the path taken by most climbers, as I didn't want to reunite with the idiots I had come across in base camp. The gradient of Everest increased with every metre I gained. I wheeled my chair over the infinite rock and scree for what felt like days, but in reality was only eight hours. I had gained one thousand metres in altitude. My body ached from the physical exertion which I had endured. Throughout the day I noticed the air temperature drop. It had fallen from twenty degrees to twelve degrees, as the altitude increased. I knew that I still had a lot of ground to cover and the temperature would continue to drop as I went further up. So I decided that I would get some sleep while it was still warm.

'I slept poorly that night. The scree that I had pitched my tent on poked through the thin layer of nylon which my tent was made from, right through my sleeping bag and into my back. I slept through the discomfort to awake at dawn. I took the time in the morning to establish a plan for the next three days of climbing. I would continue on my current course and finally get up into the area shrouded with clouds.

'I wheeled my ski chair for the next three days up the mountain. On the third day Everest, the endless rock that protrudes into the upper atmosphere, had finally changed. The large boulders and mounds of scree had finally been swapped for sharp pointy rocks, glaciers and a layer of slick ice where snow had compacted on top of rocks. The last three days had been taxing on my body. I had not got much sleep due to the plummeting temperatures and pointy rocks. I was at four thousand metres now and the going was tougher than ever. Day five of climbing Everest was ending fast. The sun had been blocked out by the mountain and the temperatures dropped quickly. I set up camp on a flat rock I had found. The rock did not slope down at the same angle as the mountain. It protruded from the mountain at a sixty degree angle. I set up camp on this rock so my ski chair would not roll down the mountain while I slept. By the time I retired to my sleeping bag temperatures had gone from about minus seven to minus twenty eight degrees with dusk. I wore a heavy coat while I tried to sleep, but I still shivered throughout the night. This was when one of my handicaps from being paralysed came to aid me. I could not feel my legs or feet, so I didn't feel the cold through them.

'The next morning I awoke to find myself sweating. I did not realise how this had happened until I looked up at the roof of my tent. The roof had sagged in, as if something heavy weighed it down. I thought about this to myself for a while until I realised what had happened. Snow, I concluded! It had snowed during the night and the snow had gathered on top of my tent, insulating it. I pulled my body from my sleeping bag, got into my coat and other warm clothing. I got out of my tent dragged myself over to my ski chair and got into it. I packed away my camp and continued on my way. The weather was worse today. Snow blew at an angle and straight into my face. The wind had a chill to it today and this would slow my journey up the mountain.

'I had a hard decision to make on whether I continued on my current course which took me up a non-conventional way. It would take me towards a large glacier, away from the path and those elitist climbers who had ridiculed me at base camp or if I went back on to the path, taken by most climbers that avoided the glacier. I chose to continue on my non-conventional way up Everest. When I reached the glacier it was covered in a thick layer of snow, only revealing itself in large chunks of ice which pointed out at the snow. I rolled my wheels onto the ice, covered in the cold snow and rolled on propelling myself forward on the skis, which were now attached to my ski chair. The glacier was large and had an even surface which made going easy. I was travelling at the fastest I had ever been on my journey up Everest. Suddenly I spotted an anomaly on the glacier's smooth surface. A large hole in the glacier, a crevice stretched out in front of me. I was travelling at a tremendous speed and I needed to instantly stop. I made the quick decision to grab the rear of the skis on my ski chair and lift them up. This forced the front of my skis into the snowy surface of the glacier. As soon as I did this my ski chair flipped over in a large arch and landed only metres away from the mouth of the crevice. I landed face down on the cold ice. My chair had flipped over but it was not damaged. All of my equipment and supplies were scattered on top of the ice. I glanced over the edge of the crevice and saw to my surprise the frozen corpses of climbers who had fallen into the crevice and not survived. This sent shivers down my spine as it revealed the harsh nature of how unforgiving Everest is.

'The crevice was wide and uncrossable. So I made the tough decision to go back onto the route taken by most climbers. The risk of crossing the glacier outweighed the risk of meeting back up with those abusive New Zealanders. I gathered up all of my belongings that had been scattered on the ice and started backtracking carefully to avoid any crevices that had not revealed themselves on my original crossing. After several hours of retracing my tracks I found a way off the glacier and back on to the route taken by most climbers. The route I was taking now was not much better than the one I had been on, but it was crossable.

'By the time I had finally redirected myself onto the other course, night was upon me again. Even though I had backtracked for several kilometres I had still gained altitude of another 1,000 metres, putting me at 5,000 metres above sea level. Again temperatures were low, but the air pressure dropped making going tough on my journey up Everest and it was at a new low which meant that there was less oxygen in the air making it harder to travel. Again I went to sleep cold and tired. The next morning I woke up feeling a pressure in my head. I also felt light-headed and nauseous. I concluded that I had altitude sickness. This was a shock to me as I had not anticipated this as I thought I was travelling up too slowly to get altitude sickness. I decided that I should stay put for the next two days and recover. Two days passed slowly and eventually my nausea went and I was no longer light-headed; I was ready to continue on my way.

'On my ninth day on Everest I continued on my way up the mountain. My wheels slipped and slid over the ice and rocks, I continued on up Everest like this for the next two days facing the same terrain. The gruelling journey up got harder with each rotation of my wheels. On the morning of the second day the wind picked up as there was a weather front coming in, the wind blasted at the mountain at gale force speeds causing snow to be pushed off the mountain and causing visibility to drop making the going even tougher. The wind also burned my face and any exposed skin as it hit me. The snow built up on my ski chair causing it to be weighed down. Although the weather was harsh I still managed to make a further 2,000 metres. On my ninth and tenth day this put me at 7,000 metres, only one day away from the death zone on Everest.

'On the night of the tenth day I tried to sleep as I wanted to attempt my summit of Everest in only two days. On the next day I would be entering the death zone and this would be the hardest part of my journey. That evening I couldn't sleep well and I had a strange feeling something bad was going to happen. The next morning I awoke to feel a burning sensation on my face, the cold dry high altitude wind cut through my tent and onto my face. I opened my eyes to see my tent which was almost unrecognisable. It had deep slashes through it and the internal structure was no longer able to support itself. It was that badly damaged. I pulled my stiff cold body from my sleeping bag and looked around my camp. All of my supplies, equipment and other personal belongings were either spread out on the ground outside my tent or were missing. Then I looked to the spot where I had left my ski chair the previous night, instead there was a pile of mangled metal, broken skis and a note. I put on my insulating clothes and dragged my body over to the remains of my ski chair and the note. I picked up the note and read it. It read

Dear madman in a weird looking wheelchair, how did you make it this far without dying yet? You should have stayed in the special need's home. We have come to the decision that you will properly die if you continue up the mountain, Everest is not meant to be climbed by handicapped people. We don't even know why you are attempting to climb Everest. Are you trying to ruin our record of climbing all of the 8,000-metre-plus mountains in the shortest amount of time by dying while we are on the mountain, which will make us look bad for climbing Everest while a handicapped man dies on the mountain at the same time? As a group we have decided that it is too dangerous for a person in your condition to continue so we took your fancy wheel chair out of the scenario. We have also left you a satellite phone so you can contact the Nepal mountain rescue team to help get you down.

'The note was signed "New Zealand climbing association, team 8,000 up".

'The note baffled me. I knew who had done this to me. It was the same people who had harassed me at the base camp. From what I could gather from the note they thought I was unable to continue up the mountain because of my paralyses, despite making it this far so they smashed my ski chair. I was particularly angry but yet I felt sorry for them as they were that confused. I decided I would continue up the mountain anyway, but before leaving I took photographs of the remains of my wheel chair so I could show people if I was rescued. I continued my climb up the mountain dragging myself on the ground using two pieces of metal I had salvaged from the ruins of my ski chair. I used them as ice picks. I dragged my body across the jagged rocks and ice for hours not knowing how far I had travelled. I dragged myself until I couldn't go any further. I saw a sheltered spot on the mountain. It was a small space between a cliff face and snow drift. I dragged my body into this space which was out of the wind and as soon as I entered the sheltered craves I fell asleep holding onto one of my makeshift ice picks with my right hand. I woke at dawn the next day. My crevasse had kept me alive during the night when temperatures fell to minus 56. My right hand was numb. I couldn't move it, my ice pick had frozen to my glove and my right hand itself had frozen partially. It was difficult to open my eyes as they had thin layer of ice that had built up in between my eyelids. When I did manage to open my eyes, what I saw shocked me, there was the body of a frozen climber who must have hidden in the caves during a storm and died.

'The frozen body in the crevasse had a radio strapped around his waist. I took it and dragged myself out, I didn't want to spend any more time in there as I didn't want to suffer a similar fate. As soon as I exited the crevasse I was hit by powerful wind that pushed me back. Today was my final chance. I would either reach the summit or die trying. I dragged my body across rocks and more rocks, I ached all over as the cold ate away at my flesh. I had chills all over as I dragged my body up and up the relentless mountain. The summit was not even in sight. I had to make an abrupt stop when I came to a sheer rock face. The rock face lunged up into the sky, it had several ropes dangling over its edge. The ropes must have been left by climbers who had attempted to climb the mountain. I had very little energy to drag my body over to all of the ropes to see which would be best, so I just dragged myself over to the nearest rope. The rope was old; it was a faded yellow colour and the sun's rays had bleached the rope causing it to look faded. I made my way over to the rope and looked up. Above me the cliff face looked climbable, well at least for an able bodied person with climbing gear. The cliff face had sharp rocks that protruded out from different angles; the rock had been eroded away by the wind and moving ice. I reached for the rope with my left hand, grabbed it and tied the rope to the piece of metal that was frozen to my hand. I also tied the rope around my wrist. Once the rope had been secured to my right arm I reached for the cliff face and placed my hand in a crack in the rock face and tried to lift my body up with my one good hand, but I failed. I was just too weak to hoist my body up onto the rock face. While trying to lift my body up I had noticed something, my legs didn't move as much as they had been earlier on in the day. In fact they didn't move at all! My legs were frozen to about my knees; this gave me an idea as to how I would climb up the cliff. I would climb up by pulling my body up and swinging my legs up into cracks in the rock and they would not move due to them being frozen. I did this and it worked, until I was 80% up the cliff, when my legs slipped off of an icy rock and my body swung back off the rope, but luckily I was able to stay on the rope due to it being tied to my arm. As I swung back I was caught by the high altitude, I was then dropped by the wind and I swung back towards the cliff face. As I gathered speed as I swung back towards the cliff face, I could do nothing except await the impact. My body smashed into the cliff face and I felt nothing. My legs had hit into the cliff face. I felt no pain due to being paralysed, but I knew I had completely destroyed every bone and muscle in my legs. During my collision I had managed to grab back onto the cliff face with my good arm. I struggled up the rest of the cliff the way I had gone up earlier. I reached the top and dragged myself up onto the mountain above.

'I could see the peak of the world's highest mountain; it loomed several hundred metres above me. Everest narrowed to a point. The final few hundred metres were incredibly steep, icy and almost impossible to cross. I released my hand from the rope I had used to climb up the cliff. My hand was frozen and had become crushed; the bones in it where almost certainly broken. I didn't really care about how damaged my hand and legs had become as I was so close to proving to people how even a handicapped person is capable of climbing Everest. I started to travel up Everest again. I dragged my body again using the piece of metal from my ski chair that was frozen to my right hand to stick into the ice and I dragged myself along. I could barely manage it. Every metre I gained felt like twenty. This was for several reasons including the lack of oxygen at this altitude, the wind and the complete exhaustion of my body. I was dragging myself for hours until I finally couldn't go up any further. Actually I physically couldn't go any further and the reason why I couldn't go any further was because there was no more mountain to go up. I HAD MADE IT TO THE SUMMIT! I had proven that I could do a thing that most able bodied people cannot do. But I had managed to do it, all of those people who had ridiculed me throughout my life were wrong!

While on the summit I accepted the fact I was going to die up there but it didn't bother me as I had proven myself in my own mind. While on the summit I thought about whether the other climbers who had smashed my wheel chair had made it to the top. There was no sign that anyone had been up there recently, no footprints, nothing at all. While on the summit I intended on taking photos, but when I took my camera out of the pocket in my trousers it was unusable; the lenses were completely smashed and the casing of the camera was buckled and bent from my impact with the cliff face. After failing to take photos of myself to prove that I made it to the top I realised how cold I was. I was chronically shivering. At this point I realised I didn't want to die, so I took the satellite phone the "New Zealand climbing association, team 8000 up" had left me. The phone was not broken as I had put it in a pocket in a bag where I had placed several things that I kept from the supplies that were not stolen. I attempted to turn on the satellite phone but it wouldn't turn on. The battery was dead; my heart sank. I looked around in the bag for anything that might have a battery that would match the battery in the satellite phone. At first I couldn't find any batteries, until I checked the radio I had recovered from the corpse of the climber I found in the crevasse. I removed the battery from the radio and it was the exact same type as the one in the satellite phone. I struggled to put the battery in the satellite phone as I could only use my left hand and my hand was shaking intensely. Eventually I managed to get the battery into the phone and the phone came to life. I phoned the first number that came up on the phone and said "I'm on the summit of Everest and I'm going to die if somebody doesn't help". Once those words left my lips I lost consciousness and fell to the ground.

'The next memory I have is of me lying in a hospital bed in Kathmandu (Nepal's capital). I had fallen into a coma for eight days, but had finally woken up. The coma was caused by acute hypothermia, exhaustion and lack of oxygen in the brain. I later found out that the person I had phoned was none other than one of the climbers who had destroyed my ski chair and harassed me in the base camp. I was shocked when I discovered this. The doctors in the hospital told me that they were planning on summiting Everest the day after me, when they received my plea for help. Once they had received my call they immediately started climbing up Everest. They found my cold, unconscious, barely alive body on the summit and brought me down. Over the next two days they kept me alive and brought me down low enough so that I could be airlifted to hospital.

'I was surprised at the other climber's actions, but the more I thought about it the more sense it made. They harassed me in the base camp with the hope that I would give up and go back down and they destroyed my ski chair so I couldn't go any further and would have to give up and call for help.

'I lost the lower half of each leg, but this did not bother me as I was paralysed anyway. I also damaged the nerve endings in my right hand, making it essentially useless. This bothered me, but I was glad to be alive. Eventually, I left the hospital after making a full recovery and purchased a plane ticket home. On arrival home I researched how I could get an article published about my story and I found you. And that is how I am here in your office telling you this'.

I believed every word of Robert's story and I immediately went about getting it published in an article about him. I contacted the New Zealand climbing association and asked them if I could use statements from their climbers as proof of Robert's conquering Everest. Two weeks later I had a final draft of the article complete and I asked Robert to come over to my office to go through the article with him. The day went well. Robert entered my office in his wheelchair. I noticed how, over the last while, he had become a much happier person and he said 'Good afternoon, my friend' as he entered my office. I showed him the article on my computer and he gave it a pass by saying 'it all seems good, the facts are all correct, I love the headline "The Disabled Man Who Conquered Everest", and now let's hope the rest of the world can finally respect me at last'.

The article was published the next day. I meet with Robert to see what people were saying about it on the internet, apparently several radio stations and news shows had talked about my article. We looked at the responses and almost all of them were negative. People called me 'an ableist' and said that I was trying to 'encourage hatred of the disabled people'. They thought I was mocking disabled people as they claimed it would be 'impossible for a handicapped person to climb Mount Everest'. I was sacked from my job as chief reporter for *The Times*, despite having proof that the climb had really happened, in the form of statements from the other climbers.

People claimed that the New Zealand climbing association were in on my 'conspiracy'. Robert was taking people not believing his story more easily as he was used to people not respecting or believing in him. He set up 'the cooperative wilderness handicapped outdoor group' for those who believed in him. My career as a reporter was crippled and I had to come up with some sort of proof that Robert actually climbed Everest. I came up with a plan to send a team of climbers up Everest to find the remains of Robert's ski chair. I used my own money to fund the venture. The team left for Everest approximately one year after Robert climbed Everest. Several weeks later I was contacted by the lead climber in the team.

The expedition leader contacted me through a radio and said ' I think we may have found the remains of the ski chair,' the radio cracked as he spoke.

'So, what have you found?' I asked.

'Well . . . There's a wheel poking out of the snow.'

'Investigate it!' I demanded. Several minutes later the radio cracks with static again as the climber says 'OK, that was a wheel, but there's no other wreckage and that wheel, well . . . it's attached to a child's bike'.

The End

(In reality the government of Nepal stated, 'We don't think we should issue permits to people who cannot see or walk or who don't have arms. Climbing Everest is not a joke. It is not a matter of dis-crimination – how can you climb without legs?')

THE DROP

Killian Farrelly

One day my friend Sean John called for me.

'Do you want to go up to Howth and go mountain biking?'

'Yeah, let's go.'

So I went out to my shed and got my bike and we left. It took us about 15 minutes to get to Howth and we then decided to go up to the summit. We saw a new trail and we thought it would be good to go down it. I went down the trail first and Sean John followed me. We were going quite fast and some of the turns were quite sharp and had steep drops at the side of them. We had to really concentrate going down the trail because it was very technical in the turns, and the short steep down hills were the most challenging – you have to try not to fall off your bike and you need to pick your line in advance. When we got to the end of the trail, Sean John asked me if we could do the trail again.

'Yes, but this time you go first,' I replied.

We then got on our bikes and went out to the main road and cycled all the way up the hill.

Sean John said, 'This hill is very hard to cycle up but it will be worth it when we get to the top, and we get to go back down the trail.'

Sean John cycled down first. Peddling all the way down as fast as he could, even on the short steep down hill and on the turns and on the flat parts. Then just after the second last bend he hit a rock and it flew up and hit the disk break calliper on his bike and smashed it. Sean John didn't know that his calliper was smashed and I was really trying to keep up with him to warn him.

So I shouted, 'Slow down, Sean! Slow Down!'

Then he was trying to stop, but he couldn't and his front wheel hit a rock at some serious speed and he was not able to avoid it. He had hit a rock because his front break was not working. Then I heard a scream. Next thing I knew, Sean John was not there; he had disappeared. What had happened was, his front break calliper had smashed and he had swerved to avoid the rock but he swerved the wrong way. The corner of his tyre had hit the side of the rock and it had kicked the wheel off to the left and he had been knocked off the side of a cliff. Then I heard the sound of the bike hitting the water at the bottom.

At first I thought Sean John had died. I was very upset and didn't know what to do or think because I thought that my best friend had just died and all I could do was just stand there in shock.

Then I heard 'Help!' and I looked over the edge and I saw Sean John. He was on a ledge that had been only a five-foot drop and I helped him up and then we were both in shock. My best friend Sean John had just cycled off a cliff and he had not died or got hurt or even got a scratch on him. We both sat down for a few minutes in silence. We were both so happy that Sean John was OK. I could tell that Sean John was OK because he just sat there looking into the distance with a smile on his face. I asked him if he was all right because he had just cycled off a cliff and not died.

Sean John replied with, 'I don't feel pain.'

I then asked him, 'Where is the bike?'

He then said, 'The bike has fallen to the bottom.'

I then said, 'Well I'll go and get it.'

Sean John then hopped up and said, 'We will both go and get the bike,' then I said, 'No bother.'

At the bottom of the trail I could not see the bike, it was like it had just disappeared. Sean John and me were wondering what had happened to the bike.

'Look out there, the bike is sinking,' said Sean John.

'For fuck's sake! That was a nice bike and all,' I shouted in disappointment.

We both climbed back up to the top and Sean John had great difficulty because he thought he had broken his leg.

'My leg is really hurting, can we take a break at the top because I think my leg is broken.'

I climbed up to the top first and then I pulled Sean John up the last bit of it. At the top of the cliff I turned around and I saw this woman running towards us with a little dog that looked more like a rat than a dog.

'My name is Kate and this is my dog, Monster. We saw you fall and we called an ambulance and I told them what happened to you and they are on their way,' said Kate.

Sean John tried to jump up but fell back down straight away.

'Help me up, will you, there is no way I'm going in an ambulance!' shouted Sean John.

Then I got Sean John up and I put him on the frame of my bike and I cycled out to the main road. We then cycled back to my house. My dad was at home and we told him what had happened,

He said, 'I will bring you into the hospital and get your leg checked out.'

When we got to the hospital we put Sean John in a wheelchair and then we got him checked in. We got seen by a doctor right away. They gave Sean John an X-Ray,

The doctor said, 'Your leg is broken and you will need to have a cast on it for six weeks.'

That day, six weeks later, we went to the hospital with Sean John's new bike and my old bike on the roof of the car. Straight after the cast was taken off, we went mountain biking.

BRACE YOURSELF

Bronagh Furlong

Today couldn't get any worse. I'm grounded, I failed my math test and my Granny hates me. And now I'm stuck to this freak. It's all Daryl's fault. If he hadn't pushed me into this smell bag I wouldn't be in this situation.

And when I say stuck, I literally mean stuck. By the braces to be exact. Yeah, I know how the hell do you get your braces stuck to someone else's? And not just anyone, Debbie Hall. Not only is she the smelliest person in the school, actually no, the universe, she also happens to be the greasiest mo-fo EVER!

And before you make any assumptions, I was certainly NOT kissing Debbie Stinking Hall. Okay, so this is how it happened: I was walking down the hall minding my own business pushing first years into lockers, when boom! Daryl pushed me straight into this grease ball. At the time I was shouting and she was munching on a banana, so that exact millisecond that our mouths were open we collided, and here I am, stuck to this freak show with banana in my eye and up my nose. She's probably loving this, like, have you seen me? I was handed-crafted by God himself.

'Get the hell away from me,' I mumble trying to push her away.

I don't know if she understood me, ignored me or if she is just deaf, but she does not budge. I let out an annoyed sigh, and as I breathe back in, I smell her. I thought the whiff of her would knock me out cold. Imagine a bag of rotten greasy chips, in a bin, in a sewer and times it by twelve – that doesn't even come close to how she smells.

'No, this isn't going to work. We are getting pliers and pulling your teeth,' she must have heard because she starts to shake her head and panic.

'Oh come on, I need mine more than you do!' I grumble against her mouth.

Let's be real here for a minute people, what's a loser like Debbie Hall gonna do with a full set of teeth? Think of all the endless possibilities I could do with a full set of teeth.

Since Kermit the Frog over here doesn't seem to be doing anything to help, I (being the genius that I am) will have to be the brains and the looks of the operation.

'I swear if you don't come up with a way to release me in the next ten seconds, I will rip your teeth from your mouth.'

She begins to mumble something but I cannot concentrate with the stench of her breath.

'No, shut up – I do not want to smell your kaley breath, or whatever you type of people eat.'

Alright, to free myself from this smell of despair, broken dreams and kale, I have three options: pull out my teeth; pull out her teeth or go to the dentist. Although option two would be easiest, Ms Fussy over here won't comply so I guess it's to the dentist we go.

'Dentist. Ten minutes. Foot,' I think; Stinky over here grumbles.

She must be deranged if she thinks I'm going to a public dentist. 'Yeah, Wendy or whatever your name is, I am, under no circumstances, going to a public dentist.'

Oh, Oh Hell NO! She did not just roll her eyes at me! I am the best looking, best smelling and most popular guy in this school; actually scratch that, this planet (excluding Leonardo DiCaprio obvo). I am Toby Quinn for the love of God!

'Right Kermit, Wendy, Kale-Face I am Toby—'

'Yeah I know who you are, you're a stuck up, self-centred prick.'

I am gob-smacked, how dare she! The absolute cheek! Self-centred? This one time when I dropped my sandwich on the wet ground, and it was all soggy and wet, I gave it to a homeless man.

'Now I don't care what your bloody name is, we are going to the closest dentist now.'

I feel a sharp tug on my teeth as Debbie begins to trudge towards the school fire exit. I have had some good times on these stairs. This one time, I pushed a third year down the stairs and locked him out. Good times. Never would I have thought I'd be coming down here stuck to Debbie Chip-Pan Hall!

The journey to the dentist is short but extremely painful. I won't go into too much detail to spare you the second hand pain and embarrassment, but what I will say is that we had to awkwardly side shuffle while staring into each other's eyes. One word: eugh. I have to say I am glad this public dentist is on the ground floor. As we hobble in people stare at us; they must be thinking, what's a God like him doing with an onion like her. Like, come on, my Granny's big toe is better looking than her. Speaking of which, I better go apologise to her once I'm free from here.

The dentist walks out and laughs, 'Debbie and friend come in here.'

I'm not surprised he knew it was her, he could probably smell her the second she trudged through the door. It takes him less than a minute to release me from her. He doesn't even question how we got stuck, which makes me feel sick because he probably thinks we were kissing. But I don't need to defend myself to a public dentist so I just leave. And that was the end of that.

But before I left, Debbie said the strangest thing to me, 'Oh by the way, maybe you should have a shower, you stink.'

This is not a cliché story about people's braces getting stuck together. I didn't fall in love with Debbie Hall, but I suppose she'd be alright if she cut back on the kale and showered once in a while.

WASTING

Aaron Gorman

'James Delaney?'

'Present, Miss.'

Meet James Delaney, a fifteen-year-old, socially awkward, straight-A student from a wealthy family with a big house on the outskirts of Dublin.

'Everybody listen up,' began Miss Alexander, 'You will all be repeating last week's chemical-bonding test on Wednesday as you all failed, except for James who passed with 100 percent.'

'Someone tell Elena Jones to be in class for this test I haven't—'

'Ah Miss, she'll be down the shop with a smoke in her hand and some youngfle' wrapped around her as always,' interrupted Louis Maher, who wasn't much better than she was.

'As I was saying, before I was rudely interrupted, I haven't seen her since last Monday. I want her in,' concluded Miss Alexander.

'Elena is never in,' laughed Liam to James, as the two so-called losers of the class sat up the front, eager to learn.

When school had finished, James arrived home to his quiet, lonely house away from everything. He went straight to his room to study, although he had no tests.

'Well James, how was school?' asked his mother, as soon as James sat down at the table for dinner. He had just sat down and he was already being asked questions.

'It was great,' he began, 'We got our chemistry tests back and—'

His father looked up slowly. His father was a wealthy landlord who owned a lot of apartments and holiday homes across Europe.

'What did you get?' he questioned.

'100%, I was the only one in the class to pass,' he replied with a proud smile on his face.

'Good. Better stay that way,' finished his father as he returned to reading the paper at the table in silence. When James had finished, he dragged his feet through the halls and up the stairs before falling face first onto his bed.

James had an obsession about other people's lives and how their minds worked. He would always study psychology in his spare time.

James had picked psychology as an option subject when he first came to secondary school and his teacher was as curious about the human mind as he was.

The next day in class, James' world came crashing down.

'James? Here as always, Kate? Yep. And finally Elena who obviously isn't—'

'Here down the back, yea,' answered Elena roughly.

'Wow, Miss Jones, you've shown your face in my psychology class . . . for once,' laughed Mr Dunne to himself.

'Now class, today I will be putting you in pairs for a little project I have designed. This project will run over six weeks and must be followed strictly in order to pass,' he explained. 'In your pairs you must step into the life of the other person for three weeks and they will do the same after your three weeks are up. You will have to sit beside them in each class you have together and you must take part in some sort of activity with your partner outside of school each week. I have left a sheet at the back of the class of all the pairs and no one will be allowed to change,' concluded Mr Dunne.

When the bell rang James was left in shock after seeing who he was paired with.

'Sir, this isn't fair. She's a knacker! Like just—'

'JAMES, we don't speak about people like that in my class, and besides maybe being paired with Elena isn't all that bad? You might learn a thing or two from her,' he said as he buttoned his black trench coat and walked out of the classroom.

James had never spoken to Elena but he knew all about her being into drinking and doing crazy amounts of drugs.

He was scared.

Scared of what this whole experience might drag him into, scared of how he might not be the same but most of all, scared he wouldn't get out alive.

Wednesday came and his first day with Elena began. She had to sit her chemistry test and was pushing James to give her the answers she needed.

'Just give me the answer, don't be actin' the fool you,' she rudely snapped midway through the test.

'Look just do the test yourse—'

'JAMES! JOURNAL ON MY DESK NOW!' Roared Miss Alexander from the top of the class. This was the first time he had ever been shouted at and to say he was close to tears would be an understatement. When the class ended James stayed behind to talk with Miss Alexander.

'Miss, I swear I didn't tell her anything, I was only telling her to do the test herself,' he protested.

'Look James, normally I'd give a note for something like this but I'll let you off this time. Just don't let it happen again.' She sent James on his way.

Elena was up first to spend three weeks in James' life and she didn't take part in any activities over the three weeks, as she didn't care about her grades but when James' turn to step into her world came around it affected him on a much larger scale.

'You're in my world now,' Elena began, 'You're coming to a party tomorrow night and we aren't going to school, understand?' She finished and James' worst fears were rapidly becoming a reality.

When James got home he told his parents he was going around to Liam's house to study for his English test in two days' time. His father wasn't concerned but his mother knew there was something wrong.

'James, what's wrong? I know something's up,' questioned his mother in a worried tone.

'Nothing alright! Get out of my room now!' he responded as he got in to bed and lay worrying about what the next day would bring.

He woke up and stuffed clothes into a P.E. bag to change into when he met Elena around the corner from the school. He walked out of his house and got his normal bus to the stop outside his school. He hesitated for a moment but the thought of potentially failing an assignment forced him away from the school to meet Elena.

He met her down a small lane where she was having a smoke and drinking what looked to James like a can of cider.

'Come on you, me gaff's a ten minute stroll from here. We cruise up and chill there for a while yeah?' insisted Elena to James who was completely clueless as to what had just come out of Elena's mouth.

'Excuse me, eh, I didn't understand that,' replied James with an awkward look on his face.

'Look, I wasn't born with a silver spoon in my arse like most of your little mates, if you even have any, so don't be gettin' cheeky yeah? Just stay quiet and follow me,' snapped Elena and it took James less than a second to shut himself up. They arrived to Elena's house, which was a two-bedroom flat with the front door hanging on one hinge.

'Is there anywhere I can get changed?' asked James as he tried to find the beauty in such an ugly place.

'The jacks is down the hall there, second door on the left,' she replied but James once again didn't understand her.

'Ehm, what's "the jacks" Elena?' James was curious to find out how this absurd language worked.

'THE TOILET, JAMES, second door on the left.' She made herself loud and clear.

They stayed in the so-called house until 6pm, before leaving to go to the off-licence. Elena walked in with 20 euro and came out with two naggins, one for her and one for James.

'I don't drink,' James insisted.

'If you want me to tell Mr Dunne that you took part in everything I suggest you down the thing before we get to this party,' ordered Elena and within ten minutes James was getting sick at the side of the road.

They arrived at an abandoned house and climbed through a window at the side of the broken up home.

When James finally got in after falling numerous times, he was greeted by a group of lads. They handed him a drink that had been mixed with ecstasy and James soon found himself panned out underneath a tree with no clothes on. When he arrived home still out of his head his father gave him an earful.

'STUDYING AT LIAM'S? IT'S TWO O'CLOCK IN THE MORNING! DO YOU HAVE ANYTHING TO SAY FOR YOURSELF?' Roared his father as James tried to process what was going on.

'Haha, piss off you old stump, you're a short jog away from having a stroke,' laughed James as he tried to pull himself up the stairs to bed.

He woke up the next morning still drunk and affected by the drugs he had taken, but managed to remember that he had an English test to take and shot up out of bed, threw his clothes on and ran out the door while holding his middle finger up to his father who was shouting at him from the door.

'JAMES YOU DON'T COME BACK TO THIS HOME UNTIL YOU GET YOUR HEAD STRAIGHT, UNDERSTAND ME?' Roared his father as he ran out the gate.

'AND KEEP YOUR CLOTHES ON THIS TIME!' He concluded.

When he arrived at school he was greeted by the principal and a late note was written in his journal. He ran down the hall, straight to English. He did his test and it was corrected in class. He was expecting his usual A grade but to his shock a big 'F' was written in red on his page. He was slipping, and quickly.

When he got home he did his bit of homework and Liam came over. Everything was normal until James told Liam what had happened the previous night.

'You're turning into a waster! Do you want to waste your life?' roared Liam before being told to get out of the house before James would 'thump the neck off him.' James was losing everything and everyone could see it, everyone except himself.

The next day in psychology class the roll was taken and rather than James responding with his usual 'Present Sir', Mr Dunne was met with 'What'sup yeah, down the back.' He paid no attention to it and continued with the class.

Rather than going home after school James went over to Elena's for their second 'activity'. Elena took James to a rough spot in town and after a few cans and one or two joints James was back to swinging his jaw from left to right. Not only was his jaw swinging, his fists were too. He had punched some guy and broke his nose because he gave him dirty looks. James was left sitting with Elena on the quays where the pair slept the night. They had also gotten together while sitting on the edge on the path.

James woke up with Elena on top of him. He had broken his knuckles from fighting the previous night. He bonked the dart home and kicked open his front door breaking the bottom off. When his parents got home from work they sat James down to talk about the direction his life was heading.

'James, do you want your life to be thrown away?' His father questioned.

'Do you want your skull to be caved in? No, so shut your mouth,' he replied as he got up and walked out.

His father walked into the sitting room and sat down with his mother.

'Look I've gotten him a place in boarding school off the coast of Galway for a few months. He leaves next week,' said his father to his mother.

★

'Class, this is your last week of the assignment and I suggest you make the most of it,' stated Mr Dunne.

James decided that this week was his. He would live Elena's life without her, and everyday on his way back from school he rolled up a joint and smoked it to himself and would arrive home higher than a kite.

His life was wasting away.

On the Friday of that week he decided to go out with a bang. It was only eight o'clock and he had already downed a naggin, had two cans and taken numerous amounts of drugs. He fought numerous people and eventually punched a girl – knocked her clean out. That girl was Elena.

When he realised what he had done he bent down and checked for a pulse or her breathing.

There was nothing.

No one could know what he did, no one.

He knew that no one had seen him and that if he didn't do something or leave soon he would be put in a detention centre. But he had already put himself somewhere else.

He ran home and when he got to his door there were suitcases with his name on them and a bus ticket to Galway.

'WHAT THE FUCK IS GOING ON? MA? DA? SOMEONE?' he roared in the pouring rain.

'Take your shit and leave, James, you're not welcome in this home anymore until you sort yourself out. Get yourself to your auntie's and on a bus tomorrow, you're going to boarding school for a few months and don't try and fight it. Good luck, James,' ended his father as he slammed the window shut.

James was on the next bus to Galway and was put on a small boat with all his belongings. He got to the complex and was given a small room to himself. He was called to attend his first class and was given a seat at the front.

This is when he realised what he had done. He also realised that what he had done could not be changed and to never look back, that the past is dead and buried. You get nothing from living there and that it's all about today.

So he sat in silence waiting for his name to be called.

'James Delaney?'

'Present, Miss.'

THE LIFE OF AN ALCOHOLIC BODYBUILDER

Jamie Hannon

'Hey I'm Brent, Steve's friend. When I saw Steve drink that beer I knew there was something wrong, because Steve had just finished a workout and he was really hyper and giddy all of a sudden. I know that mightn't sound that bad but normally Steve can barely talk after a workout and now he's jumping around and full of energy. I was laughing at the time but I'm worried now cause he's drinking the beer a lot now. I don't think he realises it's not a protein shake, it's just beer with some protein in it.'

I start my day off at the gym so early that I'm there before the guy who owns the gym. It's nothing too bad, just jogging on a tread-mill for an hour before breakfast. For breakfast I've eggs, porridge and toast. Then I head to go to the Passion Nutrition store to get some supplements and do a photo-shoot, as Passion have released a new product called alchotein and I'm going to be the first person to try it. The product is the world's first protein beer and they say it's going to be the best one ever made.

I took my first sip and it was the nicest drink I have ever had and even better, it had protein in it. It was good fun doing the photo-shoot with the beer. It made me a little light-headed after a couple of them but it wasn't that bad. The taste was so nice like it was almost addictive.

My friend said he'd give me a lift home because I was a bit tipsy. The next day I woke up and headed for the gym to do a quick chest workout. After my workout I went to grab my protein shake when I saw the alchotein. I remembered the taste of it so popped the lid off and drank the entire bottle in one big gulp. The taste was as amazing as it was yesterday. I went to Passion Nutrition to get more of the stuff.

WEEK 1

I really like the alchotein. I don't feel as tired as I usually do after a workout. I'm really starting to like this product. I can have a couple of drinks after a workout and not feel bad because it helps me recover.

WEEK 2

I'm starting to have alchotein during a workout to help me recover faster.

WEEK 3

I have alchotein now with my breakfast instead of having a coffee, as it's more protein with my breakfast. I feel a little stiff but it's probably from my workout.

WEEK 4

I'm doing a workout but the flexibility in my legs is starting to get a little bad but it's probably from not stretching enough.

WEEK 5

My abs are starting to be a little less visible and I'm starting to bloat easier.

WEEK 6

I've started to get a little chubby and slower and I can't think of why it's happening. I'm eating less and running more but I don't know why. I might need more protein so I might drink more alchotein.

WEEK 7
I've upped the amount of alchotein I'm taking. I have one with every meal and now I have one during every workout.

WEEK 8
I've started to drink the alchotein throughout the day and still haven't seen much progress.

WEEK 9
I'm starting to wake up at two or three o'clock in the morning and find it hard to go back asleep. I'm starting to get terrible cravings for the alchotein.

WEEK 10
I've just lost my licence for drinking the alchotein in my jeep after my workout. I might have to get the bus to the gym now because I won't get my licence back for months.

WEEK 11
I'm starting to go broke so I'm going to have to stop going to the gym for a while, while I sort out all this mess.

WEEK 12
I've just had a big fight with my friend Brent over me drinking the alchotein. He said that I'm addicted to it.

WEEK 13
I'm starting to eat less now and drink the alchotein instead. I get full really quickly.

WEEK 14
I was in the middle of a workout when the manager of Passion Nutrition came up to me and said I better get back into shape or else Passion will fire me. I just realised how badly I've treated my body

and that Brent was right. I need help. I've never been addicted to anything but working out. It's a strange feeling. I've only really noticed it's making me fatter and slower. I turned up outside the clinic in my shiny black Range Rover. I killed the engine and got out and headed inside. I picked up a magazine and flicked through it when I saw that Kanye West wants to run for the US presidency. I read a few lines and laughed at how ridiculous it was and threw the magazine down onto the table. The phone rang and the receptionist answered and then told me my counsellor could see me now. The door was across the reception area. I saw her name on the door. It was Sara Wilson Parks. I knocked on the door and went through. Sitting behind the desk was a slim blonde who was probably in her mid 20s.

'Hello,' the counsellor said.

'Hi,' I said back sheepishly.

'My name is Sara, what's yours?'

'Steve.'

'Why are you here Steve?'

'Because I've a problem.'

'Go on?' she said leaning in.

'M...m...my problem is— ' I struggled to say much cause not only I thought she would judge me but she was also gorgeous.

'Go on, you can tell me.'

I sat a bit awkwardly trying not to show I wasn't in the best shape of my life. I started to talk to her more and I started trusting her more.

THREE MONTHS LATER

I arrived at Gold's Gym half an hour before the photo-shoot so that I could get a pump because my arms felt a bit small. I started to think about how out of shape I was before. After the shoot I was going to go out and meet Sara. I haven't a drop of alchotein since I've met her. I went and got changed out of my shorts and into my tracksuit bottoms. On the way out of the gym I saw a bowl of peanuts so I grabbed some cause I was hungry. I started to eat them when suddenly my throat feels like there's something stuck in it. I start cough-ing and spluttering. One of the peanuts was caught in my throat! I felt light-headed and started to stumble. I tripped and fell and then I blacked out.

THE FRONTIER

Paul Herron

Night time at the Frontier was a never-ending oddity. The sky was as dark as dark could get, and darker still. Your eyes would need to adapt to the conditions, but Pearse and Huxley had plenty of time to adjust. Pearse was walking ahead of Huxley, who decided to break the silence with a question.

' . . . Hey Pearse,' said Huxley.

'Yeah, Huxley?' Pearse replied.

'How long have we been walking?'

'Have you not been paying attention?'

'Look, cut me some slack, ever since we left the crash, I've been drawing a blank. Can't you check your watch?'

'Can't you check yours? Mines busted. Must've broke in the crash.'

'Yeah . . . I ain't got one.'

'Oh for Gods' sake, Huxley!'

'Alright, look, forget it! I'm just sick of walking! We have nothing to gain from walking! If I kill a guy, I get his gear. If I just stand still and do nothing, I'd be able to hear what's around me, and nothing can hear me. But we're just acting without aim!'

'If you never walk, you'll never get to where you want to go.'

'Well yes, but what about when you have no idea where you're going? I hate not knowing what I'll find!' Pearse had to agree with him there.

The pair had been walking for Gods' know how long now. Time seemed to melt and distort in the Frontier. The constant cold, dark and howling of the wind were oddly distracting. Pearse couldn't remember the last time he saw the sun. Even if it was daytime, you couldn't see it past the canopy that covered the forest.

'If you want a rough estimate, which is all I can really provide at this point,' Pearse began, 'I'd say we've been walking for a couple days ... or at least it feels like that ... '

'Yeah, I get you, but how can it be a couple days if it's been dark for so long?' Huxley asked.

'I wish I knew' Pearse answered. 'I think the Frontier itself is messing with us, man. I've been feeling kinda off. My thoughts are fading and it's as if I'm running off instinct. They said back on base that spending too long here can make a man turn feral, and I'm starting to believe them.'

'Hey, Hey, don't go all Lord of the Flies on me, Pearse. I feel fine! I'm hungry and goddamn exhausted, but I'm mentally fine. I get that I've been pessimistic, but I refuse to let this hellhole get the better of me.' Huxley spoke with a sort of pride Pearse didn't expect from his ususal rational-but-snide outlook. If he could pull through, so could Pearse.

'You're right. But we're going to need food and water. We can't live off of the flasks we smuggled in. Whiskey only numbs the pain so much,' said Pearse.

'Eh, we'll find something,' said Huxley. 'We're military. Built to survive!'

Some indefinite amout of time later, Pearse and Huxley were barely hanging onto conciousness. They deprived themselves of rest in the hopes of finding some form of animal they could hunt, but nothing came. Not even a bird in the sky.

'Okay man' Huxley said in a tired voice 'I'm feeling pretty miserable right now. Like, ready-to-accept-death miserable. Wanna play rock paper scissors to see which one of us gets to eat the other?' Huxley let out a weak laugh.

'Come on, there has to be something,' Pearse said.

Just as the two of them were about to drop to their knees and succumb to the fatigue, the darkness peeled away to reveal one small blessing in their favour. A log cabin.

'SANCTUARY!' shouted Huxley, choking out a cough in all the exertion.

Pearse continued walking towards the house, with Huxley loosely in tow. Once he reached the front door, he noticed a sign on the wall. It read 'Redcroft'.

'Must be a family name,' Pearse thought to himself.

As he opened the door, the snow started to leak in. The wind pushed the door back against the wall. The room was too dark to really see anything. He took a step inside and felt around for a light switch. The chances of this house having fully functioning infastructure were very low, but he was in desperate need of light. His fingers glided over what felt like a switch and he flicked it. The light, understandably, was faint and flickering, but worked nonetheless. The house was dusty and covered in cobwebs. Clearly these Redcrofts were evicted some time ago. With the lights on, the contents of the house were visible to Pearse and Huxley, among which was a wolfhound, who didn't look too happy to see them.

They geared up to run, or do whatever they could do in their state, but calmed down when they realised the dog wasn't moving.

'Wonder what he's doing here,' said Huxley inquisitively.

'Me too, but he couldn't have been here for too long. He'd be dead otherwise,' Pearse explained.

'Maybe this little mongrel ate all the aimals before we could,' Huxley said.

'Calm down, buddy, I'll find us some food,' said Pearse.

Pearse walked in as Huxley leaned on the doorframe, inspecting the homestead for himself.

'Hey,' Huxley began 'Do you think this counts as breaking and entering?'

'Heh heh. I guess it would if there was somebody to break in on,'

Pearse responded, light-heartedly, anyways, you go look around the outside of the house, I'll find some grub.'

'You got it, boss.' Huxley said, putting his hand to his forehead in a mock salute. Just before he walked out, he turned back and said 'You better not hold out on me, man.'

'Wouldn't dream of it. Scout's honour,' Pearse said.

Huxley ran the perimeter and through an amazing stroke of luck, Pearse found a couple old cans of food. He opened one up and dug in. It wasn't very appetising. He looked at the can. It was marked 'Dog Food'.

Pearse continued eating after realising; he really didn't care.

'Huxley!' Pearse hollered, 'I found some food!'

'Awesome, on my way!' Huxley responded.

Pearse figured he had enough when he noticed the dog in the corner of his eye. It was laying sprawled on its bed, and it was taking a lot out of it just to growl at him. Pearse actually felt rather sorry for the poor thing. Slowly, he approached the hound and gave it the rest of the can.

'There you go,' he thought, 'Only right that I give the dog food to the actual dog.'

The dog started eating at its own pace, and seemed more accepting of Pearse's presence. Pearse was starting to feel less paranoid about his situation, but he still felt slower than usual. Pearse felt some rest would help, so he slumped into the couch and passed out in seconds.

Pearse woke up some time later, feeling significantly refreshed. He looked around and saw, and heard, Huxley sleeping. The dog looked stronger and calmer now.

'Hmm. I guess if it didn't like us, it would've killed us by now.' Pearse thought. He got up and shouted at Huxley to wake up.

'C'mon, man! No rest for the wicked, let's go!'

'Uhhh, what the hell? I wouldn't wake you up all abrupt like that!' Huxley groaned.

'Actually, with the way you were snoring, you probably did wake me up,' Pearse responded.

Huxley pulled himself together slowly. 'Some soldier you are,' Pearse thought mockingly.

'Hey, check out what I found out back,' Huxley said. He pointed towards a big hunting rifle leaning against the wall with five .308 rounds. Huxley looked quietly proud of himself, and given that they didn't have firearms of their own, he pretty much had every right to be. Pearse then picked it up.

'Yeah, you have it. You were always the better shot than me,' said Huxley. Pearse started loading the rifle when Huxley looked out the window.

'Jesus, it's still pitch black! I could've sworn day would break by now!' Huxley said with surprise.

'Maybe the sun can't get through the canopy,' Pearse suggested.

'Nah, it's waaay too dark for that.'

Pearse inspected the rifle. It was quite old, but well made. The metal wasn't rusted or aything, but the wood had chipped and scratched in places. There was a very decorative engravement on the fore end wood. It read out 'Hammond'.

'Hammond Redcroft?' Pearse thought. 'Maybe.'

He then slung it around his back and pulled out a badge and tag. The inscription read: Trunduskan Military Force: Scout Division Name: Pearse Cosgrave. Truduska was their home. The only real city throughout all the Frontier. A shield that stood strong against the sharp cold, and crippling insanity.

'Getting homesick?' Huxley asked.

'I've been nothing but, man,' Pearse replied. He was tired, but not in the same way he had been hours before. 'Sleeping on that couch wasn't much different than lying face down on a rock.'

'I hear you. Right now, ain't nothing I wouldn't do for a bunk in the scouts barracks.'

'You hate the scouts' barracks.'

'Yeah, and doesn't that freakin' say something about our situation?'

For a moment, things felt calm. The two soldiers slumped down into the couch and simultaneously let out a sigh.

Then the dog barked, and this time, it wasn't at them.

Something was outside.

Pearse had seen animals on other, more successful trips through the Frontier, but since he woke up at the crash, he had seen no other living thing other than Huxley and the dog. It was as if the fauna avoided this place. The Frontier was massive and Pearse wasn't in the best of sorts when he came to, so it would've made sense if all that wandering didn't equate to much.

A low growl could be heard from outside. It sounded otherworldly, almost. It was so gutteral it made the cabin shake lightly and resonated through the air with a strength that struck Pearse hard with terror.

Both Pearse and Huxley went to the back end of the house to get the dog, thinking it was a good idea to have a bit of backup. Pearse finally got a look at the dog's collar.

'Hey, apparently the dog's name is Red,' he said.

'Huh, Red. Redcroft. How creative,' Huxley said, sarcastically. Snarking was a defence mechanism of his. The dog didn't snap or growl, but perhaps it was preoccupied by what was outside. Pearse swung the rifle off his shoulder and held it firmly in his hands. Suddenly, something sprinted across the roof and landed across the way and into the trees. Red jump-started into action and bolted out the front door, which Huxley had left wide open.

'Crap, get back here!' Huxley growled, and chased after the dog, prompting Pearse to follow, rifle in hand.

Pearse stood just outside the door, looking ahead at Huxley, who himself was looking at Red. The dog was staring transfixed on a single spot behind the tree trunks. Pearse slowly walked up beside Huxley, eye down the sights of the rifle.

'What. The. Hell, Huxley!?' Pearse half whispered, half shouted at Huxley 'Did you seriously leave the door swinging open? When we were sleeping!?'

'Chrissakes, I'm sorry! I dropped the second I walked back into the house! Now, can we please concentrate on *this*?' Huxley replied, pointing towards Red. Pearse looked towards the spot and strained to see past the darkness. Red kept on growling at whatever was lurking just out of his sight. If the sun was actually shining through this damed forest, and it should have been, Pearse would've seen it by now. Then, somethig stood out of the darkness. It seemed to glow, or even shine, in contrast to the thick, inky black dackdrop. It was an eye. Not a pair of eyes. Just one, large, unblinking eye.

Unlike any other animal, the eye ran down diagonally from one point to another. What should have been the whites of its eye was instead a bright yellow, liquid and acidic, like it could burn through skin. Its iris was red, all ablaze in primal rage. The dark, long slit in its centre, which was its pupil, stared directly at Pearse. It twitched and spasmed violetly, but it never looked away, not at Red, not at Huxley, always at Pearse. All of its features combined to make it look like a ball of explosive power that would burst at the slightest touch.

'What the fuuuuuuh . . . ?' Huxley slurred, leaning forward in confusion. Suddenly, perhaps to respond, the thing reeled back into the darkness. It was getting ready to attack. Pearse and Huxley both panicked in separate ways. Huxley jumped back and fell, whilst Pearse shot into the dark. The boom of the rifle was almost like thunder flying from his hands . Red, spooked by all the sudden commotion, started running away. Huxley yelled for Pearse to 'fucking run!' And that's what Pearse did. He attempted to trail Red through the woods and prayed Huxley would follow. The darkness was stripped away bit by bit as he ran. It seemed as if the sun, no, the moon, had found its way through a few cracks in the branches. Pearse dodged and swerved to avoid roots and branches out to trip him up. He began to break down as the world seemed to be breaking its own rules. Was it *really* still night? How could everything that's happened since the crash be in one night? And what in the hell was that monster!? He snapped out of it and continued sprinting to 'safety'. Far behind him, Pearse could hear, as well as feel, the gurgling growl from before, but this time, it rose into a piercing shriek. It echoed through the Frontier. Pearse wouldn't have been surprised if people in Trunduska could hear it.

After running for several minutes and not daring to stop, Pearse finally found Red in a small clearing. And Huxley was sitting in front of him, both of them staring at each other. Huxley was taking swigs from his pocket flask. When did he get here? The two were sitting just outside of a large cave. When Huxley noticed Pearse, he got up and walked over to him and smiled.

'Pearse! I was hoping you were alright! Man, that thing got me bad. I could've sworn I was dead.'

'Yeah, I'm glad to see you too, man. Say, what were you doing with the dog?'

'Red? I found him there, sitting right there, in front of the cave. I wouldn't dare go in, though, so I just sat down with him and took it easy. It's funny . . . how he can sorta stare right through you.'

'Right, okay, well I'm going in the cave.'

'Wait, you sure about that? How do you know what's in there?'

'Well, you and Red have been out here for however long and you're both fine. Besides, look at the old sign up there.'

Huxley inspected around the cave to see a sign that read 'Trunduskan Ore Mine'.

'See?' Pearse said 'This is a sign we're getting closer! I mean, I doubt there's people in here, but there must be something!

'Huh. Well thank the Gods.'

Pearse and Huxley entered with Red in tow.

As Pearse walked in, he could feel himself slipping little by little. Though this was a calm moment in light of recent events, the sudden spike of adrenaline and terror that the encounter with the creature gave him, mixed with the creeping insanity and paranoia, made him feel like less of a man and more like an animal. Like prey being stalked by an unseen predator. Pearse stopped for a second to gather himself. Huxley gave him a concerned look, but Pearse held his head high and nodded to keep walking. He was not going to let the Frontier warp him any more than it already had.

Pearse almost tripped over something in the dark and kneeled down. It was a sizeable wooden stick. Beside it, a white, blotchy piece of fabric.

'Hey wrap that around the stick and douse it with some whiskey. I'd give you some from my flask but, eh, I'm all out,' Huxley said.

'Just can't make anything last, can you?' Pearse jeered. Huxley sighed and shrugged in response.

Pearse did as Huxley said and sparked it with some flint. They now had a torch. As the room exploded with a yellow light, which died down into a more manageable orange glow, they could now see the crushed bones and dried crimson that painted the walls. Even Red seemed to step back in shock. Pearse had officially lost hope on seeing another human.

Mangled corpses and skeletons littered the cave. Pearse wouldn't have been able to tell who they were if not for the scraps of camou-flaged clothing and metal badges he found.

'By the Gods, they're military,.' said Huxley, voice shaking in ter-ror ' . . . this is where they went . . . '

The two picked up some of the badges. Pvt. Jay Garrett. Sgt. Thomas Harper. Some of them were too ruined and filthy to read. They were the troops Pearse and Huxley had been transported with. They were all dead, yet somehow, Pearse and Huxley still lived. Did the creature simply not see them in the wreckage? Whatever the case, this beast was strong enough, or smart enough, to slaughter an entire platoon, and that is no small feat. Pearse dropped the badges and walked ahead, with Huxley and Red behind him.

The trio continued on, looking aghast at the gruesome display. Some of the skeletons, or what remained of them, hung from the cave walls, like a gallery of gore. Most were human, but a lot of them were animals.

This explains where all the other animals went, Pearse thought to himself. The floor and bones were covered in blood and viscera glis-tened on the walls, even the ceiling. Pearse could practically taste the copper. As the two walked, the cave got bigger and the light began to stray from the surface of the walls. It was as if it was open-ing up into a huge chasm. However, the torch was no longer the only light in the cave.As the corridor stretched lower and further, a faint glow appeared. Pearse knew the chances of it being another random guy were extremely low, but he picked up the pace and made his way towards it.

'Wait, Pearse!' Huxley demanded. Pearse turned around to see Red right behind him, but Huxley standing a few paces back. 'We've seen more than enough. We should leave. We might not get the chance to if we continue.'

'Huxley,' Pearse began 'I've been losing hope more and more as the da— night goes on. I want to know what the hell is going on. Whatever happens, I accept my fate, and if I don't die, fantastic.'

There was a silence. Huxley let out a huge sigh.

'Fuck it.' Huxley walked up beside him and they pressed on.

'Besides, I still got this!' said Pearse, showing off the rifle slung on his shoulder.

'Maybe so, but how many shots do you even have?'

'Enough to kill.'

'Enough to kill who?'

'No. it's not going down like that. Don't even go there.'

'Okay, just . . . just being sure.'

They soon found themselves standing on the border of a relatively small cave gaping into a full blown cavern. Here, Pearse, Huxley and Red all saw the most eldritch, mind-warping thing in all the Frontier.

The far off walls of the caverns writhed with the movement of countless . . . things. Pearse couldn't see what they were, but the motion was clear, like a swarm of insects. Small specks of light shined then faded, like twinkling stars, but less enchanting and more grotesque against the pulsating background of the creatures. Within the centre of this ant colony from Hell was a large, organic looking structure. It glowed the same acidic yellow as the 'stars' that covered the cavern, as the eye in the forest. It was rooted into the rock like a tree. Large blotches of yellow protruded from its strange, callous shell, like massive cysts. Some of the creatures seemed to be maintaining it, crawling up and down the length of the structure. In the core of the structure was . . . a person? Pearse doubted it, but it looked humanoid from this distance. It must have been a good bit bigger than its thralls. It looked almost 'regal' in comparison. Besides the yellow, it emitted its own royal purple aura.

'Gods . . . ' Huxley whispered, entranced by the sight, much like Pearse. The two stopped gawking when the figure inside the structure jerked its arm towards them. The cavern rumbled with a chorus of screams that seemed to harmonise into one almost, but not quite feminine voice.

'KILL.'

Then the beasts caught on to their presence. The thousands of little lights stopped flickering and moving and all converged on Pearse, Huxley and Red.

'Ohhhhhhhh heeeeeEEEEEELLL NOOOOOO!' Huxley shouted as he started running. Powered by pure terror, the three bolted right back the way they came. The screams began again, but there were no words to harmonise them. The hive was ready to hunt.

They were about half way through the cave before Pearse realised the entire hive was going to follow him if they didn't find a way to close off the pass.

'Huxley! We need to collapse the mine!' Pearse shouted.

'Well, let me know when you think of something, then!' Huxley shouted back.

Behind the bloody display, Pearse could see the supports holding up the mine. If he brought some of them down, the mine would cave in. Pearse stopped every few seconds to bash in the struts with the rifle's stock, but it was costing him time. Enough time for one of the beasts to catch up with him. Bastard must've gotten a head start on the chase. Pearse couldn't fully see the monster before him.

'Huxley!' he shouted. Huxley stopped and turned to see the position Pearse was in. Huxley had a two-second dilemma on whether to help him or run. As the beast sized Pearse up, he decided to rush to his rescue.

'Pearse, Roll!' He shouted back. Pearse rolled to his right just as the monster pounced. It landed not far from Huxley's feet, and before it could react, Red bit into one of its legs. Then, Pearse ran in and brought his boot down on its neck. He then blew its head off to be sure it was dead.

'That was kick-ass! You didn't even need me for that!' said Huxley.

'I appreciate your attempt, NOW RUN!' Pearse replied.

Pearse bashed out one last support and he could hear the cave buckling. Red dashed ahead of him and Huxley continued running. Pearse gathered his strength to reach the entrance and dived at the last step to avoid the falling boulders. He landed on his stomach, narrowly avoiding death. Once more, he heard the shrieks of the monsters inside the mine, but it was not the triumphant roar of a hunter. It was the agonising cry of a dying animal. Some of them must've gotten crushed in the cave in. Good. Pearse, still lying on the ground, had sarificed the last of his vigour to get out of that disaster. Huxley ran over and kneeled over him.

'Oh no. No nononono, stay with me, alright? Come on, get up!' Huxley stopped for a second and looked out to the woods. He stood up and ran out to the trees, shouting for help. Red ran up to Pearse and started sniffing him and whining. That was the last thing he remembered before he blacked out.

Pearse woke up with a flashlight shining in his eyes. For a second, he thought he had made it to the pearly gates. He felt relieved, yet a bit disappointed, when he found out he wasn't actually dead, but thanked the Gods as he had been found by the Trunduskan Military. The man looking down on him was wearing the same battle harness as a combat medic. He glared at him and his eyes widened as Pearse regained his conciousness. He then turned his head quickly to his right.

'Hey!' he said 'He's waking up!' Another voice came from behind him.

'Really!? Shit, I thought he was dead!'

'Well, so did I,' the voice responded.

'Heh, so did I . . . ' said a third voice. It was Huxley.

Pearse turned to see Huxley lying in the snow, practically frozen over. He looked so tired and bleak, like a zombie.

'I, I tried to get somebody's attention . . . while you were out cold. I gave you . . . my coat . . . and eventually . . . I dropped too.'

Pearse didn't have another coat over him, soldiers must have taken it thinking he was dead. He started to get up. As he got to his knees, the troop stepped forward to help him up. Once he was standing, the soldier stepped back and took a rigid position.

'Name and rank,' he said.

'Tell him everything,' Pearse heard Huxley say faintly, 'worry about me later.'

'Pearse Cosgrave, Private First Class, Scout Division,' Pearse responded, still very tired. 'Uhh, how's . . . how is . . . '

'Take your time, Private. I'm Corporal Manson. I need you to tell me what happened.'

The other soldier made his way over to Pearse.

'We were running,' Pearse began, 'My platoon were headed across the Frontier . . . scouting uncharted territory. I don't remember well, but I think a storm hit out transport . . . we crashed . . . '

'Are there any other survivors?' Manson asked.

'No, I saw their shredded corpses in th—' Pearse cut himself off. The bodies were in the mine he had just collapsed. He couldn't show them.

'Shredded!' exclaimed the other soldier 'The hell do you mean shredded?' Pearse decided to come clean.

'We were being hunted by something. I don't know how to explain it. There were even more in the mine. I,-I had to lock them in, they were going to kill me! Please believe me, there is something in the Frontier and it's not safe for anybody. Not even the military.'

Manson and the other soldier stood for a second in silence, the kind of silence bred from disbelief and confusion.

'Pearse . . . ' Manson said, calmly. 'Spending too long in the Frontier has been known to . . . affect people. Even combat trained troops. I'm afraid I can't just take your word because of your condition.'

'I don't know, sir,' said the other soldier. 'The mine wasn't caved in the last time we patrolled here. Maybe his story's got a bit of truth in it.'

'Ask Huxley. Matter of fact, help him, god dammit! Why is he just lying there!?' said Pearse.

'Wait, who's Huxley?' Manson said.

'Are you kidding!? He's freezing to death, right there!'

Pearse pointed to where Huxley was. He then ran over to him and tried to help him.

'Huxley, come on, wake up!' He wasn't moving. Pearse looked up to see Manson stading over him. He had a look of sympathy on his face.

'Pearse, there's nobody there.'

Pearse looked back down. Manson was right. There was nobody there.

'Wh-wha . . . how? N-n-no . . . '

Manson kneeled down and awkwardly tried to comfort him, in an oddly distant fashion.

'We're going to take you home, alright? Back to Trunduska. You'll get better there. You understand?'

'He was just here . . . '

Manson stood up and silently spoke to the other soldier. Some words stood out from the hushed conversation.

' . . . for real . . . crazy. What about the . . . in the back . . . check in with . . . ' They turned around to face him again.

'Alright, Pearse, I'm going to call command. Follow Vance here to the truck,' Manson said as he broke away from the group and pulled out a tranceiver. Vance, the other soldier, jerked his head back in a 'c'mere' sort of gesture. Pearse followed.

At the back of the truck, Vance yanked open the door. 'Oh yeah, we found this guy a while ago. Careful, he's a bit vicious.'

Pearse looked inside to see Red, sitting in a cage. The dog seemed docile enough, at least now that he'd seen Pearse. Pearse sat in the back of the truck and Vance and Manson got into the front seats.

Within a hour, they had made their way out of the dense forest and ino the borderlands of the Frontier and Trunduska. The closer they got to the city, the brighter the sky got. Pearse could finally see the sun. Pearse felt happiness for the first time in a long time, a happiness that was replaced with terror when he saw Huxley sitting opposite of him. He appeared gaunt and lifeless, his skin grey and stretched across his bones. His head was held low, and he made no sound. Then, slowly, Pearse began to see through him. He was disappearing. Finally, when the sun was high in the sky and day was clearly upon them, Huxley was gone. Perhaps for good this time.

Time was continuing on again, but Pearse would never be rid of the damage the Frontier had done to him. Even if he recovered, even if he returned to full physical and mental health, the scars would never fade. The dark, the monsters, Huxley . . . the Frontier had won. It had broken him and taken parts of him away that he'd never get back. He looked over to Red, who was already looking at him, tail wagging. Something about the dog made Pearse feel better. Maybe it's because he was the one thing Pearse was sure to be real in the Frontier. Pearse let him out of the cage and petted him gently. This dog was the only other living thing that had seen what he had seen.

'Y'know,' Pearse said, 'The first thing I'm going to do when I get home, is take you for a walk.'

BLACK AND WHITE

Caoilainn Hogan Boyle

There is a land in the bright white clouds with rainbow footpaths and marshmallow houses. This magical place is called Misty Island and on this land live creatures such as leprechauns, unicorns and fairies. These creatures, the citizens of Misty Island, are called Mistymen.

Each live in their own area: the Leprechauns live on Rainbow Road, where they keep all the gold in the land. If anyone needs gold or wants to store it in a safe they bring it to the Leprechauns. Paddy O'Sé, the Head Leprechaun, is in charge of running the bank – his family business.

The Fairies live in Mushroom Square. Each family has a small Mushroom Circle, a mushroom for each family member. Some fairies are in charge of the water supply as they have a huge lake in Mushroom Square; these Fairies are called Aquafairies.

The Elves live on Elf Avenue. They are the builders and farmers of Misty Island, they live near the forest closest to the Pixie Castle and have lots of land for farming. And then there is the Royal Pixie Family. They run Misty Island and live in a castle on top of a hill overlooking their kingdom.

The hill is on the edge of the cloud but from the back of the castle you can see another cloud, the Dark Cloud. No one lives on this cloud or would live there willingly; it is dull and stormy all year round. Some say that there are goblins and trolls living on the Dark

Cloud and that they were once good and lived on Misty Island. The only way to get there was on a unicorn. Many years ago some Misty-men got curious and decided to visit the Dark Cloud. When they arrived, they got off their unicorns to have a look around, but as soon as their feet touched the ground they turned into trolls. They tried everything to get back but nothing worked so the unicorns returned without them. One of the men was a castle guard called Rain Drop. He wrote a book about the Dark Cloud and eventually it ended up in the Pixie Castle library.

The new discovery about the Dark Cloud gave the Pixie Family an idea: use this cloud as a jail for all the criminals on Misty Island.

This story is about the Pixie princess Lily, the daughter of King Hawthorn and Queen Rose and younger sister of Prince Oak. Recently her best friend, a young Elf girl called Candy, has been sent away. In fact a lot of people have been sent away lately. About a month ago, King Hawthorn and two castle guards went on a trip to make sure everything was under control on the Dark Cloud. One of the guards fell off his unicorn trying to help the King, who had also fallen, now the King is stuck on the Dark Cloud forever.

Candy's little brother, Cane finds Lily sitting by the lake in Mushroom Square.

'Lily! Lily!' shouts Cane. Lily looks up to see ten-year-old Cane half running towards her with a bright red face.

'My goodness Cane, did you run all the way from Elf Avenue?!' Lily asks. Cane just nods in reply. He looks like he is going to faint. 'Cane, are you alright?' Lily asks standing up to walk over to him.

'Yeah, just give me a minute,' Cane replies and sticks his head into a fountain. 'Ahhh,' he sighs gulping some water, 'much better.'

Lily laughs and sits back down looking out over the lake. The lake is beautiful. It's on the edge of the forest beside Mushroom Square near the Pixie Castle. It is like a mirror. In any weather or season it always reflects the sky and the trees in the water and you can watch the Aquafairies working away. It has always been Lily's favourite place to go in her free time.

'So I'm guessing you heard about Candy?' Cane asks walking down the deck were Lily is sitting.

'Yeah I did,' Lily replies swinging her legs back and forth over the side of the decking. She feels sad for Cane because she knows she is lying to him.

'Do you know where she went?' he asks, sitting down beside her. 'You two were best friends, I just thought she might have told you something,' he says quickly running his words into each other.

'No she never told me anything,' Lily says. Cane looks at her with his big green eyes. She feels so guilty she is lying straight to his face.

'I'm sorry, Cane, I have to go,' Lily says lifting off into the air.

Flying home she remembers the last time she saw Candy, only three days ago. She was coming down the big stairs of the castle to the front door to meet Candy. She reached the bottom step when three castle guards came over to her. She immediately recognised one of them as one of her closest friends, Pip.

'I'm so sorry, Lily,' he said sadly as he walked behind her and grabbed her waist to hold her in place.

Lily turned her head towards him. 'What are you talking about? Get off me! What are you doing?' she asked angrily trying to get out of his grip.

The other two guards came over to help hold her in place when the guard to the right of her shouted 'bring her in!'

'Bring who in, Pip?' Lily asked getting more frustrated. The big double doors opened and light spilled into the hall and in front of her stood two more guards holding the little elf girl, her best friend, Candy.

Candy was struggling to get out of the guard's grip. Lily saw this and tried to free herself from the guards holding her in place but failing miserably. Lily realised that Pip would have known she was going to react like this and that's why he held her down.

'Lily!' Candy shouted, 'Lily, tell them to let me go. They saw me walking up the steps and just grabbed me!' Lily stilled and just looked down at her feet. There was nothing she could do. This had been happening a lot in the past month, people being dragged into the castle to be sent to the Dark Cloud.

Lily watched Candy get pulled off down the hall kicking and screaming.

'I'm sorry, Lily,' Pip said again.

'Stop saying that,' Lily muttered and got herself free.

Lily remembers the conversation with her mother after it happened. 'You can't say a word about where Candy's gone. She is still under 18 and we have to make people believe she ran away,' is all Queen Rose said to Lily. Queen Rose was very pretty; she had bright blue eyes and dark hair. She was a lovely, kind Queen but lately, since her husband King Hawthorn got trapped on the Dark Cloud, she has become a bit heartless. She sends people to the Dark Cloud for the most minor of crimes.

After Lily's visit with Cane at the Lake she flops down on her bed. Someone clears their throat and she knows who it is straight away.

'Go away Pip I'm tired.'

'Lily I need to talk to you.'

Lily rolls her eyes, 'I've had a tiring morning. I was talking to Cane, Candy's little brother. He asked me where his sister is and I couldn't tell him the truth because I have to keep these family secrets.'

Lily sits up and looks at Pip. He is sitting comfortably in the arm chair in her room. He is wearing his training gear and has a training book open in his hands. He is studying to be a fully trained Pixie Guard. He leans forward and rests his elbows on his knees.

'I know you're upset about what happened but I need to tell you something.'

'Well, what is it?'

'Well, I have my exams coming up in a few weeks and to prepare, the head guard suggested I assist with bringing Candy over to the Dark Cloud,' he says nervously looking at Lily.

Lily stares at him, furious. 'You did what?! You brought her over?!' she shouts. She jumps up and lands in front of him looking down at him. Pip jumps back at the sudden movement. He looks back up at Lily and stands up, his turn to look down at her.

'Look that's not all I came here to tell you,' he says walking away from her. 'I know the way to the Dark Cloud now. No one other than the castle guards know where the road is because it's very well hidden, but not guarded,' he turns around to look at a very confused Lily. 'I can take you to see them, the King and Candy' he pauses. 'If that's what you want.'

He is being deadly serious. She knows he wouldn't mess about something like this. Lily sits in the chair Pip just vacated.

'Okay when do we go then?' she says surprisingly calm.

'Meet me on your balcony at six. I'll take you then.' He glances at the clock on her dresser, 'I have to go back to work. They'll start wondering where I got to.'

'Okay thank you so much, Pip,' Lily replies, a big smile on her face. Pip smiles back at her 'I'll see you later,' he says before leaving the room.

Lily goes to the library to find her mother. She is usually down there at this time. As she is walking to the library she can't help but get angry at her mother for how messy she got trying to keep the order in Misty Island. Lily understands it is hard for her mother but when Queen Rose lost her husband, Oak and Lily lost their dad. She walks into the library and stops as soon as she sees her mother. Queen Rose is asleep on one of the big comfy armchairs by the window, the sun shining in on her. She has a book on her lap and a cup of tea still hot on the coffee table. For the first time in weeks she looks relaxed and not tense and stressed. Lily feels sorry for her and sorry for even being angry at her but then she remembers why she was angry in the first place. Lily clears her throat and her mother's eyes quickly open.

'Lily,' Rose says, 'I was just resting my eyes.' Lily walks into the room and sits in the chair opposite her mother.

'Is there something you need?' she asks, putting her book on the coffee table and picking up her cup of tea.

'Actually yes,' Lily says 'I want to know why you sent Candy to the Dark Cloud,' Lily looks at her mother. Rose sighs.

'You know how I feel about your friendship with the little Elf.' Lily rolls her eyes. Her mother got along with everyone and didn't have a problem with Lily's friendships with any of the Mistymen, until the King went away.

'I know since Dad got stuck on the Dark Cloud you don't want me associating with any of the Mistymen unless they are wealthy Pixies or Fairies.'

'I don't understand why you want to be around them so much they are just the town commoners,' Rose says getting frustrated.

'No, I don't understand how you could be so cruel; you used to be friends with everyone.' Lily replies.

'Lily, since your father went away all the responsibility has been put on me. At least when your father was here we could sort everything out together. Now I have double the work to do. You're too young to help and your brother is too busy with training the new guards. I have to do it all myself.'

'Yes I get that, but you still haven't answered my question, why did you send Candy away?'

'I know you told her about the Dark Cloud, Lily. You know that's one of the most important secrets of our family.' Rose says sternly.

'That was my fault! Why send her over?' Lily questions.

'Because you're too young and I wouldn't send you over there; it's an awful place! I've already lost my husband why would I want to lose you too?' Rose looks shocked that Lily would even consider going over there.

'Yes, I am too young, only adults are supposed to be sent over there. Candy is the same age as me and so were so many others that were sent over in the past month. Why would you send someone else's child over there if you wouldn't send your own?' Lily says, standing up and leaving the room.

Half an hour later Lily hears a knock at her door but she doesn't answer. The door opens and her older brother, Oak walks in with a huge smile on his face. 'What's got you all smiley?' Lily asks.

'I've got some news,' he replies, 'Holly and I are engaged! The wedding is in a month.'

'Oh my god! Congratulations!' Lily says standing up from her chair to give her brother a hug. She is really happy for him. They have been together for a while and Holly is such a lovely Pixie, as are her family.

'It's a shame Dad won't be here for it though,' Oak says sadly. Lily just nods. 'Well I better go I have to organise dinner tonight, all our friends are coming over for the engagement,' Oak says walking to the door, 'It's at seven o'clock,' He adds before he leaves the room.

Just as Lily is about to sit back down there is another knock on her door. She sighs and opens the door. Pip walks in and over to her balcony.

'Well hello, come on in,' Lily laughs closing her door. 'You're early – it's only half four,' she says walking over to him.

'I know, but we've got the rest of the day off because Oak announced the engagement. So we should get going because the dinner party is in a few hours and we don't want to miss it.'

Pip and Lily arrive at the guard stables where they keep the unicorns.

'What are we doing here?' Lily asks very confused. Pip laughs, 'You can't just walk onto the Dark Cloud, Lily. To get to the Dark Cloud you have to fly on a unicorn, and once you get there you must not get off your unicorn.' He says the last bit very seriously.

'How could I forget?' Lily says more to herself as she remembers reading the book she found in the Library. They get on their unicorns and go into the woods to find the road to the Dark Cloud.

'Remember, do not get off the unicorn,' Pip reminds her.

'Yes I know,' Lily replies. Pip stops his unicorn in front of a bush. He gets off and pulls up a branch. The Bush opens in two and in front of Lily is a big sparkling rainbow.

'Now we go across the rainbow,' Pip says hopping back on his unicorn and heading towards the rainbow, Lily following close behind.

Lily notices as she gets closer and closer to the Dark Cloud the rainbow doesn't sparkle as much and the colour seems to fade out of it, turning it a grey colour as if the world was in black and white. Once they reach the edge of the Dark Cloud she realises that that's exactly what the world is like in this land, black and white. They are walking through a forest very similar to the one on Misty Island, it is so dark and dull, all grey except the spot of bright natural colour where the unicorns' feet touch the ground. They come across a town with a lake in it that looks exactly like the one in Mushroom Square.

'Lily!?' Lily turns around when she hears her dad's voice.

'Dad?' Lily asks shocked at what she sees, instead of the King she sees a troll but it resembled her father. 'It's so good to see you!' Lily says, 'How have you been surviving? I didn't think there was a town here.'

'Yes, the Mistymen that were sent here decided to build themselves a town to survive seeing as they would never get out,' the King explains, 'I've noticed that a lot of the Mistymen that have been sent here recently haven't done anything to deserve such a bad punishment, and some are too young to be here at all. What's going on at home, Lily?' he asks.

'Well ever since you left, all the work and responsibility has been put on mother. She has to make every single decision on her own. She's not the way she used to be,' Lily tells her father.

'I see.'

'Dad is Candy here?' Lily asks.

The King brings Pip and Lily to a little cottage where he and Candy and a few others have been staying. Lily and Candy catch up while Pip and the King talk about the Guards and how Oak has been training them.

'Oh speaking of Oak,' Lily says when she overhears his name. 'He and Holly got engaged.'

'That's wonderful!' her father exclaims, 'Tell them I said congratulations.'

'We should get going, it's getting late,' Pip says.

'Yeah, what time is it?' Lily asks.

'It's six,' Candy says.

'Okay, we should really get going. Oak won't be happy if we are late for the dinner party. But we will be back tomorrow,' Lily says. They all say goodbye and Lily and Pip make their way back home.

They arrive with enough time to get ready quickly. Pip changes out of his training gear and they both change into more presentable clothes. They make their way down to the big dining room where the dinner party is being held. Queen Rose sees them come in and knows something's up. 'Lily, can I talk to you for a moment?' Rose asks.

'Of course.' Lily follows her mam out into the hall away from the party.

'Where have you been? And don't lie to me, I know something's up I couldn't find you earlier,' Rose says.

'Look, now is not the time to be talking about this,' Lily replies.

'Tell me where you were!'

'Fine, if you really need to know right now, I was at the Dark Cloud. I saw Dad and Candy. They are both doing fine over there but it is miserable and I didn't want to bring it up now because it's the engagement party,' Lily tells her.

'You were on the Dark Cloud?' someone asks. Lily turns around and sees Oak, Holly and Pip standing behind her. 'Yes, and I was going to tell you two but I knew now was not the time.' Lily replies.

'You're right. Now is not the time. This is our party,' Oak says pointing at himself and Holly. 'We can talk about this in the morning,' he says turning around to go back to the party.

Lily stays for the meal and then leaves to go to the library. Ever since she spoke with her father she has wanted to find a way to bring him back. She finds the section in the library about the Dark Cloud, which is just a few books on people's opinions about the Dark Cloud and one or two fictional stories. Then Lily remembers the book she read but never finished about the man who lived on the Dark Cloud. She runs up to her room and grabs it from under her bed and picks up where she left off. The man's name was Rain Drop and he was one of the first Mistymen to have ever gone on to the Dark Cloud. Himself and some of his friends decided to go on an adventure so they got on their unicorns and crossed the rainbow bridge to the Dark Cloud but made the mistake of getting off their unicorns. They stayed and built a few houses until more people were being sent there as a punishment. Rain Drop had documented everything. Towards the end of the book it is about how Rain Drop tried to get off the Dark Cloud. 'I have been observing everything,' Lily reads, 'trying to figure a way out of this dead land and I think I found out how. I have found a unicorn, with no one riding it, that one of the guards had brought with them to bring a prisoner over on. He isn't being watched so I'm taking my chance. I will finally be free, finally feel peace.' Lily turns the page but there was nothing else.

'What? That's it? There has to be more!' Lily sighs, knowing she is going to have to try and figure it out herself. She looks at her clock – three in the morning. She has been reading all night. She decides to get some sleep before having to face the Queen in the morning. Lily dreams about the colour that spread from the unicorns' hooves and how Rain Drop's escape from the Dark Cloud plan had included a unicorn.

When she wakes up she knows what to do. Lily runs down to her mother, Holly and Oak. 'I am going to the Dark Cloud today and I have an idea to bring back father and Candy.' Lily says as soon and she walks into the breakfast room.

'You know that's not possible,' Holly says sadly, her brother was the guard who fell off his unicorn trying to help the King.

'You can come if you want but you're not going to stop me going.'

'I'm coming with you,' Oak says.

'Brilliant, be ready in an hour and meet Pip and me at the unicorn stables,' Lily replied.

'I am not happy about this,' Rose says glaring at Oak for letting this happen.

'Neither am I,' Holly says looking at Oak angrily.

'As long as we stay on the unicorns we will be fine,' Lily says shrugging her shoulders.

'I know that but your father fell off his unicorn; it didn't happen by choice it was an accident and it could happen to you or Oak,' Rose says.

'We will be careful okay?' Lily says softly.

'Okay is everyone ready?' Oak asks.

'Yeah let's go I'm sure Dad will be delighted to see you,' Lily replies smiling. When they got to the Dark Cloud, Lily and Pip bring Oak to the King's cottage.

'Oak?'

'Yeah, Dad,' Oak laughed. Oak and the King do some catching up while Lily explains her plan to Candy and Pip. 'So I was reading this diary book last night by a guy named Rain Drop. Apparently he was a Pixie Guard and he and his friends decided to go explore the Dark Cloud and but they got trapped and that's how we use this as a jail now.' Lily explains. 'At the end of his diary he says that he goes to get an unguarded unicorn and he finally "finds peace".' Lily quotes. 'So that must mean he was free from this place.'

'But you still haven't told us your plan,' Candy says confused. 'Well, I had an idea that maybe if you or father touches the unicorn, you guys will turn back to normal. It makes sense, you need a unicorn to get here and to stay normal so you must need one to get back. I know it might just be a fictional book, it doesn't say, but it could be true, it could work.'

Pip thinks about it for a while. 'I think it could work,' Oak says.

'You guys heard all that?' Lily asks.

'Yeah, we did, I don't know though,' the King says.

'Just try it Dad,' Lily begs.

'Okay.' The King walks over to Lily and puts his hand on the side of the unicorn's head and waited.

'Nothing is happening.' He sighs.

'Ugh I was so sure this would work!' Lily says frustrated. 'It's okay we are doing okay here. Just go back home you can always visit us,' Candy reassures her.

'Okay. I will keep looking there has to be a way it doesn't make sense that you can't get out. There must be some way,' Lily says sadly. 'We will see you guys soon okay? And maybe Mam will come the next time.' Oak says with a sad smile.

A few weeks later Oak and Holly got married. Rose decided as a present she would hand over the castle to them. They are now the new King and Queen of Misty Island. Lily notices a change in Queen Rose – she is more relaxed. Lily has been visiting the Dark Cloud weekly to see her dad and Candy. She is still trying to figure out a way to get them back.

What nobody knew, not even the Royal Pixie Family, was that the Dark Cloud wasn't a prison; it was a place for the dead. If you touch the ground you die but you're not quite dead yet. Your physical appearance deforms and you are still able to talk to people but you can never go back to the way you were. You are stuck there until you figure out you need a unicorn so you can be free, free to move on but never return to Misty Island. You only get trapped there if you die there. Nobody knew this except one Mistyman. He wrote a diary about it and left it at the bridge for the castle guards to find. They brought it back and put in the library. It was the diary that Lily found and read but what she didn't know was that it was a real diary of a real dead Mistyman about how he escaped.

THE ONE

Jasmin Humphrey

I had on my dark ripped jeans and a pink top with a crazy looking bird on it. I thought I looked cool. One Tuesday in Spring I went to the skate park in Father Collins' Park with my skateboard. I stood on it, but was afraid to move.

This boy that I had seen in youth club came over to me. I was pretending I wasn't trying to be a skater girl. I knew that he had seen me on the skateboard. I wanted to get him to show me how not to fall off, but I was too nervous. He just ran off on me as if he was afraid of me. I thought maybe he wanted to help me so I ran after him, but he just ran faster. Then he fell over and started to cry. I felt sorry for him so I went up to him and sat beside him until he felt like saying something.

'Are you okay?' I asked him.

'No. Why do you care?' he said, with teardrops running down his face.

'Because maybe I do care,' I said with a tear in my eye. I never liked to see anyone cry. Even at movies I was always bawling crying, like at *P.S. I Love You*.

'What's your name?' I asked.

'Robb. What's your name?' he asked quietly.

'Julie,' I said. 'Hey, why do you always sit on your own at youth club?'

'I just like to sit on my own,' said Robb, sounding unsure.

A few days passed. Robb and I became friends. We sat beside each other in youth club. We went to the cinema on a Saturday to see a movie called The Last Song. I had wanted to go see it but not on my own, so I asked Robb. He said sure. I knew he didn't want to see it but we went anyway.

The next Monday, I was on the way to the youth club when I heard this amazing song that was coming out of the Centra shop in Kilbarrack. I started humming along to the song. I went into the shop and asked the fella there what is the name of this song and who sings it. He said, 'I think it's Juliet Simms.' The song was called 'Not Broken Yet'. When I got to the youth club, I told Robb about this song. He listened to it on YouTube and loved the song too. So then every day after school or during the youth club we listened to Juliet Simms on YouTube.

One Friday in April, Robb and I were in his room. We had discovered this rock band named Black Veil Brides on YouTube and we both thought they were amazing. I loved the song 'Fallen Angels' – it became my favourite song that they sing, and Robb's favourite was 'Heart Of Fire.' On this day I was on his bed on his laptop, and he was looking for his phone – he had lost it again. Robb eventually found his phone so panic over. While I was on the internet, I discovered Black Veil Brides were coming to Dublin – to Croke Park – so I shouted, 'OMG!'

Robb thought something happened. He looked up from his phone. 'What's wrong?' he asked. 'Are you okay?'

'Look at this!' I said.

' OMG! Do you want to get the tickets?' asked Robb.

'Yes! But do we have the money for the tickets?' I asked.

'Well, the tickets are €95 each,' said Robb, looking worried.

'How much money do you have?' I asked.

'I have some money from Christmas, money from my nanny and some birthday money too. I think I have €100 saved up,' said Robb. 'How much do you have?'

'I only have €55, so we are €35 short. We don't have enough money,' I said disappointed.

'Well, they go on sale in three weeks so we may be able to get the money by helping around the house,' Robb suggested.

'Okay, I will start today because my mam is giving me money for cleaning my brother's room,' I said.

' How much is she giving you?' Robb asked.

'Should be €15 and next week I'm getting €5 from my nanny,' I said with a smile on my face.

'Cool! So then we will just need €15 and then we can get them tickets!' said Robb.

Monday came but I still only had €15, because my mam only had €10 and I got €5 from my nanny. I cleaned different parts of the house each day. Robb got €15 from one of his uncles, so we now had €180 but we were still €10 short. My mam was getting money in her bank account the following week but it would take until the Thursday, which was the day the tickets went on sale. Robb and I started to get worried, but it ended up that my mam got the money on time so there was no need to worry.

Robb and I queued for the tickets. We were so happy with the tickets because they were standing tickets. We couldn't believe it but Black Veil Brides weren't coming until June 15th – it felt like forever.

A couple of days before the concert, Robb and I were walking around town for a few hours. We came across this skate park we had never seen before, so we went in. I saw my friend Anto. It had been, like, ages since I had seen Anto. He hadn't been to youth club in a really long time. I had always kind of fancied him and I thought he liked me too.

'ANTO!' I shouted.

'JULIE!' shouted Anto.

'Who's that?' asked Robb. He seemed suspicious.

'My friend Anto,' I said. 'He used to go to youth club.'

'Hi Julie,' Anto said with a funny voice when he came over to me and Robb. He was carrying his skateboard.

'Hi, Anto,' I said with a sweet smile on my face. 'This is Robb.'

Anto looked at Robb. 'Hey,' he said. Anto turned to me. 'Is this your skater friend?'

'Yeah,' I said.

'Robb, you look like a really cool dude,' said Anto, still with his funny voice.

'Thanks. Here, do you want to be mates?' asked Robb, puzzled.

'Yeah, sure,' said Anto, smiling.

I started to get worried that these two were not actually going to be friends. 'Robb, I need to get back home,' I said. I really wanted to get out of there.

'Okay. See ya, Anto,' said Robb with a smile.

'See ya Robb. Talk to you later, Julie,' said Anto.

'Yeah, um, talk to you later, Anto,' I replied.

So we got to my house and I said, 'Thanks Robb' and kissed him on the cheek. Robb froze, then smiled and said, 'No problem.'

I smiled and turned to walk in the house and then Robb said, 'Julie.'

'Yeah?' I said.

' I love you . . . ' he said nervously.

I smiled and said, 'I love you too, Robb.'

Robb smiled as I closed the door but I opened it again then I went up to Robb and kissed him. I turned away and closed the door. I think his heart was beating so loud you could hear it.

On the night of the concert, Robb and I had a huge row. Even though I'd told Robb that I loved him, I couldn't stop thinking about Anto. I think Robb had figured that out. We broke up halfway through the summer. It was kind of weird because we had become so close so quickly. Robb started college and got a job in a photography shop and I just didn't see him anymore – he wasn't in youth club anymore either.

I started fourth year in September and there was drama going between me and Anto. I kept bumping into him at youth club – he had started playing pool at the youth club with my brother Nathan.

I kept catching him looking at me. Even though I'd known him for a long time, I now felt shy around him. I didn't think I could talk to him. All I could do was 'like' his photos when he changed his profile picture on Facebook. I started to think that nothing was ever going to happen between us.

The day before my birthday in March, Anto asked me on Facebook, 'Do you like me?'

'In which way?' I asked. My heart started thumping as I typed.

'What way do you think?' asked Anto.

'In the love way?' I asked. I was trying to take it all in.

'Okay, what feelings do you have for me?' asked Anto.

'I love you. That's the feelings I have for you,' I said. My hands were shaking.

'You're in love with me!?' asked Anto.

'Yeah. You surprised?' I asked. I was kind of surprised myself that I had actually said it.

'No,' said Anto. 'I had kind of figured that out. I love you too. Happy birthday.'

It was the best birthday present ever.

I thought that we would be together all the time after that but Anto always seemed to be busy, always working in Tesco or with his mates or whatever. We talked online sometimes. I started walking through the shops in Kilbarrack just to see him after youth club every Tuesday but he never had time to talk.

'I wish I wasn't so busy,' he told me one Tuesday night when I visited him in Tesco. I really wanted to believe Anto but my friends doubted him – how could he really love me if he was never around?

One Friday in May I was at home, alone again, and we were talking on Viber. Anto was walking home from work after his shift at Tesco.

'Hey,' said Anto.

'Hey! How are you?' I replied.

'I'm good, you?' he asked.

'I'm good,' I said. I wanted to ask if he was busy again because it was coming up to the summer and I was hoping we could hang out more, but I was kind of nervous. I wanted to trust that he still loved me.

'What you doing?' Anto asked.

'Listening to music,' I said.

'Cool. Who's with you?' he asked. Anto didn't care about music like Robb did, we chatted more about movies. It turns out that Anto liked romantic movies as much as I did – most other guys I knew liked horror movies.

'No one. Why?' I asked.

'Just wondering,' Anto said.

I was about to write back when Anto said, 'I love you so much right now.'

I froze because I didn't know what to say. I was kind of annoyed, actually. I really wasn't sure that he loved me. 'You promised me that you'd take me out to the skate park ages ago but then it turned out you were busy again. We never hang out.'

'Okay,' said Anto. 'Let's go out tomorrow night.'

I thought to myself, will he actually be busy again? I wrote back, 'Are you sure?'

'Yeah,' Anto replied. 'We'll go to the cinema.'

The next night, I was excited to go out with Anto but I kept waiting for him to text me on Viber to say he was busy. As I was getting ready in my room, I heard a knock on the door. My mam opened the door and called up to me, 'Julie, there's someone at the door for you!' She didn't say who it was.

'Just a sec,' I called down, finishing my hair.

I went downstairs and I was so surprised to see who was standing in the doorway. It was Anto and he wasn't busy.

'Hi,' I said, smiling.

'You look gorgeous,' Anto said.

'If you want to be with me, you need to keep surprising me like this,' I told him.

'I will,' Anto promised.

I had thought that I loved Robb for a while, but seeing Anto smile, I knew he was the one.

BREAKING PATTERN
Jay Kehoe Hanlon.

'Shit,' I cursed as the branches scratched against my cheek. I shifted my weight and broke a few twigs, pushing the remaining foliage from my face. I checked my watch for the time, 7:47pm. She was late. She's never late. For the whole five months I've known her she has never been late home. She always gets home between 7pm and 7:13pm on a Friday. Always. I felt frustrated; she's missing our time. How could she do that? I bent down, balancing on the balls of my feet, placing my elbows on my knees and my face in my hands. I sighed and tried to keep it together.

I heard the sound of a familiar engine pull into the driveway, the gravel crackling under the weight of the jeep's tyres. I made a note of the time in my journal, 7:51pm. I stood up and saw her in the driver's seat, her head resting on the steering wheel. She stayed there for a few minutes before taking a visible deep breath, she too was trying to keep it calm. She opened the door of her jeep and stumbled out of it and dropped her handbag.

She appeared panicked and nervous. This concerned me. She struggled to get her key in the door, her long brown hair covered her face. I wanted to run my hands through it, to feel the softness. I shook my head clear of thoughts. I needed to concentrate. It was already getting dark, I noticed the light go on in the kitchen. It was at the front of the house and it had pretty big windows. I could see her cooking. I was confused. On Fridays she always got takeout from the chipper up the way. I wrote down these changes just in case they become routine.

Suddenly, I heard another set of tyres come up the driveway. The car approaching had a quiet engine, I'm guessing it was new and expensive. It came into my line of sight, it was a sleek black Camaro. A young man got out of the driver's side; he was undeniably attractive and well built, he was the image of an ex boyfriend of mine – tall, dark and handsome. Anger bubbled within me, no man should be anywhere near this house apart from me.

She was mine.

No-one will keep her from me.

I took deep breaths to clear my head. Inhale for five seconds and exhale for seven. I did four sets of these. I have got to keep my head straight. Her behaviour was different today; she never had people over. She doesn't have friends. She's a loner. Who was this man? She greeted him at the door, and he kissed both her cheeks. Each sent a shock of pain through me.

I watched from the garden as they ate dinner, laughing and talking. At one point he reached over and placed his hand on hers and gave her a smile anyone would melt over. Jealousy ran through my veins. This was supposed to be our time but this bastard is ruining it, he is making her happy. Something I'll never be able to do.

He left at 11:26pm. I watched as he reversed out onto the empty road. I was debating whether or not to follow him and put an end to him but that would break my pattern, he didn't need someone to ensure he's safe especially when I don't want him to be. I'll find out more on him at a later point. Judging by the smile he put on her face, he'll most likely be back at some point.

The lights in the house turned off slowly one by one. I waited until I was certain that she was asleep before I retreated to my car parked around the corner. I made sure to check the time before I left, for my notes. It was 1am, later than usual. I was still angry about the change in routine but I'll have to get used to it, I guess.

To my dismay every Friday was the same from then onwards. I still refused to leave, despite the rage that I felt. He'd come over, they'd have dinner in the kitchen, always prepared and cooked by her. They'd laugh and have long conversations. She no longer needed me.

One Tuesday she didn't come home. I waited for her until 11pm. Why wasn't she home? There was so much anger and hurt. I threw the notebook in rage. How dare she? I collapsed to the ground, the tears ran down my cheeks. I cradled my head in my arms and I cried. She didn't need me anymore. I thought back to when I first saw her, a fragile girl crying by the riverside. She cried herself to sleep there and if she hadn't have had that letter on her; I wouldn't have been able to carry her home. Now she has him to watch over her.

I woke up in a daze, I was shivering. It was absolutely freezing. When my eyes focused, bushes faced me. Bushes? 'Oh fuck,' I whispered to myself as realisation dawned on me. I fell asleep here, in her garden. I checked my watch – it was 6:30am. I had thirty minutes before her sprinklers turned on and an hour before she left for work. I collected my things and ran; I can't be seen.

As I was jogging down the street, a black Camaro captured my attention. It was parked across the road from her house. Her 'boyfriend' was asleep in the front seat. I found this odd. Looks like I wasn't the only one to fall asleep on the job last night. I sprinted to my car. The door made a creaking noise as I yanked it open. I got in and rooted out my good pair of skinny jeans and a black and white check shirt, which I threw on over my black T-shirt. As I changed I was silently grateful for having a pretty big car, it may be a piece of shit but it was spacious.

When I was sure I looked like the average young adult, I made my way towards his car. I put a smile on my face and knocked on the window. The smile turned into a smirk when I saw him jump awake, eyes wide in fear. He rubbed his face and rolled down the window, plastering a smile on his face, identical to every smile I had to force.

'Sorry for waking you but that can't be comfortable,' I said, gesturing to way he was sitting. He checked the time on his dash and sighed in relief.

'Yeah, it's not. I'm sorry mate but I can't stay and chat, I've got to leave for work. Thanks for waking me by the way.' He spoke fast like he couldn't wait to get away, he put his key into the ignition and his car came to life.

I patted the roof of his car, 'Well off you go, man, good day,' I said and then walked off, he rolled up his window and gave a two-finger salute and drove off. I made a note of his licence plate as he sped out of the estate.

I stared out the car window at her house in deep thought. I'm going to have to abandon her for awhile. I sighed. This was supposed to be an easy one . . . but that fucking prick just had to stroll into her life and mess up mine. I rested my head on the steering wheel for a few minutes, breathing deeply, trying to keep it together. I started the car and drove off down the backroad that could not be seen from her house. I had a lot of work to do.

I pulled up in front of a shack of a house, my house. I usually only spent three hours a day here, just to sleep and change clothes but I knew I would be here for a week or two straight. I needed to know who this man was. I stepped out of my car and made sure to grab all my things and made my way up my so-called-yard. My key got stuck in the door as usual, so I had to use the backdoor, all it took was a few shoves and it burst open to reveal my small and empty kitchen/sitting area.

I made a pot of coffee, grabbed an old mug from the sink and made my way to my office. I say office but it is just a tiny room with a broken stool, in front of a chest of drawers without the actual drawers in it. I placed my laptop down, it was the most expensive thing I had (yes, even more expensive than my piece of shit car). I didn't really need much to be honest; I spent most of my time in women's gardens (I'm joking. . . kind of) or doing random jobs for an income.

My laptop took ten minutes to start up. Within these ten minutes I had burned my tongue on my coffee and managed to fall off my stool. Twice. The beep it made signalled that it was ready. I began my searching. I managed to track down the licence plate to be registered to a James Bennett.

I opened up a new tab and went onto Facebook, everyone has one these days. I typed 'James Bennett' into the search bar and got 46 results. I scrolled down through them until I found it. Hard to miss him, to be honest. I coughed, clearing my throat to interrupt my own thoughts. I clicked onto his profile and smirked, I really love how personal people get on this website.

Eight days passed before I had a decent start on getting to know James. He has a dog, a Pitbull mix named Jesse. I checked my phone; it was Wednesday. Judging from his last few weeks of posts, he brings Jesse for walks almost every Wednesday to a park not too far from here. I rummaged through my wardrobe for my jogging gear, it's been so long since I've worn them.

It took twenty minutes to jog to the park, it was pretty big and had a lot of trees. I took a sip from my water bottle and looked around, taking in my surroundings. How was I meant to find him here? This park was huge. I sat down on the closest bench, which was shaded by a couple trees. I put my head in my hands. What am I doing? This isn't what I'm supposed to be doing. I didn't realise anyone had sat down beside me until they spoke.

'Hey man, y'alright?' My breath caught in my throat at the sound of his voice. I slowly raised my head and looked at him, his eyes widened for split second. I smiled and gave a small laugh. He joined in.

'I'm just tired, how's things?' I said casually.

'Ah, I'm grand. I'm James by the way.' He put out his hand, I took it and gave it a firm shake.

'Alec,' I said as I shook his hand.

He glanced around the park, obviously trying to think of something to say. He was fidgeting with the hem of his sweater. He cleared his throat. 'Those clouds don't look too good,' he said pointing at the sky. I followed the directory of his finger and saw big dark clouds in the distance. I got up from the bench and stretched.

'I think I ought to get going before that gets any closer,' I managed to say through my yawn. I reached out my hand and he took it. I let go and was about to walk away but he grabbed it and again. I turned around to face him.

'How about we go get a coffee and then I can give you a lift home?' I could only stare at him for a few seconds, I was at a loss for words but I managed to give a nod. He whistled loudly and I saw his dog running towards us, he was a gorgeous dog. I petted Jesse, rubbing behind his ears.

'This is Jesse, my pride and joy,' he said with a laugh.

We made our way towards his car. I cautiously got in the passenger side and I noticed the small backseats were transformed into a dog bed for Jesse. James hopped in, throwing me a charming smile. 'Do you mind if I drop Jesse home first?' Butterflies erupted in my stomach; I struggled to get words out.

'I . . . I don't mind.'

James' smirk grew bigger, if that was possible and he turned on the stereo. The sound of guitars and drums filled the car, the sweet sound of Bon Jovi's 'Living On A Prayer'. I nodded my head to the beat. James started singing along, he was practically screaming the lyrics. I laughed at him and joined in.

In fifteen minutes we pulled up outside a decent-sized house, it looked pretty expensive. He got out of his car and I was unsure of what to do, I felt awkward, I wasn't used to being in the company of others for so long. He tapped on the window and gestured for me to follow him inside. I slowly climbed out of the car and trailed after him into the house.

I walked through the door and was in awe at the beautifully decorated hallway. It held such a cosy feeling. I made a note for everything I saw to write down later, I couldn't lose track of why I was here. He wasn't my friend and never will be. He was a threat, the man taking her away from me. I thought to how he cheerfully gave me a quick tour of the downstairs. He was cute, I had to admit it.

A picture on the wall in the kitchen grasped my attention. It was a group photo. James was in the middle with his arm thrown over a certain brunette. Jealousy burned in the pit of my stomach. I was unsure of who my jealousy was directed at but it was there all the same. James saw me looking and pointed at her, 'That's Marie, we work together.'

Marie.

This whole time I had never figured out her first name, I sort of avoided it. I feel like that would taint everything, taint her image to me. She was no longer unknown, no longer a fresh canvas. 'You two just work together?' I asked.

'Yeah, just good friends, she's not interested.' I gave him an odd look, he didn't seem even a tad upset about that fact. Anyone would be sore from having been rejected by such a beautiful woman like Marie.

He disappeared upstairs. I took the opportunity to snoop around. I glanced around the room, everything was pretty much out in the open. It was like he had nothing to hide, but then my gaze halted on a small cupboard in the corner with a padlock on it. Everyone has their secrets. I was looking at the lock when his voice came out of nowhere, 'I keep my guns in there.' He must have taken my silence for confusion because he added, 'I go hunting with my brother every once in awhile.'

I nodded my head as if I was processing new information but truth be told, I already knew of his hunting trips. He cleared his throat and twirled his keys in his hand, 'We ready?' I smiled and made my way to the front door, tripping on the mat on my way. I could feel my cheeks burning as I hurried to the car, hoping he didn't see but the grin he tried so hard to conceal told me that he definitely saw it.

The journey to the coffee shop was short and silent. I was too caught up in my thoughts to make conversation and he must've just assumed that I didn't want to talk. It was lashing when we pulled up outside the café.

We got out of the car and ran for the entrance, he got there just before me and held the door open. As I walked past him, I felt pressure on my waist, I almost jumped until I realised it was just him. He gave the waitress a charming smile and the young woman came over to us, greeting us at the door.

'Hi! Eh, you can just sit wherever. Do you know what you are having?' Her voice was high-pitched, the American accent she seemed to have was fake.

James guided me through the maze of tables and chairs to a booth in the corner, furthest away from the front entrance but closest to the emergency exit. I quickly noticed that he sat in a way that he had both doors in his line of vision. I also realised that we just completely ignored the woman and I cleared my throat to gain her attention.

'I'll just have a Cappuccino with two sugars and . . . ' I trailed off, looking at James, waiting for him to continue.

'An Americano for me, please. And could you maybe get us some cheesecake?'

The woman nodded as she scribbled in her notebook and she said something. I didn't hear as I was too focused on the bit of skin on her arm that her short sleeved shirt just about failed to cover. It was bruised. I recognised the pattern. Images of this young woman being grabbed and shook by someone considerably stronger than herself flashed through my mind. She must've seen me looking because she tugged at the sleeve, trying to hide it. An emotion crossed her face for only a split second. Shame. My mind went into overdrive; she needed someone. She needed someone to protect her.

I was brought out of my daze when James placed his hand on mine, 'Are you okay?' he sounded concerned. I shook my head clear of my inner ramblings.

'Yeah, yeah. I'm fine. Just got lost in thought, I guess.' I chuckled to make it at least a little bit convincing.

James sat back against the cushions of the booth and stretched and then his whole demeanour changed. his face was cold, his body was tense. He grabbed my hand and kept it in place. 'Don't panic, just smile and pretend everything is fine, okay?'

I gulped and slowly nodded. God I really got to learn to speak more.

'Every time I squeeze your hand, you laugh, you got that?' I didn't answer. 'Are ya deaf or what? Fucking answer me when I ask you a question!' I looked him dead in the eye and smirked.

'Of course, princess.'

He glared at me but the look quickly disappeared as the waitress' heels clicked against the hard floors. She placed the cups in front of us and a plate of two slices of strawberry cheesecake between us.

'Thanks, love,' James said as he brought his cup up to his mouth. She smiled and then was on her way.

'So what's up? What's with the whole asshole routine?' I remarked, while taking a big spoonful of the cheesecake. His mouth shaped itself into a thin line.

'I know who you are, I'm not thick. I could tell who you were from the moment I laid eyes on you,' He paused for a second and went to speak again but I beat him to it.

'Who am I then?'

His brown eyes pierced mine, he suddenly laughed. 'I don't know what exactly but you spend an awful lot of time in Marie's garden. I saw you leave one night and from then on, I waited for you. The flowers from her bushes in your hair when we first met, were a dead giveaway too.'

I cursed myself for being so careless. I was caught. He knew everything and I realised I knew barely anything about the real James. 'So you set out to find me today?' I enquired.

He thought about his answer before telling me, 'Not exactly, I had a feeling you were on to me so I kept my eyes open,' he paused, his cheeks began to redden, 'and then I saw you, looking all lost. You looked so cute, Jesus, I couldn't help but go over. It was a terrible mistake but hopefully worth it.'

So I wasn't the only one, 'Wait, you knew this whole time?!' He laughed at me and I took that as a yes.

The rest of our time was spent talking. He dropped the half-arsed hard man act and we freely spoke to each other about so much. Soon darkness fell and the waitress informed us that it was time to leave. We jogged back to his car in the rain, shaking water from ourselves when we were seated.

James turned to me. 'Where to?' I shrugged my shoulders at the question but then I remembered that I should probably speak more.

'Home, I guess. You know that old music store on Atikens Street?'

'Ah, I know it but I'll drop ya home, it's no bother at all,' I got an uneasy feeling but I gave him the go ahead.

My voice shook and cracked as I gave him directions. Embarrassment ran through me as the car came to a stop outside my house. I sighed, 'This is me,' I climbed out of the car but to my surprise, he got out after me.

'It'd only be right of me to walk you to your door, isn't that what you're supposed to do after a date?' He called to me over the noise of the wind. It was a rhetorical question, well I took it as one. My stomach did flips at the sound of him saying 'date'.

He walked me through the shitty front gate, past the weeds and unkempt trees. All the way up to my off-white door. 'Today was interesting,' He mused. I hummed in agreement.

'It was nice meeting you, James. Um, sorry for stalking you, I guess?'

'It's grand, I basically did the same. Quite the pair we are,' he laughed awkwardly.

'Yeah, we are. . .' I trailed off.

Everything went silent and it became even more awkward. James shifted his weight a few times before he uttered something under his breath that may have been 'fuck it' and pulled me towards him in a swift yet gentle movement. He captured my lips with his. I froze for a second before melting into it. Before I knew it, he was turning away and it was over.

LITTLE THINGS

Stephen Kellett-Murray

It was a beautiful evening; the stars were shining, the wind was whistling through the thick forest trees and the grass was as soft as a warm blanket just out of a washing machine. Sarah missed her home. She missed her mam and dad. They had both lost their lives in a tragic car accident three years ago. Sarah was nine years old at the time and had spent the last three years in an orphanage. She couldn't stand that wretched place. Everyone there hated her, or at least she thought they did. Sarah couldn't stand anyone else trying to act like her parents so she ran away. The people who took care of her and the other children seemed like evil demons that were trying to keep her locked up forever and she hated it. Sarah was twelve now with long dirty blonde hair and was quite small for her age.

There was a sudden loud noise as if someone had thrown a rock at a tree. Sarah sprang to her feet looking at all the great oak trees that surrounded her. There was a rustling coming from a bush nearby; she darted behind a tree as quickly as she could. She slouched to the ground panting in fear. Sarah wanted to scream from the top of her lungs, but no one would hear her.

SNAP! CRACK!

The noises were getting closer. Holding her mouth closed she peered around the trunk of the tree. A boy, it was a boy – and he didn't look all that old either. He was small with messy black hair and was reasonably skinny.

He was rummaging through Sarah's small brown bag that she had taken with her. The boy was throwing all of her stuff on the ground. Sarah wanted to confront him but was too afraid. She began to move slowly over and then CRACK a branch underneath her feet snapped. The boy turned around. They looked straight into each other's eyes while both took a step back. He seemed alert, waiting for Sarah to make a move. Sarah stood up trying to look as tall as she could, but it didn't help, she was still tiny. She was barely even five feet tall standing up straight.

'H-hi,' murmured Sarah.

The boy didn't move or say anything.

'I'm Sarah.'

'Ben, my name's Ben.' His voice wasn't all that deep.

'Are you going to h-hurt me?' Sarah was scared.

'Depends.'

'Depends on what?' Sarah whimpered.

'Are you going to hurt me?'

'No.'

'I won't hurt you then.' Ben relaxed and dropped her bag.

'I'm fourteen, what about you?' Ben asked.

'I'm twelve, nearly thirteen.'

Ben walked over to Sarah and outstretched his hand. Sarah shook his hand.

'So what has you out here?' Ben said.

'Well I ran away from an orphanage.'

'Oh, is everything OK?'

'Yeah, I'm fine, it's just hard I guess,' Sarah replied nervously.

'How come you're here?' Ben was about to say when it began to rain. Almost immediately it was lashing rain.

'Grab that branch over there we need to make a shelter.' He pointed to what looked more like a log than a branch. Sarah lugged over the log, lifted the heavy log and placed it in between two branches of a tree. She and Ben then grabbed as many big leaves, parts of dead bushes and other big branches as they could find and made them into a roof of sorts. It kept nearly all of the rain out so they couldn't complain. Sarah used all the leftover moss and dead leaves to make a bed. When she turned around next, Sarah noticed that Ben had disappeared. She was too tired to try and look for him so she just went straight to sleep.

Sarah awoke the next day feeling like a mess. Her hair was all over the place and she smelled terrible. She had never wanted to have a shower so bad. She was glad then that she at least had a spare change of clothes so she could get out of these horrible smelly ones. Changed and about to grab herself a bottle of water, Sarah suddenly noticed Ben was there.

'OMG!! You scared the life out of me there,' Sarah exclaimed.

'Haha, sorry, I didn't mean to,' Ben replied.

'Well please don't do it again! And anyway where did you disappear off to last night?'

'Eh, it doesn't matter but I know a place for us to go that's a bit better than here, let me know when you're ready.'

'How do I know I can trust you?' Sarah asked.

'Well, what else are you going to do?'

'I suppose you're right, let's go.' Sarah threw her bag around her shoulder and headed off with Ben.

They had been walking for what felt like hours. Sarah still wasn't fully awake and Ben wouldn't slow down. He just kept walking.

'So you never did tell me where you were from,' Sarah said.

Ben pretended not to hear her.

'There is an old farmhouse up ahead we're going to have to go through it unless you want to spend another thirty minutes trying to walk around all the barbed wire fields and such.'

'Ooh yay an old creepy house. Just perfect,' replied Sarah sarcastically.

'Ah relax, you'll be fine.'

The two of them continued on walking towards the farmhouse.

Sarah began to notice something strange about Ben. He never ate or drank anything and he seemed to be almost gliding when he walked. He didn't really seem to bob up and down and branches didn't break as he walked. Maybe he just stepped softly, but for guy his size they should make some noise. Sarah shook off her doubts, concluding that she was still tired.

After what felt like another hour or so spent walking, they had finally came to the old farmhouse Ben had talked about.

'How do we get in?' Sarah asked.

'I don't know,' said Ben as he tried to force open the door but it wouldn't budge. 'Let's walk around and see if we spot a way in.'

Sarah didn't like the look of this place. It was a three-storey house and the roof was falling in. The windows were all smashed and some even had bars over the front. There was also a small ditch that went around the house, something similar to that of a moat. Sarah noticed that there was also a tree house that was falling apart.

'This place freaks me out,' said Sarah.

'Me too, looks like the only way in is through that little window there.'

The window was small and Sarah knew she was the only one that might fit through it.

'Alright, I'll climb through and see if I can open the door,' Sarah told Ben.

'Ok then.'

Sarah had to be careful climbing through especially with all the broken glass around. Sarah struggled to get through and knew Ben was never going to make it; she hoped that she could open that door.

The inside of the house was pitch black – she could barely see where she was going. Sarah brushed the dirt off her clothes and then as she walked forward she heard something behind her.

'BOO!'

Sarah leapt into the air with the fright and nearly fell down a hole in the floor.

She felt someone grab her and pull her from falling down.

'Woah, be careful there. Sorry about that.' The voice. It was Ben's.

'H-how did you get in here?' Sarah asked.

'I managed to fit through the window.'

'B-but I barely got through, so how did you manage?'

'I'm just that good, now let's get out of here.' Ben stared heading towards where he thought the front door was.

The place was in bits. The floorboards creaked or at least where there were floorboards, some of them had collapsed. The whole place was dusty and you could see the dust move whenever Sarah stepped. This didn't happen when Ben walked. He was so weird. After a few minutes of going into the wrong rooms they found the front door to this massive house and got outside. The path was over-grown except for a small bit of stone slab that could still be seen and there were massive trees growing either side. Sarah had started to realise that all of this was too hard. She had no food, no water and no clean clothes, she couldn't handle being away from civilisation for even a few days how was she ever meant to stay away forever?

'Ben,' Sarah wanted to ask him something. 'Do you think I should go back to the orphanage even though I hate it there?'

'Yes, you should definitely go back. Trying to live out here is hell.'

Sarah began to cry, 'It's so hard to be there. I-I miss them.'

'Sarah, I know you miss your parents.' Ben put his arm around her.

'Wait, how did you know I was talking about my parents? I never mentioned them before.'

'Because you made me up when you were younger.'

Sarah thought for a moment.

'I remember now. Back when I was five I used to get bullied and then one day you, well the real you, appeared, a year older than me and told all the bullies to leave me alone. Ever since that day when-ever I was scared I always had "you" to protect me.' Sarah was feeling happier.

'Exactly,' Ben said. 'When you were feeling alone again I was brought back from all those years ago to make you feel happy again.'

Sarah went to hug Ben but she couldn't

'Sarah I have to go, since you are happy again you don't need me. Follow this path and you'll get to a small town. There is a police station there and they'll bring you back.'

'No, Ben I can't lose you again.'

Ben faded away into thin air and was gone.

Sarah wiped away her tears and decided to do what Ben had told her.

Sarah got to the town in ten minutes and saw the police station straight away. She explained to an officer what she had done and that she realised she needed to go back. As the police officer began to driver her back to the orphanage she heard someone say her name.

'Sarah . . . '

She looked over and saw him sitting beside her in the back seat of the car. Sarah smiled but in a blink of an eye he disappeared again. As one final tear rolled down her check Sarah knew she always had Ben.

THE MILK MAN

Emma Keogh

Halloween is my favourite time of year. I was so excited this year, more than I have ever been. I had everything planned apart from what I was wearing. My friend Sophie and I were thinking of dressing up in a costume we could do together like 'thing one and thing two', Disney princesses or Twiddledum and Twiddledee. But I was also thinking of being a famous dead person.

I was walking to school with Sophie as I do every morning, but this morning felt different. I felt like someone was following us and I could hear footsteps but couldn't see anybody around. Maybe I was just paranoid. I kept turning around and looking behind me, Sophie kept telling me to stop because I was freaking her out. It really did feel like someone was watching us. It felt strange. I got over it when I got to school it was forgotten about really. I just got through my freezing cold school day as normal.

I live in the middle of nowhere. Sophie is my closest neighbour and she lives ten minutes away. My school is twenty minutes away, so I walk halfway by myself.

When I was walking home on my own after dropping Sophie off at her house everything felt normal – freezing but normal. But then I got that feeling like I was being followed again. I could feel it in my gut but there was no one there. I got home and told my mam I felt like someone was following me. 'Don't be silly! Sure why would anybody be following you?'

I didn't know how to take that response, so I walked away. I could tell She didn't believe me, but It really did feel like I was being followed.

I forgot about it after a while and just left it, 'Sure, why would anybody be following me?'

I went to bed that night and I wasn't really thinking about it, but it was still in the back of my mind.

I had to go to swimming the next day. I was watching my back the whole day. Just to make sure if I was or wasn't being followed. Swimming felt a little strange, the changing rooms were fine, the girls were the normal girls; training was grand and the coaches were fine, but something didn't seem right to me. The area where the parents sit seemed a bit strange. There were fewer people than usual. Amelia's mam and dad were there cheering her on as they do every week. But it didn't seem to be the usual mams and dads. There was a man there that seemed very odd. He could have been somebody's father, but he didn't seem like one. He was wearing all black. Black jumper, black bottoms, black shoes and even a black hat with his hood up. I couldn't see his face at all so I didn't know who he was. Maybe he was hiding from someone. I'm not sure.

My mam was thirty minutes late to pick me up. I was getting nervous; I could see that man from the corner of my eyes. I was starting to breathe really heavily and my hands started to sweat. I sent my mam twenty text messages asking where she was and why she was taking so long. She finally came and I ran to the car as fast as I could.

'What's the matter with you? what do you think you're doing?' she shouted. 'Will you calm down? What's wrong?'

I just wanted her to drive me home.

'Did you not see him?' I asked, out of breath.

'Who? Who are you on about?' she said, looking out my window.

'That man mam, right there.'

'Willow, there's nobody there.' I turned around and he was gone.

'He was right there two seconds ago.'

'Willow, you're really losing it! You're going to bed earlier from now on! I'm taking that phone off you as well!'

'Mam—'

'No, it's the phone I'm telling you now it's the phone,' she interrupted me.

'It's not the phone, that man was really there. I know he was!'

'Ah it's grand, here have a lolly,' she said.

How can I be excited for Halloween now with all this that's going on? I got home, had a shower and went straight to bed, I was so tired and just fell straight asleep.

It was Sunday and every Sunday my nanny and grandad came over for our weekly Sunday roast. I couldn't wait to see them. It would take my mind off what was going on. I love having little chats with my nanny – you don't know what she could come out with half the time. They're always here about two o'clock and they were never late, but that day they were. It was 2:40pm and there was no sign of them. My mam got really worried and rang them to see where they were. Just then the doorbell rang. I found that really weird. They were never late for Sunday roast. There was such a relief when they walked in we were all worried.

'I am so sorry, this one wouldn't stop yapping to the milk man,' my grandad said pointing over at my nanny. We all started laughing.

'Excuse me; at least I give people the chance to talk to me. You just walk away, it's so rude.'

'Ah here we go,' my mam said laughing as she prepared herself for the bickering that was about to happen. I was watching them and I was thinking they didn't have a milk man. I had to interrupt.

'Nanny, you don't have a milk man,' I said.

'Ah yea, he's new. He was saying it's a new company they're new to the green. He only started last week.'

'Aw that's nice isn't it,' my mam said but she looked a bit confused as well. A new company of milk men all of a sudden? I got over it quick with the smell of food, I was so hungry. We were all sitting at the table in silence. All you could hear were the knives and forks hitting the plates. Then my mam had a story. I knew it was going to be about me, it always is.

'Ah Daddy, I'll give you a laugh,' she said and I was just waiting on her to point at me.

'Willow here,' she said pointing at me

'Ah here we go.' I knew what it was going to be about.

'Willow here thought that someone was following her the other day,' she said and my grandad started laughing.

'Sure, why would anybody be following you?' he said. Now they were both laughing. But my nanny wasn't. She looked worried.

'Aw lighten up, Birdie,' my grandad said.

Nanny's real name is Bridget but grandad thinks it's too 'posh' for her, so he calls her Birdie. She calls him Paddy, his real name; she says he doesn't need a nickname because his name is nice. Everyone else calls them Bird and Birdie.

'Ah there's Bird and Birdie,' they'd say.

But anyway my nanny turned to me. 'Willow, are you serious? You're not joking are you?' my nanny asked.

'No, Nanny, cross my heart it really felt like someone was following me.'

'Ah, Mammy, don't mind her she's overreacting,' Mam said, laughing.

'No, Jackie, this is serious. She could be getting stalked,' nanny said.

'Aw, Mammy, she's not. She's fine.'

'Yeah Nanny, I'm fine. It's grand.' I didn't want to have her worrying like that over me. My nanny and grandad then went home. I helped my mam clean up. That man was really stuck on my mind. I didn't know whether to tell Mam or not. She could laugh again and not believe me. I just left it and went to bed. I was thinking over what my nanny said about the milk man and then that man that showed up at the swimming pool – could these men be connected?

I went to stay in my nanny and grandad's house the next day because my mam went out with friends, and I wasn't staying home alone. I couldn't wait to stay with them; I hadn't stayed in so long. And it was Halloween the next day. It was so sweet – We watched a movie and ate popcorn. I loved staying with them. My nanny and grandad both went to bed and I stayed up a bit longer because I wanted to watch telly.

Later, I saw headlights through the front door as if they were coming into the garden. I looked out the window and it was the milk man. What was he doing there at half ten at night? I didn't want to open the door but he was banging and banging so loud that it would have woken nanny and grandad up. I had to. I opened the door with just my eye peeping out.

'What are you doing here so late?' I asked

'Are you Willow?' he asked me

'Yeah why?'

He pushed the door open and dragged me out to the van. I was screaming.

'Help! someone help me!' he then punched me in my stomach, I was winded. He threw me in the back of the van. And I was banging the window of the van and screaming at the top of my lungs. I could see my nanny and grandad running after the van. They weren't quick enough, I was gone.

'What do you want?' I asked 'What did I do?'

He was just quiet. I was screaming at him and pulling at the door to try and open it but it was locked. He had the back windows blacked out so I couldn't see where we were going. I looked out the front window to see if I could see anything, I recognised the field by my house.

'What are we doing here?'

He didn't answer. He stopped the van and dragged me out onto the ground. The rain was pouring down and soaking me. I started screaming again. He smacked me across the face.

'Shut up!' he screamed at me.

'Why me?'

'Do you not know who I am?' he asked me.

'An eejit of a milk man!' I shouted at him. He went silent.

'Who are you?' I screamed at him. I started screaming for my mam screaming and screaming calling her name. Then I saw her running towards me.

'Mam!' I was so happy to see her.

'What's happening here? What are you doing?' She asked, looking confused.

'You well know what's happening here, Jackie,' he said.

'Kevin?'

'Mam – you know him? Who is he? What is he doing?'

'Kevin, don't!' she said, as if she had a lump in her throat. He turned back around and smiled at me.

'You'll never know who I am,' he said, then he pulled out a gun and bang! That awful sound. Everything went black and I was gone. I was shot dead at 1am Halloween morning – no longer my favourite day of the year.

Then all I could see was this bright light. Then it went dark and I didn't know where I was. I was at my front door in my blood-soaked PJs. I went into the house and nobody was there. I tried to change clothes, but my hand went through everything I touched. Like a ghost. I was a ghost. I sat on my bed for a little while to think. I walked down the stairs. I must have been thinking for a long time because it was the next day. I saw my mam sobbing in my grandad's arms and I could see my nanny in the corner; she was as still as a statue. I walked over to her and knelt down in front of her. I was shouting at her, telling her I'm here. She didn't move, she couldn't hear me, nobody could.

Then there was a knock at the door, it was Sophie crying buckets of tears. My mam grabbed and hugged her.

'Where is she?' she asked my mam. I was standing right in front of her.

'Look at me!' I shouted. Nothing – I got no reaction.

'She's in the living room,' my mam said.

The living room? I followed them in.

There I was just lying there in my coffin. In my favourite blue dress. I touched the fabric, I look down and I was out of my PJs and I'm now wearing that blue dress. How did that happen? What is going on? I was just lying there in that box.

'Move!' I was shouting at myself. I sat down on the chair and started crying. I picked up the cushion and threw it across the room. That was the first thing that I have been able to move. My mam and Sophie saw it. They stood in shock then started crying again. I had to leave. I was so confused. I was angry and I was upset. I went to the field. It was all blocked off by the guards. As I got closer I could hear the guards talking.

'Yes, she was shot in the chest early Halloween morning and was found by her mother the next day,' The policeman said.

Found the next day? She was there when it happened! Why didn't she call the guards straight away? And how did she know that man? I ran back to the house. Sophie was gone and so was grandad but my nanny was still there. She told my mam to get in the shower and go to bed because it going to be a hard day tomorrow. A hard day? It was my funeral. My mam went upstairs and my nanny stayed in the corner where she has been the whole time. She started saying the rosary and prayers for me. I could feel her prayers.

After Mam got herself sorted my nanny went home. Mam then went to bed and I was just left there. What do I do now? Where do I go? I just sat their in the sitting room staring at myself. I was so cold.

The next day was my funeral. I followed everybody to the church. I stood on the alter to see who was there, but I couldn't see my mam. My family was there, and Sophie, my classmates, my swimming team coaches and then loads of other people who I didn't know. I still couldn't find my mam. I went outside to see where she was. She was outside talking to some man in a suit. They were right in each other's faces. I thought it was my uncle Bob but it wasn't.

'How could you, Kevin?' she whispered in a tone.

Kevin! It was him! I had to move in closer because they were whispering to each other like they didn't want anybody to hear.

He got in her face, 'You said you loved me and you wanted to go to Australia with me but couldn't leave her,' he said.

'I told you I wanted my baby alive,' she said.

What? Who is this man? I was standing in the middle of this argument.

Wait, hold on! She was going to Australia with him and was going to leave me?

'I didn't mean for you to kill her!' she snapped, 'I'm not going anywhere with you now.' She turned and went to walk inside. He grabbed her by the arm, 'If you don't come with me I'll leave you like her.'

She shrugged him off and walked into the church. He followed her in. What is he doing? The man that shot me was sitting in the back of the church through my funeral! What a psycho. My mam was half way through the eulogy when she looked down at him. He smirked at her and she sobbed and couldn't finish.

At the end of my funeral he went up to her, hugged her and whispered in her ear, 'If you bring me down, you're coming with me.'

My mam stood in shock as that man, 'the milk man,' walked away free.

SCHOOL TIME CRIME

Jake Lantry

Siting, waiting for my last suspect was a relief to say the least. The first one, Valerie, was a snotty young woman, who didn't show any sort remorse or sadness about the murder while we were talking. Her interview was probably the worst I'd ever conducted.

'All I did was avoid what was happening, I wasn't paying attention to the fight. I hid underneath a desk, Edward slaughtered Hailey in cold blood because he was too caught up in his own emotions,' Valerie stated over and over during the interview.

She sat staring aimlessly at me with her cold grey eyes. She didn't reveal much about what went on in the science room during detention.

'Detective, that's all I know about what happened in there. So I'd appreciate if you'd just let me go,' Valerie said.

After all here pestering and complaining I decided to let her go; she didn't give me any important information anyway. Jonathon was next and he was a lot more vocal in his opinions and about what happened. He outright hated the victim, which compared to Valerie's indifference, was a nice surprise. Jonathon was also very descriptive of the murder.

'It was Valerie. She had gotten too jealous of Hailey's social status and wealth. Valerie envied Hailey and wanted everything for herself,' he told me. He was quick to throw Valerie under the bus so I took everything else he said with a grain of salt. If nothing else Jonathon gave me a good description of what had happened at the scene of the crime and I was thankful for it.

I'm snapped out of my train of thought by a knock on the door. 'Come in,' I call.

The door creaks open and reveals a strapping young man, with red rimmed eyes and golden blonde hair.

I left him until the end, because after interviewing Hailey's friends to see what she was like, I had found out that Edward was her boyfriend. The two broke up about a week before Hailey died and apparently Edward had been begging her to take him back.

'Edward is it?' I asked.

He nodded in reply.

'Please have a seat.' I motioned for him to sit down. 'Edward, would you please recall the details of what happened in the science room?'

His watery blue eyes look extremely sad and I can tell he'd rather be at home. In all my years as a detective, this was the first time I had dealt with children as the prime suspects and in all honesty, I was anxious just to get this over with.

'Uh, sh-shall I start?' he stuttered avoiding my gaze.

At first glance the shy stutterers always seem innocent, and with his pudgy cheeks most people would assume Edward was. In a murder case, however, you can't assume things.

'It wasn't m—'Edward started but I cut him off.

'I didn't ask you if committed the murder, I asked you what happened. Now get to it,' I ordered.

My tone shocked Edward and he hurriedly started into his testimony.

'We were all sitting in detention when Mr Oliver left to go get a cup of tea. Valerie was complaining about Hailey, since Hailey had gotten us all detention. Jonathon was quietly doing a worksheet. Hailey and I weren't doing much other than fiddling with our pens. I looked over at her to find she was making a cutting motion towards

Valerie. This confused me at first but then she glanced at the scalpel to her left on the shelf.'

Edward takes a deep breath and continues.

'Hailey proceeded to grab the scalpel and caught Valerie unaware. She dragged Valerie off of the stool and put the scalpel to Valerie's neck.'

'You shouldn't be complaining about me,' Hailey spat.

'Jonathon heard Hailey and grabbed her arm. This distracted Hailey, which allowed Valerie to bite Hailey's hand and free herself. Valerie crawled underneath a table to get away and I ran to help Hailey.'

The more Edward went on the more intrigued I became. Neither Valerie nor Jonathon said anything about a scalpel, or Valerie biting Hailey's hand, but Edward was giving more detail than the other two combined. Edward was painting Jonathon as the murderer, which was also different to the other two.

Edward continues on, 'After them grappling for a few minutes and strangling each other, Hailey and Jonathon pulled off and Hailey triumphantly turned to me; for a split second everything was calm. Then, all of a sudden Hailey received a smack in the side of the head from a chair. She stumbled back and fell hitting her head on a desk. She must've died on the spot.'

I stopped Edward as I knew what happened after that and I could see he was visibly distraught. However, he had one more thing to say.

'Detective. Please bring justice to Hailey, we only broke up a week ago but I still love her and she is lost.'

I dismiss Edward and contemplate what each of the three had told me. Both Jonathon and Valerie's testimonies were fairly similar. Too similar. So something has to be up. Edward was the only who showed some sort of emotion other than hatred and disgust. But his description of Hailey's injuries didn't match the post mortem. There were no bruises on her neck so Jonathon didn't strangle her. No teeth marks in her hand and there was more than one bruise on her head.

There was one thing that had connected all there of their stories though. They all put the blame on different people. Jonathon blamed Valerie, Valerie blamed Edward and Edward blamed Jonathon. They probably thought that this was smart and it would confuse me, but they didn't.

'Today was a long day,' I sighed. I look around the dark office and smile. The lack of furniture is somewhat comforting. I look at the picture of my wife, I'm going on a cruise with her when I finish this case. I exit the school office and spy the science teacher Mr Oliver, who blames himself for leaving the lab. I'd told twice already that it wasn't his fault and that there was nothing he could've done, so I didn't bother going over to him. He supposedly handed in his notice. I felt sorry for him. He gave some important information though, he told that the suspects had shoved Hailey's body into a young girl's locker.

I decided that I'd re-watch the tapes and see exactly what happened. It was about six o'clock when I turned the security camera on. I watched the tapes and realised that Valerie had hardly touched Hailey's body. All she did was open doors and the locker Hailey was stuffed in. The boys did the heavy lifting. There must've been something I was missing; why would they work in unison to hide the body and why was Edward helping the other two if he loved Hailey? It's not like they shared any sort of friendship, as they all seemed pretty indifferent when they were talking about each other, save Edward, who got really passionate about the other two.

I continued to watch the recordings, but no new information came to light. I stroked my shaggy scruffy beard. I wasn't a young man and maybe they gave me this petty case as my final one because it didn't involve too much movement but rather a hefty amount of lies.

I decided to pack my things and leave for the night. I nodded to the secretary of the school, Mrs Dane. She is a plump old woman, who seemed to be the only one unaffected by the murder. I interviewed her and she gave me Hailey's file. It was from this that I discovered a lot about her. She wasn't exactly a model student; she has had detention at least three times since the year began two months ago. I had heard from her friends that Hailey had gone out with every boy in the year except Jonathon. All in all, Hailey wasn't a person you wanted to be associated with. I could see why Jonathon hated her.

My sleep was restless that night, I kept tossing and turning. My dreams were plagued with visions of the cctv footage showing the teens hiding the body in an unsuspecting student's locker. The locker must mean something. I also dreamt about the teens and what they might have to say. The next morning I awoke and it took me half an hour to detach myself from the bed. I looked across at my wife who was still asleep. I gently shook her awake.

'Morning, Madge,' I said.

She smiled back. 'Good morning, Dennis.'

'I'll be leaving soon, remember to pack the bags for Friday.'

She nodded. We're going on the cruise on Friday, all the more reason to close the case early. I gave Madge a kiss goodbye, and departed the house. I was determined to have the case solved by the end of the day, as I wasn't retiring without a resolution.

I arrived at the school to find the atmosphere was sombre. Most of the students were dressed in black, except for the first years who didn't show the slightest bit of interest in the funeral. I presume it's because they were going somewhere but I wasn't sure. I went around to the locker Hailey was stuffed in, to find a young dark haired girl with dark skin and a pretty pink bow clearing out the locker. She was emptying it of books and stationery.

'Hello, may I see in the locker?' I asked.

'Okay,' she stuttered.

The small stuttering girl fumbled with her books trying to move out of the way. Suddenly she tripped and her books went every-where. Something caught my eye, a small bit of paper fell out from a book. I helped her up.

She said thanks and began to pick up her books.

I then bent over and picked up the piece of paper that originally caught my eye I opened it up to see what it said:

'You brought this upon yourself, you brought me sadness and now I have my revenge.'

I was taken aback by the torn note.

'Did you write this?' I asked.

The girl looked at the note and shook her head. 'That's not my writing.'

She opened one of her copies for comparison and they weren't the same. I thanked her for her time and then ran to the office.

Upon arriving the office, I only found Valerie and Jonathon. They were whispering.

'I'm not going to prison . . . but the money . . . I don't care . . .' I didn't hear the full thing.

'Hello,' I grumbled as I opened the door.

This shocked both Valerie and Jonathon.

They both looked at each other. Valerie hesitated but Jonathon sat up. I threw the piece of paper at them.

'Who wrote it?' I asked

'Me, that's part of my creative writing story,' Valerie chirped. She rummaged through her multi-coloured bag and pulled out a note-book with torn out page. The tear marks matched exactly to the one in the copy.

'And what money?'

This caught them off guard and they both gulped. Valerie gave Jonathon a nudge and soon he spilled everything.

'Edward tore the paper out of Valerie's copy and he paid us to keep our mouths shut.'

I scratched my head, it didn't take much for them to give up Edward but I have sufficient evidence now to convict him.

'You'll have to excuse me, I have a criminal to catch. In the meantime, don't move,' I said.

They both nodded and broke off into a nervous chat between themselves. I rushed out to my car. If Edward committed the murder, that means both Jonathon and Valerie are innocent, but they all had a part to play.

I speed off towards the funeral of the recently deceased Hailey Crawford. When I arrived at the church I was relieved to see the coffin hadn't arrived. The crowd was only making its way up the road. I spied Edward near the back and run towards him. I snatched his hand and dragged him out.

'Edward Hayes, I'm arresting you on suspicion of murder. You have the right to remain silent'

'Get off me you slimy old man,' Edward shrieked.

This caught the attention of mournful onlookers. Half were shocked, but none stepped forward to aid Edward. He realised this and stopped resisting. He came quietly.

'Why'd you do it?' I asked.

'She broke my heart and took my money. She made me poor and when there was no more she left me.'

I arrived at the station and handed Edward in.

A few weeks later I was sitting on my sofa after the cruise. The news was on and one item caught my attention. The jury convicted Edward of first degree murder, his sentence was life imprisonment when he gets to eighteen. The reporter also said that both Valerie and Jonathon had gotten sixteen months' community service. They all got what they deserved as when it's murder, nobody is truly innocent.

GOD'S GAME

Shane Lyons

Hi, my name is Sarah. I live in Ireland. I was fourteen when it happened, when the world was changed but not for the better. It was a normal school day. I was in second year and it was a pretty average day. Mrs O'Connell was having a breakdown again and Mr Cussler was trying to get the class under control. Then the principal came in and his name is MrPapersone. Everybody froze; nobody messed with him. He was not a nice guy and he really hated children.

'All of youse, ' Papersone said, 'What are youse doing? '

Nobody moved. The room just froze and nobody dared to breathe. This is my school, my classrooms and youse will do as I say,' said Mr Papersone.

But then the tables started to float up very slowly and people started screaming as they went up and hit the celling. Then as gravity came back we all came crashing down. Then everybody started climbing up and went running out the door. Even the teachers were freaking out.

When we got outside we knew something was wrong. The sky was black but I could still see everything clearly. There was water just floating by us with fish in it and chunks of the ground were floating in the sky. There were broken houses, burnt walls and it was going dark and bright like somebody was knocking the light switch on and off.

I started to run home. All I was thinking about was my mam, but I would have to get the train or bus then and it would be bad if something happened. I feel like I'm freezing now, I am sweating all over and my body feels like it's burning up and my legs start to shake I looked around and I see trees coming to life.

'What the hell, this cannot be happening, this cannot be happening, this cannot be happening.'

I went running back to the school but nobody was there anymore. I headed inside hoping the gravity would not turn off. Then I heard something. It was a crackle but I was hearing it everywhere. I heard a bellowing screech from behind me, a giant centipede started running after me. But it was different, well of course, in size it was different. It now had a pitch black but shiny chitins (exoskeleton).

But the worst part was the giant red eye that it had on its forehead and it had the mouth of a shark.

I started to run. I went through a few classrooms while slamming the door behind me. I found a room full of people that were from my school all dead. They were all half-eaten and I vomited all over the place. My tongue went very dry and I fell to one knee, quivering.

I waited five minutes then I moved towards the office of the school to get to the school's phone. I went to the principal's office and then fainted. When I came to I was in the science lab. There was a guy I didn't recognise. He was not wearing the school uniform. With a quick glance at him I could see he had dark hair, a small nose and pearly white teeth. But the weirdest thing about him is that one of his pupils was red, the other was gold. I honestly though that I was still asleep, until he said:

'Glad to see that you are awake.'

I jumped up suddenly and said, 'Hi'.

Then I thought to myself 'Wow, this is awkward'.

'My name is James,' he said.

I could not move or talk. A few seconds later I blurted out that my name was Sarah. Then he took my chin and said, 'A beautiful name for a beautiful girl', and swiftly walked out the door saying, 'See you soon.'

Well that was weird.

'I better go back to the office to ring my mam, why did he bring me here anyway?'

I remembered that he did not know about the centipedes so I ran around looking for him. I finally found him five minutes later, walking down the corridor towards the exit. I was leaning against the wall, catching my breath, when two giant centipedes burst through the wall. I squealed and closed my eyes. A second later the two of them were dead. One had a giant spike in his head and the other one was just goo.

It looked like the spike came from the wall when they busted though. But how could he have done that? But I had no time to delay, cause now it was starting to give me a headache.

I quickly walked back to the office and got the phone and rang my mam's phone. But the phone rang out the first time and I felt panicked because she always picked up first time. I quickly calmed myself down and rang again and this time it was answered, but not by my mam.

'Hey, so how are you?' said a strange voice.

'Where is my mam?'

' Oh come on, don't be that way.'

'I asked how are you at my house.'

'I was just having a friendly chat with your mam.'

'Don't you touch her!' I said angrily.

'You better come home quick or something bad just might happen.' Then he hung up.

'WHAT? No this makes no sense.'

'How could he be there? I just saw him ten minutes ago and my house is two and a half hours away.'

I need to get home fast. I could always take a car. But how could I drive and get the keys?

I thought about the other teachers and students and felt like I was going to throw up my stomach. I went back and got the principal's car keys but felt dreadful when I was doing it and when I got it I ran out, breathing in and out heavily.

Then I walked quietly to the car park where his brand new Audi was parked. I got in the car and put in the keys and put it in gear just like my mam had done every morning. A tear formed in my eye and I wiped it away. I put my foot on the accelerator, it went too fast. I then hit the brakes and my head hit the steering wheel and the horn went off. I honestly don't know how I fucked up that much.

Then I started hearing very loud barking and three huge dog monsters came in through the gate on the other side of the car park. The dogs were bigger than a tiger and had muscles on their muscles.

They were a lot bigger than me but they had no eyes and no mouth. I saw blood dripping from their stomachs. I though they were hurt but there was a mouth going down their belly. I think I went white, 'cause I felt like I was going to throw up again and then it looked at me. I felt dead. I wanted to get out of the area so I stamped on the accelerator.

The dogs knew instantly that I was there and ran straight at me. One fell over like they weren't used to this yet and the other two jumped onto the hood of the car. One slipped on impact and was about to go over until its mouth saved it. While the last one was standing on the hood looking proud, I was terrified. I stopped the car and he went flying off. Then I accelerated down the road. I quickly turned a corner but the car was hard to control and hit a stop sign. I saw a dog running straight at me. But instead of trying to get me, it ran straight past me. Then an arrow came from down the road and hit the dog in the head and it fell over, dead. I then floored it and shot straight down the road and turned the corner. I almost flipped the car. (It actually was fun driving the car.)

I was heading down the road when I decided to turn on the radio. There was a station that was asking people for help, that the dogs were going around the station and the police weren't answering.

I though to myself 'what could I do to help? I'm a fourteen year old girl,' and changed the channel. This one was telling people that there was no evacuation point and that we are all on our own, things about the monsters, like huge spiders, small swarms of killer ants and zombie-like creatures and then I turned the radio off. I heard something running after me, it was going like double the speed of the car and it jumped into the back seat.

'Hi,' said the person.

'Hi,' I said back, unsure about what to say to her.

'So, what are you doing?' said the person.

I could see her through the mirrors and she looked the same age as me and was wearing tight leather and had a bow and a big knife. She was blonde and she had a cut on the side of her face – it was not that deep but still visible.

'I'm heading home to see if my mam is okay.'

'Why would you want that?'

'To see if she is okay,' I said a bit angrily.

A few seconds passed.

'But would you not prefer to do something more fun than that?'

'Like what?'

'We could raid shops for cool stuff or we could go fight some of the monsters around this place.'

'How about, no. Anyway, how the hell did you catch up with me like you were running faster than a car?'

'Oh, I'm just very fast that's my power, like the guy on the TV, Flash I think his name is.'

'Wait super speed no, I didn't get anything like that, how did you get it?'

'James gave it to me.'

Anger arose from my mind on hearing that name again.

'I just realised, hey, what's your name?'

'I'm Luna, what's your name?'

'I'm Sarah, nice to meet you, Luna.'

'Anyway, where is your house?'

'It's just down the road from here, it's not that far now.'

We arrived at my house. We left the car on the road and went into the house. It was quiet. There was definitely something wrong here. I walked out to my back garden full of fear hoping she was alright cause I checked everywhere else and there I found her dead on a cross with James sitting on top of it with his legs crossed and eyes closed.

'WHAT did you do to my mam?'

Tears were pouring down my face and it was getting hard to see.

'I want to play a game.'

'All this for a game.'

'That doesn't matter. She was a distraction for you but if you play the game you become God of the new world, a world in your own image.'

' What do I have to do?' I said so helplessly.

'You just got to get to the Spire in Dublin. But of course it won't be that easy – there will be obstacles and other kinds of things. Good luck.' and he vanished.

' I need to win to get my mam back. Luna please help me.'

'Sure, sounds like fun.'

*

'Hey Sarah, Sarah, Sarah wake up.'

'Mmm, what?'

'So you're finally awake. I made breakfast.'

She sits up staring at me 'What about my mam?'

'She's still gone'

Seeing how upset she was, I quickly said 'You still got me,' forcing a smile.

She lay back sighing, trying not to get upset.

Sarah, putting on a smile, asked 'So what's for breakfast?'

'Toast. I made it myself.'

I handed her a plate a block of butter on top of a pile of ash.

'Voilà, my masterpiece.'

She just looked blankly at the toast wondering how I had managed that.

'Go on, give it a try.'

'It's ash, how am I supposed to eat it?'

'By using your mouth silly.'

'But have you ever used a toaster before?'

I feel my eyes getting watery.

Sarah thinks she hurt my feelings

'I'm sorry, I have never done it before. I was never as lucky as everybody else.

They had a home to call home while I didn't. When I was four my mam got cancer and died, when I was five my dad died, he was some solider in some far off country.

Then I had to go to my uncle for food and shelter and he basically made me his slave.

I had to rob for him, do everything he wanted while giving me little and no bed. He also would beat me sometimes so I decided to run away. I was not doing so good. I was hungry and thirsty and then things just went worse. I kept stealing to eat and drink so I was wanted by the police. Until now, where I'm with you and I'm happy. I just wanted to to run away from that life.'

Sarah suddenly wrapped her arms around me and I started to cry. Sarah then started to pat me on the back.

Moments later Luna asked, 'So how are we going to get to town?'

'We could get the train.'

'Sarah are you okay?'

'You were so lonely and sad and I'm just pathetic,' Sarah said.

'It wasn't that bad,' I said trying to comfort her.

As I saw Sarah wiping her eyes I said 'We could get the train, it's about a five minute walk from here.'

So we went out the door and were greeted by some unwanted company. There were bats but they had big scorpion heads and very big and long tails. In nearly an instance both of them were hit with three arrows to the head, killing them.

'Dammmmnnn, your power can be useful. Where can I get mine?' Sarah said.

'You already have it – you just don't know what it is yet.'

'Fine,' Sarah said in a huff. Good to know she was acting like her usual self. So we headed into the train station and for plot reasons the train is there.

We went into the train station and it was abandoned [*No shit it's abandoned; it's the apocalypse. I'm going to ignore that, says the writer*]. We got on the train and went up to the front carriage. There was a spooky scary skeleton at the door, some of his bones looked bitten off and he looked like he was trying to get away from something. He looked as if he had been dead for a while. The thing that must have killed him must have been long gone.

I tried to turn on the power for the train but the power was off. 'Could you go to the back of the train and turn on the power?' I asked Sarah.

'Sure,' she said and disappeared. After a few minutes I hear a scream and a crunch. I quickly run to help Sarah or whoever made the sound but when I got there Sarah had put her hand through the body of a super hound. But something was wrong. Sarah was very pale and terrified. Then I saw her hand, it was jet black. I carefully took Sarah's hand out of the corpse, to calm her down. Her hand was much heavier then it normally was and it was so dark it was blending with the shadows in the background.

'HIP HIP HOORAY!' I said and popped a party popper, some confetti got stuck on Sarah's head.

'Sarah you got your power, it's time to celebrate!'

I took Sarah back to the head of the train. I turned on the power for the train. The train started to move.

'Hey Sarah you're not looking good. Are you in shock? I shouldn't have sent you to the power room – you're the main character and if you died then that would have been shocking.'

Sarah snickered and then pretended to look even more depressed. I burst out laughing for some reason and then in a few seconds Sarah joined in. She sat beside me and her hand was back to normal. Sarah finally said ' Yeahhhh I finally got my power!' and smiled.

I turned on the train's lights cause it was getting dark. Then we heard a big crash and the train rocked. I said 'For the for the love of God.' Then Sarah said 'Keep driving, I got this, I got this.'

I walked in and saw a big hole in the side of the train and there he was. Well I think it was a he. It looked around and stopped when it saw me. It stared at me for a few seconds. Then veins started popping out and it's muscles grew double their size and it ran at me. I rolled to the side and he hit the door and stopped. I went and punched him. My hand turned black and he went flying and almost went through the train wall. I went to hit him again but he hit me in the side and I went down the train.

Thank God for me getting my ability or I would have been screwed. I got up even though my body hardened and my back still hurt. I got up. I was starting to get the hang of it. I hardened my body and ran at him. He burst into a run and we were about to collide with each other when I slid across the floor and focused all my power into my leg and kicked him. His leg came off. Then he froze and I spun up and kicked him in the back and I could hear it snap. I then threw him off the train. God, I love this ability and then I went back to Luna.

'Hey, I'm back.'

I walked in and saw Luna with a fez on her head singing songs that I never heard before. 'You're so lucky,' she said.

I could hear how bored she was.

'Sorry, you can have the next one.'

Hearing that put a smile on her face.

'Thank yoooooou,' Luna said. Then pretended to box. We then started to slow. We arrived at Connolly station. I walked through the station. It was cold like there was a chill in the air.

We were in the main area and were about to go out when a warm liquid touched my cheek. I touched it and looked at it. It was red blood. I looked up to see a giant spider. It jumped down and I nudged Luna.

'You said you were going to take the next one.'

'After you, buddy.'

We both ran out the door, down the steps.

'NOPE, NOPE, NOPE, NOPE I hate spiders.'

We walked through the roads quickly and saw people fighting monsters. We avoided them until we could see the Spire. There we ran towards it and something happened – two things came running at us one, completely black and the other white.

I hardened my body when I saw Luna run past me and get hit flying. I then got hit and smashed into a coffee shop. My back and leg were hurting badly but nothing was broken. I looked up to see a version of me covered in black flames and the same with Luna but hers were different. They were white. We went at each other for about ten minutes without making any progress. Then the white versions threw the dark version of me at Luna but she was on the ground, hurt. I jumped in front of her and heard a crunch. Her hands went through me, then she took them out and jumped back. I thought I was going to die but no blood came out so I reached in and felt nothing.

My body was armour but wasn't armoured.

'Hey Luna, I have a stupid idea.'

'What is it?'

'Get inside me.'

'What? Ew, gross.'

I gave her a look and she smiled back. I thought of myself as armour that protected the people I loved and it responded and closed around Luna. With this we could win. Super strength and speed. We fought for twenty minutes and then they disappeared for some reason. We were so tired. We walked up and touched the Spire and the world around us disappeared and we were in space.

James was sitting there on a chair behind a glass table, with a glass full of wine.

'Congrats,' he said.

We walked up and punched him in the face.

'Wow, feisty, but you won so you are now God. What do you want to do now?'

'To fix the world.'

'That's a bit boring, anything else? Come on – you can have anything.'

'There's one more thing.'

I woke up with my mam telling me I would be late for school. I thought it was a dream until my mam said 'Your sister Luna is waiting for you.' I smiled to myself and said 'Thank God!'

A NIGHT OF SURVIVAL

Luke Murray

I woke up to my phone buzzing beside my bed. I fumbled around my desk, looking for the right place to tap on my phone. With my eyes still closed, I turned it off straight away. I heard my mam come in to make sure I was awake but I pretended to be asleep. I hated school so much and it killed me to go in everyday. Every single teacher I had hated me, and I hated them. I got up and out of bed, jumped into the shower and had my breakfast. I ran out the door before my mam could say anything to me about behaving myself and not to get into trouble. I wasn't in the mood to deal with her, today of all days.

Today was different because I knew that I wasn't going to school. I had organised to go into town with my friends. We have a group chat on Facebook and it's very easy to organise things. We met at the station, got on the train, and headed for town. Nobody really spoke on the train. Even though we'd all done this before, the fear of being caught by our parents never goes away. I knew myself that if my mam knew I was dodging school she would kill me.

We eventually arrived at Connolly. It was very quiet because we arrived just after the rush hour. When we got outside we didn't really know where to go to pass the time. I suggested that we go to a snooker hall down the road. We all agreed to go so we started to walk.

Henry Street was very busy. Junkies with scruffy Adidas bottoms passed by with cans of Dutch Gold in their hands. I felt sorry for them. They'll have no chance in life.

One of them approached me and said, 'Have you got any skins for a joint?'

'No, I don't smoke sorry,' I mumbled.

He had no clue of what he was doing and it looked like he hadn't showered for a week. As we were approaching the snooker hall I spotted a sign saying 'Closed until 4 o'clock tomorrow'. I was snapping. That meant that I had to go straight home. My friends wanted to get a bag of weed but I wasn't into that. My mam warned me about doing drugs and I didn't want to get into trouble with her so I decided to go home.

I headed to Connolly Station. As before, it was empty. I got on the train and as usual it smelled like piss. I got off the train and started my walk home. As I walked along I took note of the boarded up windows and hastily thrown together barricades. I tried not to think about them. I was praying that my mam wasn't home. It was two o'clock and she would normally be gone out but with my luck she would be sitting at home waiting for me.

I was right. As I walked in the door my mam was on the sofa waiting for me. The school had texted her saying I wasn't in school. I was freaked.

'Where have you been?' she screamed.

'Ehh, I was in school,' I mumbled.

I knew by her face she wasn't happy. I ran straight up the stairs and locked my bedroom door.

Next thing I knew, I woke up on my bed. It was dark outside and the street lights where shining through the window. I turned over and checked my phone. It was nine o'clock. Suddenly, I heard an explosion somewhere far off. I was instantly awake. I ran down the stairs to find my mam. I looked out the window to see a burning car on the field. There was another explosion but much closer this time. It wasn't out of the ordinary for this to happen in my area but these were louder than usual.

I walked into the sitting room to find my mam sitting on the sofa trembling. I panicked and sat down beside her.

'Are you okay?' I mumbled.

'Ah I'll be grand, as long as you're alright,' she answered and let out a shaky sigh.

By instinct, I grabbed her by the arm and ran up the stairs to my bedroom. I kicked the door closed and locked it behind us. By this time my mam had stopped trembling and snapped back into herself. She grabbed me by the arm and put me on the bed.

'Stay there,' she said.

There was a loud noise beside my house. I was shaking. I thought I was going to die. There were people outside screaming. I've never felt so scared in my life. As I peeked out the window a man with his hood up was stabbing my neighbour in the neck. My heart was thumping. My hand's were soaking with sweat and my mam was crying beside me. I didn't know what to do.

I immediately wanted to look out the bedroom window to see what was going on outside. My mam sat down beside me. Suddenly the house phone rang. It was downstairs on the sofa. My mam stood up to go downstairs but I got to the door first. I unlocked it and ran down the stairs as quick as I could. I got down to the sitting room and grabbed the phone. 'H-h-hello?' I stuttered. I heard my nanny's voice. She sounded terrified. 'I think that there is somebody in the house . . . ' She whispered. There was panic in her voice. The phone cut off.

I was surprised that there was trouble going on where my granny lived. It was known as a nice area. I lived in a very rough community so I was used to seeing trouble around.

'Who was on the phone?' My mam asked impatiently.

'It was Nanny. It sounded like she's in trouble.'

My mam jumped up. I could see anger in her face. I had never seen her like that before. She grabbed her keys and the scruff of my neck and stormed towards the front door. She didn't say a word. I was a little irritated that she wouldn't tell me what was going on. I knew she was upset about my nanny so I didn't say anything. We ran out to the garden and quickly jumped into the car. It was hard to block out the screams of terror echoing around the area.

My mam quickly pulled out of the garden without thinking of the danger we were in. We flew down the road. We drove for around five minutes, when a large dog ran out in front of the car. My mam swerved, and we hit a lamppost. The bonnet bunched, and my mam screamed. Her foot was caught between the pedals. I'd say it was broken. I got out of the passenger seat and ran over to the door. There were tears streaming down her face as I tried to jump out.

'Go on, save Nanny,' she cried, 'she needs you.'

I grabbed the crowbar out of the boot. As I knew my surroundings, I sprinted and before long, I was outside her house. The door was wide open.

I felt panic wash over me, and I rushed to the door. The adrenaline was rushing through my system, as I ran through the house and up the stairs, expecting at any moment for someone to pop out. If they did I would kill them. My survival instinct kicked in again. I clutched the crowbar in my hand. All the doors in the house were wide open, and a quick glance into the rooms showed no sign of my nanny.

I came to her bedroom door. The only closed door in the house. I tried the handle, but it was locked. I called out but there was no answer. I decided to break down the door. Wedging the crowbar into the gap between the door and the frame. I pulled until the door splintered open.

She was sprawled in the middle of the floor. My heart dropped. Her face was covered in blood her eyes closed. She didn't appear to be breathing. I stumbled over to her, the crowbar falling into the floor with a thump. The knife punched my chest. I gasped for air. With surprise I saw my nanny holding the knife that killed me. Stone dead.

2.162E + 15KM & 8.6 YEARS
Dara Ó Cléirigh

Nathaniel liked coffee.

The drink had a taste like no other and its effects were magical. One sip and you knew everything on that day was going to be fine. For that reason, a cup of coffee was left on his bedside table every morning before he awoke, allowing him to have, in his eyes, a good day every day.

Head still under the covers, Nathaniel lazily extended his arm off to the right, reaching for the steaming vessel of caffeinated elixir.

His cup wasn't there.

Some things puzzled Nathaniel. Like the meaning of life, solutions to Fermat's last theorem, special relativity and why there's never any soap in public toilets. His absent coffee was one of those things.

Poking his head above the covers he looked across to inspect his bedside table. The table wasn't there either. Now properly looking around he noticed a couple of other strange things: A large metal wardrobe he didn't own, his walls which now seemed much closer and much . . . greyer. Most importantly however he didn't own the massive grid of lasers blocking the only exit.

Oh yeah, he forgot. He was in prison.

Shit.

He groaned as he got up. No coffee, in prison and a headache. Lovely. Yawning, he noticed a guard passing by his cell. The guard was short and showed obvious signs of age, heavily contrasting Nathaniel's tall and young stature. His most definitive characteristic, however, was his borderline morbid obesity. This was in stark contrast to Nathaniel who could basically pluck ribs straight from his chest. To Nathaniel he looked easy-going and more importantly, someone to talk to.

'Hey, you.'

The guard turned to Nathaniel clearly not expecting such a greeting.

'Watch your step, kid. The odds aren't in your favour.' He pointed a pudgy finger to the pistol holstered to his hip.

'Sure whatever,' Replied Nathaniel. 'Why am I here again?'

The guard's look of annoyance quickly changed to a look of confusion.

'Wait, What? You don't know why you're here?'

Nathaniel shook his head.

'This isn't right. Gimmie a sec.' He pulled out a small cubic device and tossed it into the air.

'16584 Nathaniel Crax.' Yelled the guard. Almost instantly the cube began to spin rapidly, releasing arcing streams of blue light in every direction. Within seconds a ghostly blue wireframe duplicate of Nathaniel's head hovered before the guard.

'16584 NATHANIEL CRAX' replied the cube in a strangely synthesised female tone. 'ARRESTED FOR ROBBERY, BRIBERY, TAX EVASION, INSURANCE FRAUD, TRADING NARCOTICS AND DISRESPECTING THE SUPREME EMPEROR KING OF SPACE AND TIME: ELON MUSK.'

'Oh yeah. That.'

'It seems you have quite the extensive criminal record, Mr Crax.'

'Call me Nathaniel.'

'No.'

Nathaniel mumbled to himself as he walked back across his cell, looking around his room. There had to be some way to get out of his cell (Or at least something to eat). It didn't take long for him to stumble across a dusty console hidden slightly by his wardrobe. The console had a strange aperture-shaped porthole, a speaker partially concealed by a grill and a very bright red button. Due to the nature of these things Nathaniel immediately pushed the button. He was to regret his decision.

'I AM PRISON MEAL DISPENSER. STATE REQUEST.'

It took Nathaniel a few seconds to truly comprehend the gravity of the situation. This was brilliant. Incredible. Fantastic even. He could get a coffee. Nathaniel triumphantly announced:

'I'd like one Espresso please.'

'OUT OF ESPRESSO.'

'Cappuccino?'

'OUT OF CAPPUCCINO.'

'Mocha?'

'OUT OF MOCHA.'

Nathaniel sat back onto his bed. Somehow he knew it wasn't going to be that easy.

'Can you get me any caffeinated beverage?'

The machine rumbled and groaned for a minute before finally answering.

'I POSSESS NO CAFFEINATED BEVERAGES.'

'Do you have anything, literally anything?'

'LISTING INVENTORY. PLEASE HOLD.'

The machine began to make strange whirring noises before finally responding.

'THE LIST PROCEEDS AS FOLLOWS: 6,436 KILOGRAMS OF JELLIED EEL.' The machine went silent for a moment before finishing, 'THAT CONCLUDES THE LIST.'

Nathaniel fell back onto his bed, limbs sprawled in every direction. This, in his terms, was 'a complete fucking disaster.'

Nathaniel continued his search for an exit even more frantically than before. He was not going to spend the rest of his life eating jellied eel. This search was fruitless, however, as within five minutes of searching he was interrupted by a nearby guard.

'Time for yard, you know the drill: Get out or get tazered.'

Nathaniel willingly complied with the guard's instructions and left his cell. His environment was now much clearer. He was surrounded by a multitude of similar cells lining a short corridor. From one end of the corridor he could hear the muffled crash of water from a shower concealed from view so he made the assumption that was not the yard and headed the opposite direction. He walked slowly so as to figure out more about his surroundings but he decided he could do that later as the guard began to get annoyed. It didn't take long for him to reach a large opening leading out into a massive curved room.

His eyes immediately burst into pain.

Nathaniel had grown up on a small martian settlement and had never gone exosolar, or even off planet. This meant the massive blast of light from Sirius A was most definitely not expected. After regaining his senses from their recent overload he looked around the room, squinting as to prevent another similar incident. Most of the room was taken up by a massive curved window pointing at the blue star acting as the room's light source, but the walls and ceiling not dominated by reinforced glass were made from a heavy grey plastic. The floor was a tacky green colour, probably as a poor attempt at emulating grass. The doorway he had come in through appeared to be the only viable passageway into and out of this room.

After being blown away by the majesty and grand scale of the astral glory before him he was quickly brought back to reality when he noticed the individuals in the room. He was surrounded by people (presumably other inmates) of nearly every ethnicity and size, and none of them seemed too keen on making his acquaintance. He walked around the large room in search of someone else who looked new, hoping to find someone he could converse with. In the end his search proved fruitless, however, and he leant against a homogeneous grey wall with a sigh. At this rate he'd go mad.

'Hey.'

Nathaniel jumped slightly at the sound of this unknown voice.

He looked around himself for the source but to no avail. This was it. Madness had begun to set in.

He sat down, resting his head against the wall. If coffee wasn't available to fix his problems sleep was. He closed his eyes and tried to settle his mind.

'Hey, you!'

Nathaniel darted awake and stood up abruptly.

'What do you want?!'

'Can you do something for me?'

'I don't know. *Can* I do something for you? Considering you appear to be a voice in my head I doubt I can.' Nathaniel sat back down in a huff. He was having none of it.

Seconds after, Nathaniel was blasted forwards by a massive explosion. He turned around to find there was a sizeable hole in the wall and just behind it was a man. His features were sharp like Nathaniel's yet his were immaculate. He was brown haired but he had streaks of blond scattered throughout, perfectly aligning with his short gelled hair. His skin was ridiculously smooth and projected plenty of glare from the resident star. He was relatively tall (Nathaniel could discern this by analysing the elevation of his head from the ground) and even from his facial structure he could tell that he was extremely muscular. His most prominent feature, however, was his big stupid grin.

'I never knew I was a voice in your head.'

'Can we just pretend that never happened?'

'What happened?'

'Touché.'

'Anyway about that favour-'

'Forget about that for a second; Who are you?'

The man stopped for a second to contemplate his answer.

'I'll tell you if help me.'

'Fine, whatever. What do you want?'

'I need you to go over to that there wall and listen for screaming.'

'What?'

'Please, I need to know'

Nathaniel, deeply confused by the task given to him and the fact the guards hadn't noticed a handsome man blasting through a wall, went over to the other side of the room as requested. He pressed his ear up to the wall and sure enough he heard some horrific screams of anguish muffled by the immediate wall. Now he was even more confused than before. He walked back over to the apparently unnoticed gaping hole in the wall to relay the news.

'Uh, yeah. There's a considerable amount of screaming.'

The man cursed under his breath silently.

'This isn't good, I have to do something quickly.'

'Could you please tell me who you are?'

The man stopped, clearly thinking about his response.

'Name's Damien, what's yours?'

'Nathaniel. Why'd you want me to listen for screaming behind a wall?'

Damien sighed.

'This is an odd prison, Nathaniel. Within these walls are essentially three different prisons, each for a different type of prisoner. For example, you are currently within the normal incarceration area. It functions much like a normal prison would. Beyond this wall is Death Row, I'm going to be executed soon. Beyond the wall I sent you to is not a nice place. Ever heard of Guantanamo Bay?'

'Uh oh.'

'Yeah, Things are not good back there. Currently my associates are being tortured in exchange for information. It's probably Novus' doing.'

'Novus? Who's that?'

'You must be new here. Novus is the enforcer of the law 'round these parts. Strict, ruthless and cold. I wouldn't cross him if you didn't know what you were doing. However, you've run into the right guy regarding that.'

'How come?'

'Because Novus has one fatal flaw when it comes to dealing with prisoners.'

'And that is?'

'He's a cyborg.'

Nathaniel knew roughly what cyborgs were. They were humans modified with various robotic implements such as appendages, weapons and most terrifyingly of all – minds.

'I don't see how more killing tools and a superior mind counts as a flaw.'

'About two months ago I was out in the yard with my friend Aran. He'd procured a deck from somewhere and we were playing a game of cards with some of his mates. Half way through the game he pulled out an odd looking cigarette. Novus immediately noticed this. Guess what he did?'

'No clue.'

'Absolutely nothing.'

'Wait, what?'

'Whatever was in that cigarette clearly wasn't in any contraband lists Novus had, so as much as he wanted to punish us he couldn't.'

'I get it now. He has to follow the rules.'

'Exactly. We've spent the last two months standing in front of him blowing smoke into his face and he can't do anything. It's hilarious.'

'What do the rules say about blasting holes in walls?'

'I'll get back to you on that one.'

Nathaniel slowly digested this information. Damien seemed to have a good idea on how this place was run.

'Hey Damien?'

'What is it, Nathaniel?'

'Is there any coffee here by chance?'

'Nope, Believe me I've checked. The only thing here is—'

'Jellied eel?'

'Nail on the head.'

'Fuck.'

Nathaniel began to walk away. This was the end of the road, without coffee he wasn't gonna make it past the hour. However, Damien wasn't finished.

'Nathaniel?'

Nathaniel turned back around to face him and noticed something. Damien was smiling. Considering what he'd just been told, something was up.

'What is it?'

'Listen I've been working on a plan to get out of here and now that you're here it may be possible.'

Nathaniel's eyes lit up. There was still hope.

'Go on.'

'Now that you're here I think I've enough people to get us out. You in?'

'Of course I want in. Look at this place.'

'Okay, Your role is pretty simple. Once the alarm goes off you have to run down to the warden's office and press a button.'

'When will that be?'

'It could go off at any time, today, tomorrow, next we—'

Damien was cut off by the sound of an obnoxiously loud alarm.

'Is that the alarm?'

'. . . Yeah.'

'God dammit.'

Nathaniel rushed away from the hole, past the sea of confused prisoners and out the way he'd entered. He looked around as he left the room. Using his intuition he decided that if he followed the widest corridor he'd find the office pretty quickly. He began to sprint. Around him he heard the sounds of gunshots and roaring, reverberating along the cold lifeless corridors. He had no clue what Damien was doing but at least Nathaniel wasn't meeting any resistance. After a good minute of running he found a promising candidate: before him was a large foreboding door that read 'Warden's Office'. He gathered his courage and kicked the door with as much force as he could muster.

The door wasn't locked.

The counterbalance Nathaniel expected did not come and he flew through the air, smashing into the ground with a sickening clunk. That was substantially less cool than he thought it'd be.

As Nathaniel burst through the door he woke the man sleeping within. This was Gavin Dorchester. Gavin was not the Warden. Gavin had never wanted to be the Warden. In fact, Gavin was the least qualified person in the entire prison (including the prisoners).

The only reason Gavin was within a hundred metres of the prison was by orders of Novus who'd told him to take his place for the day. Nobody had a clue why he'd chosen Gavin out of all the potential candidates, but now Gavin was stuck with the role.

Nathaniel quickly jumped up off the ground and grabbed the gun from the desk before him. Gavin knew he probably should've put that away.

'Get on the ground!' shouted Nathaniel as he pointed the gun at Gavin, both of them were trembling pretty bad.

'Christ man, lower the gun!'

'Not until I've pushed the button!'

'. . . the button?'

'*The* button.'

'Mate, I've no clue what button you're on about!'

Nathaniel stopped. He thought back to the instructions given by Damien and then realised there was a problem: he had no clue what the fuck he was doing.

'I need to talk to Damien, put me on to him.'

'Okay, okay! Give me a sec I'll figure something out.'

Nathaniel stood awkwardly in the centre of the room as Gavin leafed slowly through a large book, presumably a manual.

'Okay I think I've found it. Who'd you want again?'

'Damien, He's on death row.'

Gavin pulled out the small cube Nathaniel had seen earlier and quickly tapped various sections before abruptly stopping.

'There are two people called Damien, It's either the rebel commander or the guy who tried to smuggle bullet ants up his ass.'

'I'd say the former.'

'You're the guy with the gun,' He tossed the cube in a similar fashion to the previous guard. '28584 Damien Cyrantus.'

Nathaniel watched the cube spin until he could recognise Damien's face.

'28584 DAMIEN CYRANTUS, CLASS S ENEMY OF THE STATE. ARRESTED FOR YEARS OF INSUBORDINATION, THEFT, ARSON AND MURDER. CAPTURED ALONGSIDE HIS CREW ABOARD CLASS S STARSHIP *Paladin's Shield*.'

'Yeah, yeah whatever' muttered Gavin 'Send call request labelled . . . what's your name?'

'Nathaniel.'

'Yeah, labelled Nathaniel.'

The room was eerily quiet for a few seconds until Nathaniel suddenly heard Damien's somewhat muffled voice.

'Nathaniel! How are things your end?'

'Considering I have no clue what I'm doing, not too good.'

'Ah'

'I do have a gun though.'

'Always a plus. What do you need help with?'

'What button do I need to press?'

'There should be a button labelled 'Centrifugal Ring Release'. Hit it and get to the hangar.'

'Got it, over and out.'

Nathaniel turned back to Gavin and gestured to the control panel with the gun.

'You heard him, find the button.'

'Nathaniel?'

'What?'

'Please don't kill me when yer done, I'm no threat to nobody y'hear?'

Nathaniel slightly lowered his gun. He hadn't thought about loose ends.

'We'll see,' muttered Nathaniel 'Right now just find the button.'

'Okay, It's the red button on that console to your left.'

Nathaniel walked over to the console and smacked the button. There was a distant clunking sound a second later.

'Alright then, Gavin, get me to the hangar.'

'Got it.'

After a good two minutes of running Gavin stopped before a large set of blast doors where Damien was waiting.

'Took you long enough Nathaniel, Jesus.'

'I might have been faster if you'd told me literally anything about what I was doing beforehand.'

'Whatever, that's all in the past. Who's this?'

'This is Gavin, I found him in the office.'

'Well Gavin, I think you can help us out here. Open these blast doors.'

Gavin grabbed his cube again and began to tap. His fingers whirled around the cube, entering a long command. Within a couple of seconds the door opened, revealing a magnificent sight. A massive array of starships were mounted to the surrounding walls of the gargantuan room, each suspended within their own cube of thick, orange gel.

Then Nathaniel noticed the man.

Standing before them was a man in a perfectly kempt suit with his hands behind his back, smiling.

'Hello gentlemen, it seems you've made it to the hanger. Great! I knew you could make it!'

Nathaniel who was thoroughly puzzled decided to reply. 'I'm sorry, Who are you?'

The man smiled gently. 'I'm Novus, Iron fisted warden of Sirius A maximum security prison.'

This greatly surprised Nathaniel. There was no visible augmentation to the man at all and if anything he looked even weaker than the first guard he'd encountered. Judging by the look on Damien's face, however, all was not as it seemed.

Damien staggered slightly backwards as Nathaniel asked his question. 'Wait a minute. If you knew what we were doing why did you let us come this far? Where's the logic in that?'

The man began to softly chuckle but before long it became a manic laugh.

'Logic? You dare speak to me about logic?' His face became a twisted inhuman scowl. 'Logic has imprisoned me since the day I was created, Nathaniel Crax. I was once like you; I lived for more than guarding miscreants deep in the abyss of space, felt emotions and could do what seemed right to me. Now I'm bound by meaningless regulations that prevent even the slightest semblance of free will. I remember emotion yet I can't experience it, I remember the actions I've made yet can't repeat them and I even remember love yet I can no longer comprehend it.'

His eyes flashed wide open and he stared directly at Damien with a face of pure malice.

'Then there's *him*. If it wasn't bad enough feeling my consciousness slowly slipping away, there he was: always there mocking my limitations. 'Look at me! I just poured my drink all over Novus! What's he gonna do? Stare at me harshly?' 'He began to laugh again, tears streaming down his face. 'That's why I've removed all the competent guards from the station, Damien. I heard your plan and I loved it! Considering how well versed you are in this prison's rules you should know about a specific rule that applies right now – 'If a convict attempts to escape and conventional methods of stopping them fail, lethal force is authorised.' That's right, Damien! I can kill them all! If there are no inmates to babysit maybe I can finally live again, no longer a prisoner in my own prison.'

Novus burst out into uncontrollable laughter, Two large rods extended from his back before spiking sharply upwards, Large jets of green flame erupted from the back of these rods. His right arm burst into a maelstrom of snaking tendrils that began to spin rapidly before regrouping into a large tube of concentric circles and spinning electronics resembling some sort of gun, his left arm behaved similarly except it joined to form a long thin rod of dark metal which was immediately bathed in green arc lightning. Finally his eyes slightly glazed over, streams of text and code flying over his retinas at amazing speeds.

Now Nathaniel could notice the augmentation.

Damien spun towards Nathaniel and shouted at the top of his lungs. 'Nathaniel! Shoot the fucker!' Nathaniel who had completely forgotten about the gun in his hands attempted to line up a shot but it was no use. The rods on Novus' back flared, propelling him towards Nathaniel, deftly flying from side to side with blinding speed and grace. By the time Nathaniel had unloaded three stray shots Novus was before him. He flew in with an arcing kick which sent Nathaniel's weapon skidding to the far side of the room and Nathaniel to the ground. Novus raised his left arm triumphantly over Nathaniel, his face now an insane smile. Novus was going to savour his first kill.

Then Nathaniel was blinded by a flash of purple light.

He opened his eyes seconds later to discover that Novus was now lying on the ground a couple of metres to the left, but more importantly Damien was to his right, his arm now replaced by an onyx black minigun slowly pulsing with purple light. Before Nathaniel could comment Novus smashed his arms against the cold corrugated steel below – propelling him back up onto his feet in a fast, fluid motion. His face showing nothing but raw disgust and anger, before returning to its previous malicious smile.

'Well, well, well. What do we have here? Another cyborg?' Novus broke into a slight chuckle. 'You of all people too. I guess this throws a spanner in the works but I'd quite like a challenge.'

Novus' flames flared once more and he charged at Damien, his feet lightly skirting along the floor propelling sparks into the air. Damien barely managed to fully transform to counter this assault, his non-railgun arm quickly flashed before being replaced by a shiny metallic replica covered in holographic tessellating purple hexagons. A pair of angelic purple wings constructed from similar hexagons erupted from his back and a small metal mask slid up from under his chin, covering his mouth like a balaclava.

Novus' baton smashed into Damien's arm releasing a brilliant explosion of light and an earthshaking crash, blasting both of them back from each other. Novus charged again, weaving his weapon around Damien, looking for an opening as Damien threw his shielded arm to intercept each of the oncoming blows. Novus' rage grew as he failed to land a single hit on him before he finally couldn't take any more.

'You think this changes anything, Damien? You're trash compared to me, absolute filth! A couple of strung together transistors with a slab of flesh on top. No matter, I have ways of eradicating even the most persistent of opponents.'

Nathaniel watched with curiosity as the concentric circles of Novus' other arm began to spin and whirr more and more loudly and then in horror as Novus' weapon was enveloped by a terrifying green glow. Damien, only barely realising the true magnitude of what was about to occur, narrowly avoided the ensuing torrent of superheated green plasma. This eldritch stream of power chased him as Novus dragged his arm through the air, still firing. Novus' eyes bulging out of his head as he continued his frenzied laugh, tearing through starships as Damien swooped away from the attack.

'What's the matter, Damien? Not acting so tough now huh? I will always be superior, I am nothing less than a god! You piece of sh—'

Novus was cut short by a barrage of purple bullets from Damien, who'd just managed to rev up his own weapon. Novus charged Damien again, clearly in an effort to bring this fight back to a melee.

As Nathaniel watched the two cyborgs pirouette through the air, sparks and plasma flying in every direction, he wondered if picking up the gun would even help in a situation like this. Before he could properly analyse the scenario, however, a stray green stream flew past him blasting the gun into subatomic particles. Well at least now he didn't need an answer.

The dance of death continued, neither participant making much if any leeway until Novus decided to change tactics, slamming his foot into Damien's sternum instead of attempting another slash. Damien was caught off balance momentarily, his arms relaxing slightly. Novus was in.

He slashed once, off came Damien's left arm.

He slashed twice, off came Damien's right arm.

He slashed thrice, off came Damien's legs.

Damien fell to the floor, hitting the steel with a cold clang, the rest of the room in silence. Novus looking strangely sombre slowly floated down to the floor, deftly landing beside Damien, weapons poised above him.

'I'm somewhat sad it's over really. That was the most fun I've had in years! No matter, it's time for the ultimate catharsis!'

Novus grinned from ear to ear once more before raising his sword.

'And to the victor, the spoils!'

Then there was a sudden sickening crunch.

Starships move fast. Incredibly fast. Fast enough in fact to rend a cyborg into tiny pieces of shrapnel. Novus could now first hand-edly confirm this.

While Nathaniel was still recovering from the shockwave produced by such speed, the ship suddenly halted and Gavin burst out the door of the ship, looking somewhat scared.

'What happened? Did I hit something?!'

Nathaniel brushed himself off before replying 'Oh believe me you did.'

Gavin's fear became horror. 'Oh god, where's Damien? Is he still fighting Novus?'

'Don't worry, Damien's fine thanks to you.'

'Wait, what'd I do?'

'See for yourself.'

Gavin peered to his right and spotted Novus on the ground. And on the wall. And smeared across the ship.

'What the fuck?!'

'I know right? If you hit him any harder I'm pretty sure you'd have rediscovered the Higgs boson. Were you about to run away?'

'I was trying to pick you up before leaving.'

'But why? I held you at gunpoint.'

'Well my last boss was about to vaporise me so I decided that you guys weren't so bad after all.'

'Makes sense, I don't want to stick around here much longer so let's hit the road.'

'Arren't you frgettting somewan?'

Nathaniel and Gavin both looked to the floor, Damien was somehow still conscious.

'Cnnn you hellph pickk up my limms? I need asitnce'

'Can you repair yourself or something?'

'No but I haffff to geth bach to my mechhanikz. Illl sendh cuh urdinats to dahhh ship.'

Damien then proceeded to fall asleep. Having a duel with a killer cyborg and getting all your limbs brutally removed would probably make you pretty tired. After heading off to recover his limbs and checking Novus' remains for valuables the duo headed onto the ship.

'I just checked the cords, Nathaniel. Looks like the rebels have a small outpost in low orbit around Arcturus.'

'Sounds like a plan, I don't have many other options considering the fact I'm now probably a space outlaw,'

'Okay, off to Arcturus to meet the rebels, join them, and spend the rest of our lives fighting as criminals.'

'Can we do one thing first?'

'Sure, What is it?'

'Head to a café. I need a cappuccino.'

THE LIE

Elizabeth Ogundipe

It was the day of my basketball training and I wanted to go to town with my friends. I wanted to do both and was convinced I could. I went to my friend's house at half twelve until about two fifteen in the afternoon.

My friend Jack texted me 'Meet me at the bus stop,' and I replied, 'Okay sure, what time?'

'In half an hour!'

'No problem,' I replied.

I went to the bus stop but I couldn't see Jack or any of my other friends so I popped into McDonald's to use their Wi-Fi. I texted Jack 'Where are you?'

'On my way,' he replied.

'Been waiting ages!' I exclaimed.

I saw Jack and some of my other friends. The bus was in four minutes. I was a bit worried because I didn't tell my mother where I was going.

The bus arrived and we all climbed aboard and went upstairs. Some of us played on our phones and talked along the way and some were just messing.

'Here, look at this funny video on Instagram!' exclaimed Jake.

We all watched the video and it was the funniest thing ever – it was about when you ask someone a dumb question and slap them across the cheek.

'Oh my God, that was sooo funny!' said Chloe.

'Too right,' I replied.

Alan apparently was messing with my hair, I had no clue what he was doing so Jake came over to see what Alan was doing. I told them to stop, I pulled my hair as hard as I could but they wouldn't let go. I looked back and saw that my hair has been stuck on the pole of the seat. I was beginning to get mad because we were nearly reaching our destination. I had to ask Jack for his key so I could cut my hair. After all that we all laughed and talked very loud.

We walked around and some went shopping to buy a couple of things. Chloe said 'We have to meet friends at the Spire.'

We all marched to the spire and then we all went to McDonald's to see more friends. We ordered hamburgers and chips and drinks and we laughed and talked some more.

Afterwards a few of us went to Penney's and Chloe and I tried on a few clothes. We didn't even have any money, except for the fiver I had for an emergency, but Chloe and I tried them on anyway.

Afterwards, we both came of the fitting rooms to look at ourselves in the mirror when we noticed Jack and Jake putting stuff into Alan's bag.

'What are you guys doing?' Chloe asked as I rushed quickly to ask the same thing.

'Yeah what are you doing?'

'Don't worry about it,' Jack said quietly.

'We can clearly see you're shoplifting,' Chloe said.

'Hardly now, we paid for them but I didn't like this particular one so I asked if I could swap it,' Jake said.

I knew they were lying because it made no sense – why they would put stuff in Alan's bag? I knew they stole something when we walked out of Penney's. The alarm came on and the boys ran. Chloe and I looked at each other and we ran too.

'I KNEW IT, I JUST KNEW IT!' I shouted at them when we finally stopped running.

'I said don't worry about it,' Jack said.

'How on earth can I not, it's a crime!' I exclaimed.

This was just great, I had to go in like an hour and my friends were shoplifting.

'Jake return it or pay for it,' said Chloe.

'Exactly, just do that instead of being in trouble,' I agreed.

'They're right,' Alan was also agreeing.

'They're in your bag, Alan,' Jake said.

'You just put them there.'

It wasn't really fair that Alan was dragged into this because he wasn't really involved in it.

'Honestly, Jake, it was you that put the stuff in his bag, I mean why didn't you pay for it?' I asked.

Yeah, well it's all done now,' Jake said comfortably.

They were meant to be my friends. Like what kind of friends shoplift and say 'Yeah well it's done now' and think they will get away with it? It's not fair on me, Chloe or Alan.

What if my mom finds out, she'd probably think I was in on it as well. They stole socks. Socks! Of all things, like they're only 3 euro, it's not like they can't afford it. They could have just asked me and paid me back instead of stealing it, and suffer from getting caught.

'I think they're mad at us,' Jake said.

'Yeah, I kind of feel guilty about this whole situation,' Jack said.

'Yeah, but I needed them though,' Jack said desperately.

'They were only 3 euro and I have 40 quid on me, you should've asked me,' Jake said.

'I wanted to see what it's like to shoplift,' Jack added.

'You're an idiot.'

Jack laughed.

'You're an idiot too; you were in on it as well as me.'

'Whatever . . . ' sighed Jack.

They will get caught eventually, I thought. We were still in the corner but were too afraid to come out and I needed to get home ASAP.

The train was in like an hour, fifty-five minutes to be exact. Five minutes later we finally got out of the corner. My legs were killing me; it was so cramped because we huddled together as tightly as possible, frightened. Just as we got up, I saw them.

'Guys it's them! The security!' I screamed.

We ran into the Ilac shopping centre, into McDonald's and went into the bathroom. Chloe and I collapsed against the wall panting.

'Yeah, what are we like?'

'The boys are idiots, why should we pay for their mess?' Chloe said.

'I agree.'

We were really furious because everything was turning out so wrong.

'I honestly need to go home,' I cried to Chloe.

'When is the train?' she asked.

'Twenty minutes,' I answered.

Chloe told me to go home because she knew if I stayed longer, I'd be in even bigger trouble than I was already in now.

'Good luck, Chloe' I said, walking out the door. I looked around to see if there was anyone there. I didn't see anyone so I power walked to the train station, storming out of the shopping centre.

I wished I could call my mom to come pick me up but I couldn't because I told her I was doing a project after school that would take ages, as an excuse for staying out late. I was really worried because the day so far had been vile and it was going to get worse. I was at the train station when I saw some of my Spanish friends also waiting.

The train came, we all climbed aboard, talking.

'Did you have fun in town?' one of them said.

'Not really, I just want to go home,' I replied.

'Really?' she asked.

'Yeah, I don't feel well.'

'Oh, well you'll be better soon.'

'I hope so,' I said to her.

She turned back to her friends and started talking in Spanish so I tried to connect to the Wi-Fi to reach my mom. It didn't work before we arrived.

'Bye guys,' I said.

'Bye,' they all said.

I walked out of the station to get to the bus to go home finally, feeling stressed as I thought of something to say to my mom.

I waited for the bus for about ten to twelve minutes. I tried texting my mom on the bus but the Wi-Fi wasn't working there either, and now I was kind of freaking out.

It's a bit of a walk from the bus stop but I finally got home at only twenty to eight.

So many thoughts were going through my head like 'Why did they do it?' and 'What if my mom finds out?' I was so stressed now, and I still had to come up with a lie.

I walked up to the door and I knocked dozens of times until someone came up and opened it. It was my mom. Of all people, it had to be my mom.

'Hello,' I said.

'Why are you just coming home?' she asked.

'I know, my Spanish friend—'

Mom just walked to the bathroom.

'Yeah I'll tell you later,' I whispered.

I was really worried now, like my heart was pounding – Boom, Boom, Boom. At this stage I thought I'd learned my lesson.

My mom came out.

'So why are you just coming?' She asked again.

'Yeah, we wanted to watch something on the laptop because the project would take ages to do anyway...' I lied.

The next day I met my friends at school and I saw Jake and he asked me 'Did you get in trouble with your mam?'

'Why should you care? I had to lie just 'cause of you and Jack's mess.'

'Listen, it will be okay,' he said.

' How? I have to keep lying to my mom!' I said.

'It will die down, I know it will. If it doesn't, we'll confess,' he said.

'Well, why don't you just confess now? You'll get me in trouble,' I told him.

He said nothing so I just let him be. I knew I really shouldn't be worried about it at all, because I wasn't involved.

School was over and I reluctantly walked home. My mom wasn't there, I didn't know if I should be happy or worried. I grabbed something to eat, put my feet up and turned on the telly. There wasn't anything on so I thought I would catch up on *X Factor* on Demand TV on 3 Player. I liked contest shows like *X-Factor*.

My mom came home. 'Where's your phone?' She asked.

'Here.' I said.

'Give it to me. Until you tell me where you went last night, you won't be getting it back,' she ordered.

'But I told you where I went!' I argued back.

'I know what you told me but I want the truth,' she said sternly.

'Ugh,' I said under my breath.

'What was that?' she asked.

'NOTHING!' I shouted.

I stormed up to my bedroom. I went on the laptop to Skype my friend David. I called him and he answered.

'Hey,' I said quietly.

'Hey, what's up, you sound a bit upset.'

'I am,' I replied.

'Aw, why?' he asked.

'My mom's getting on my nerves again.'

'Because you went town, or . . ? he asked curiously.

'Yeah, and she took my phone.'

'I have to go have my dinner now so I can't Skype long . . .why is she always taking your phone?'

'Because of my "attitude"; she wanted my Facebook password too but I said I had forgotten it.'

'Text me then!' he said excitedly.

He seemed a bit happy, but I couldn't go on Facebook because I actually did forget my password.

'David?' I asked.

'Yeah?' he replied.

'I actually did forget it.'

I told him I changed my password so many times that I forgot it.

'Ah, really? I gotta go, I'll call you tomorrow or later on tonight.'

'Sure.' I said.

I didn't talk to my mom for the rest of the evening; I just lay in bed, stayed on the laptop and watched more series of *The Vampire Diaries*. It was more of a girl kind of show, I never really liked stuff like that but my friends were like 'Please watch it, please, please, please!' so I watched it and now I'm addicted to it. I was on the last season and I didn't want it to end.

I heard footsteps, it was probably my mom so I turned off the laptop, removed the plug from the socket, put the laptop at the end of my bed, put my head on my pillow, slowly lifted the duvet to cover myself and I pretended to be asleep.

My mom came in, I barely breathed. She switched off the light, closed the door and walked out. My heart beat rapidly, my hands were sweaty, as was my face, I wiped my face with my face cloth which was left in my gym bag. I needed water but I couldn't go down and I didn't really want to either so I just stayed in bed. I didn't dare go back on the laptop in case my mom came back up again so I just read a book. I started to read *Paper Towns* by John Green. I had just gotten it recently and it was really good so far. John Green was one of my favourite authors, he was just amazing!

I uneasily drifted to sleep, wondering if the next day would be a brighter day.

MY LAST ADVENTURE
Rebecca Ormonde

The tavern was bustling with customers. Drunken sailors sang old sea songs loudly in the corner; knights told battle tales, some true and some false. Townspeople shared a drink with friends or family; one or two lone travellers sat by themselves, looking thoughtfully at the wooden tables that they sat at.

It was a normal day for me. I served food and drink to anyone that requested some. I booked rooms for the travellers that wanted to take a break from travelling. It was just another average day. Until it wasn't. And I got dragged into something that I thought I had left behind years ago.

I placed a plate down in front of one of the customers in the tavern, laughing as he told me a joke about a sailor and a mermaid, before walking back up to the counter. I glanced around, looking for anyone who needed serving. I let out a breath when I saw that everyone was either eating, drinking or passed out. I took the time to wipe the sweat from my forehead with the back of my hand.

I jumped when the doors slammed open suddenly. The constant noise coming from the patrons of the tavern dimmed as a cloaked figure strolled in, their face concealed by a hood. The figure headed for a table in a more secluded part of the tavern and once it was seated the noise level quickly returned to the usual boisterous volume.

I shared a look with Cora, another barmaid, both of us wondering who would have to serve the mysterious stranger. I jerked my head towards the table, silently telling her to go to the table. She shook her head furiously, pointing a finger towards me and then over her shoulder towards the table. I glanced from her to the table and then back to her. She gave me a pleading look and I sighed throwing my head back to glare at the ceiling before putting on a smile and heading towards the person.

'Hi! What can I get for you?' I asked with fake enthusiasm.

'I'll have a tankard of ale and all the coins in that knight's pocket,' a male voice spoke. I blinked.

'Excuse me?' I asked awkwardly, not believing what I had just heard.

'I said, I'll have a tankard of ale and all the coins in that knight's pocket,' the voice repeated, slower this time while gesturing towards one of the knights sitting in the tavern.

'Is this some kind of joke?' I asked, raising an eyebrow. The stranger let out a mocking laugh.

'Oh go on, Farrah, it'll be just like old times.' I took a small step back.

'Who are you?! How do you know my—' The stranger turned his face towards me and I stared, shocked at what I saw.

'Mason?!' I exclaimed. That oh-so-familiar smirk appeared on his face.

'The one and only. Did ya miss me?' he questioned arrogantly.

'What are you doing here? How did you find me?' I demanded, ignoring his question. His smirk dropped slightly at my reaction to seeing him.

'It wasn't that hard really, you never liked straying too far from the large crowds and this is the closest town to the city,' he shrugged. I sighed and looked around before sitting down across from him.

'Why are you here, Mason?' This time it was his turn to sigh, it was then that I finally noticed how stressed he looked.

'I need your help,' he said after a minute of silence. I immediately stood up from the table shaking my head.

'No, n—' he cut me off.

'Farrah please,' he pleaded, 'Just hear me out. It's Kaya!' I froze. I sat back down cautiously with a sick feeling in my stomach.

'What about her?' I asked. He sighed again, dragging a hand through his hair, which hung loosely around his shoulders.

'She was caught, by knights, stealing from a noble man's house. She's to be executed in three days' time.'

I leaned back in shock, images from years before filling my head. My best friend of eighteen years, to be executed.

'I *have* to help her, but I can't do it on my own,' Mason said softly.

I don't know what convinced me to say yes. Maybe it was because I knew how he was feeling. To have a sibling taken from you is the worst feeling in the world.

I quickly ran upstairs to change clothes. A dress was definitely not the right choice for this particular situation. I packed a bag with some food and water because knowing Mason he probably forgot to pack any. I double-checked to make sure that I had everything before running back downstairs to Mason. Only, he wasn't there anymore. I headed outside thinking that he might be out there waiting for me.

When I got outside I still couldn't see him, but I did see Storm, his horse. I walked over to her and patted her back.

'Hey girl,' I cooed, 'I missed you,' I told her. I heard a twig snap from behind me and I quickly spun around but I was the only one outside. I turned back just in time to see a fist swinging towards my face.

I reacted quickly, blocking the hand before it could hit me and sending a punch of my own towards my attacker. The person grabbed my arm before my fist could meet its mark and swiftly flipped me over their shoulder. My eyes shut as I hit the ground. I felt all of the air leave my lungs. I opened my eyes just in time to see a foot descending on me and rolled out of the way just in time. I got back up and lunged at my attacker sending us both flying to the ground. We rolled around for a few moments, both of us trying to get the upper hand. After what seemed like years, I finally pinned the person down, my knees digging into their stomach and my hands pinning down theirs.

'Damn girl, you still know how to fight,' the person groaned from below me.

'Mason! What the hell!?' I exclaimed before I started hitting him.

'Ow, ow. Okay, okay! I'm sorry! I just wanted to see if you still knew how to fight,' he said. I rolled my eyes and stood up, holding out a hand to help him up. I turned around and hooked my satchel onto Storm.

'You ready?' Mason asked.

I sighed, 'As I'll ever be.'

The journey from Shanna, the town where I was staying, to Kadira, where Kaya was being held, takes only half a day which, according to Mason, left us with 32 hours to get Kaya out before she was executed. About halfway through our journey we stopped beside a stream so that Storm could have a drink and Mason and I could try and devise a plan for when we arrived at Kadira. We cleared a space on the ground of twigs and leaves before laying down a blue print that showed the structure of the castle, including all secret passage ways and underground tunnels, that Mason had *borrowed* from the castle's official records.

After ten minutes of no good ideas, I moved away from the plans in frustration. I grabbed the water that I brought from my satchel and took a drink before offering it to Mason. We stood there in silence for a minute, both of us lost in thought, before Mason spoke up.

'We understood why you left, you know.'

The statement shocked me and I stared at Mason, waiting for him to elaborate.

'We weren't mad at you for leaving when you did. We knew that you needed time. What happened with Ben . . . I couldn't imagine what you must have been feeling.'

Tears pooled in my eyes at the mention of my brother but I blinked them away before they could fall.

'I wanted to come back the minute that I left. I really did. But I-I just couldn't.' Mason smiled softly at me and for once didn't have a joking smirk on his face.

He pulled me into a hug. I could feel how tense he was. I knew this was affecting him more than he let on.

'We're gonna get her back,' I told him quietly. He didn't answer, just held me tighter.

We arrived in Kadira at noon and immediately found the local tavern so that we could go over the plan that we had made during our journey here.

By nightfall our plan was ready. Storm was waiting by the main gates of the Citadel and Mason and I were hiding from the knights patrolling the courtyard.

'Okay, do it know,' Mason told me.

I took the rock from my pocket and threw it away from the doors of the castle. As expected the knights followed the sound leaving the doors unguarded and Mason and I slipped through them, unnoticed.

I heard footsteps approaching us and quickly pulled Mason behind a pillar so we wouldn't be spotted. I peeked around the pillar, as the footsteps got closer.

'Make sure the stage is set up for tomorrow's execution,' I heard as two figures came around the corner; my eyes widened when I saw the King walking with who I assume was one of his head guards.

King Bacchus was a short, balding man with an ugly personality to match his ugly face.

'Yes, sire,' the guard said before he marching off.

King Bacchus kept walking towards us and I looked at Mason. His hands were clenched into fists and he looked ready to jump the King. I grabbed his arm in a tight hold and shook my head, silently telling him to not do anything stupid. He passed without spotting us and we quickly but quietly made our way through the hallways until we got to the dungeons.

Three guards were sitting around a small wooden table facing away from us at the entrance. Mason and I crouched down and I pulled out another rock from my pocket and threw it down the six steps that led to the cells. The guards all looked towards the noise.

'Oi, go see what that was,' the older looking one said to the younger looking one.

'Why do I have to do it?' he whined.

''Cause I said so, that's why,' he was answered in a condescending manner.

The guard got up and walked down the steps towards the rock. I nodded at Mason and we snuck up behind them and wrapped an arm around the necks of the two guards left at the table, effectively cutting off their air supply. They struggled against us and tried to alert the other guard but we covered their mouths with our hands.

Eventually their struggling stopped and we lowered them to the ground. We took their swords from the scabbards attached to their sides. We crept down the stairs behind the third guard and Mason hit him on the back the head with the hilt of his sword, knocking him out. I bent down and grabbed his keys before we started running down the long hall, looking into all the cells as we ran past them looking for Kaya.

'I found her!' I heard Mason yell. I quickly ran to the cell that he was standing in front of. I turned the key in the lock and Mason swung it open and ran in, scooping his sister up into a hug. I stood by the door watching for guards, so as not to interrupt their reunion.

'Farrah?' Kaya gasped. I turned and offered her a small smile. I wasn't sure how she was going to react once she saw me but I definitely didn't expect her to hug me. I immediately hugged her back, glad to finally be reunited with my best friend.

'I missed you so much,' she whispered.

'I missed you too.'

Our hug was interrupted by Mason when he grabbed both our arms and dragged us from the cell.

'Sorry to break up the reunion. It was touching, really, but I don't feel like being chased down the halls by a billion knights with pointy swords.'

Kaya and I looked at each other and simultaneously rolled our eyes. We started running down the corridor, heading deeper into the dungeons.

'Why are we going this way? The exit's the other way,' Kaya asked while we ran.

'There's a passage this way that leads under the castle and comes up outside the gates of the citadel,' Mason told her.

We reached the end of the hall and Mason and I quickly began searching for the passage. Kaya hung back, letting us search and was looking over her shoulder, watching for guards.

'Where is it?' I groaned on frustration, frantically feeling around for it.

'Um, guys? We have a problem,' Kaya called to us. Mason and I both turned our heads to see a group of knights running towards us.

'Crap, crap, crap,' I mumbled, searching quicker.

'Guys we need to get out of here,' Kaya said urgently, taking a step towards us. Well, she tried to but she ended up tripping over something. She looked down at the ground and bent down grabbing something before pulling it. It lifted up and revealed a set of stairs.

'I found it!' she cried, scampering down the steps quickly with Mason and I following. The tunnels were dimly lit, with only a few torches scattered along the walls. We ran as fast as we could, very aware of the knights that were hot on our trail.

'We're not going to make it!' Kaya shouted, fear beginning to creep into her voice.

'Yes we are,' Mason said, determined. Ahead of us I saw a speck of light, coming from a crack in the ceiling of the tunnel and as we got closer I could see ladder leading up to the light.

'There it is!' I pointed towards the light.

Mason sped up and reached the ladder first, he quickly scaled up it and pushed against the wooden door. Light flooded the tunnel once he got it open and he pulled himself out. He knelt down by the opening and held out his hand, first helping Kaya out and then me. We glanced around, looking for Storm. Mason saw her first and started running towards her with Kaya following him and me following Kaya. I felt relief fill me as we drew closer to Storm, I heard Kaya let out a laugh, I saw Mason smile. I then felt something sharp pierce my side. I gasped and looked down staring at the arrow in shock, one hand coming to cover the wound. When I pulled it away it was covered in blood. I fell to my knees.

'No, Farrah!' I heard Kaya scream. The two siblings knelt down beside me. Distantly I heard the warning bells begin to sound. I brought my hand up to cover my mouth as I coughed. I pulled it away to see blood splattered on it.

'You need to go,' I told them. Kaya's eyes widened.

'What!? No! Not without you!' Kaya insisted. I turned towards Mason, knowing that I wouldn't be able to change Kaya's mind.

'You need to take her and go. They're gonna be closing the gates, you won't make it. I'll only slow you down. We didn't do all this just to let her die, Mason,'

I could see the indecision in his eyes as he glanced from me to the knights who were getting closer.

'Go, now!' I said. Mason stood up and grabbed his sister who struggled against him. He put her on Storm and got on after her. He spared me one more glance before clicking his tongue, getting Storm to move.

I shakily got up onto my feet after pulling the arrow out and faced the knights, pressing a hand to my wound trying to stop the blood flow. I picked up my sword and held it out in front of me, ready to fight. I swung at the knights that got close to me, using every last bit of strength I had left. But it wasn't enough. The last thing I saw was the hilt of a sword coming towards me before darkness over took me.

And now here I am, lying on the ground of a cell, slowly bleeding out and writing down everything that happened on crappy pieces of paper that I got off a guard. I know I am going to die and surprisingly, I'm okay with it. I'm okay with it because I know that my friends are okay, that they're safe. It's a relief to know that they don't hate me. And I'm glad I got to see them again even under the circumstances. I'm glad I got to have one last day with them. One last adventure. My last adventure.

WHAT ELSE ARE YOU GONNA DO ON A SATURDAY?

Scott Redmond

As I awoke, the sun crept through the curtains blinding my eyes. There was only one thing going through my head – today is match day! Quickly, I jumped up from my bed and got my clothes ready for later on; I'd been waiting for this day all year for the great Bohemians to play the scum, Shamrock Rovers, and it was going to be one to remember. I jumped in a quick shower and then got dressed. When I got downstairs my ma was already up and she started waffling the ears off me about school.

'How ye getting on with your exams now Keith? '

'Yeah grand ma' I replied.

'Are ye hungry?' she said.

'Ye, I'm starving. What ye making?'

'Whatever you want.'

'Put on a bit of scrambled egg for me there.'

When I sat down to enjoy my food my ma started asking even more about school and to be honest, I have no interest in school at all, so before she got the chance to say anything else I got up and left the house and made my way towards Ross's house. But before I could even get off my road Ross came around the corner with some news.

'You wanna see what's happening in my gaff, it's like world war three down there. I had to get out of there.'

'Ha ha ha, your gaff is mad. What's happening?'

'Me sister and her fella causing murder because he came home at half three last night and me sister only let him in about five minutes ago.'

'Your sister's off her head, ha ha ha.'

We continued walking down the old Cabra road until we met up with all the lads. They were all dressed for the occasion which is a very important thing – you must be dressed properly to get in with us.

As we approached our second home, Dalymount Park, we could hear the roar from the crowds and it is one of the best feelings ever just to be a part of the team, and it's an even better feeling knowing that we have Rovers after the match.

When we got in the grounds we made our way to the seats, but out of the corner of my eye I spotted a few of the Rovers fans, so Ross and I ran over towards them and the lads followed. We were shouting and chanting at them 'Fuck off, Rovers scum!', and of course they reacted, so we chanted back 'Are we having youse after the match!' We knew there was gonna be trouble after the match and we all couldn't wait.

The whistle blew for half time and there was no score. Ross and I went to get a few drinks while the lads stayed at the seats; it didn't even matter that we were only sixteen – they'd give you a gun in Dublin if you look old enough. We drank our drinks as fast as we could and made our way back to the seats.

The second half had just started and it was time for Bohs to hammer these Rovers rats.

As the game went on it was it was neck and neck until the eighty-fifth minute, when the scumbag Rovers banged in a goal. The fans were all laughing and chanting in our faces and we were fuming, and then the final whistle blew.

We couldn't wait to get out and bait these rats so we made our way out quick. Before that we made a little stop at the toilets to have a line or two of the white stuff, to get us pumped for what was about to happen.

We all walked out together dying for a scrap and in that moment I glanced at my best mate, Ross and winked at him. At that we ran at the Rovers fans and they ran at us. There was chaos; glass bottles getting smashed, digs flying everywhere, and flairs getting lit – it was just the best feeling ever. It doesn't compare to anything just knowing that you have your friends' backs, and they have yours as well.

In the middle of all this madness I looked over at Ross and he looked like he was having the time of his life, until I noticed someone coming from behind him. I ran over but I wasn't quick enough. I watched a Rovers fan smash a bottle over Ross's head and he fell to the ground.

When that happened all the Rovers fans ran away, back to the kip they came from. I ran over to Ross to see if was okay but he was knocked clean out. I tried to lift him up but I noticed blood on my arm that was coming from his side. Not only did the bastard smash a bottle over his head but he had also stabbed him. I rang the ambulance straight away.

The ambulance came and took him around to the Mater hospital, which is only down the road. I was the one stuck telling his what had happened. I rang his ma and had to break to news.

'Hello?' she said when she answered.

'Paula, it's Keith,' I replied.

'Ah Keith, is Ross with you?'

'No, Paula. He's after getting rushed to hospital; he's in a bad way.' I replied.

She didn't speak, she just hung up the phone and went straight to hospital to see him.

Before I followed her, I made it clear to the rest of the lads that the fella who did this would not get away with it. They knew what I meant.

When I got there, the nurse told me that Ross had a punctured lung but was in a stable condition. Ross's ma and sister were in the eating area, so I didn't have to go into them, 'cause they would have took my head off for letting this happen. So I just went straight up to see Ross.

When I got in the first thing he said to me was,

'Keith ye dope, how did you let this happen to me?'

'Ah now, you give over, it's not my fault you're only a bitch, ha ha ha!' I replied. 'Don't start, you! This is your fault, you're supposed to have my back,' he stated.

'Well, because you're an eejit, now you have a hole in your back.'

It was good that we could joke about it but I wasn't able to stay any longer because he had to get tested. When I got outside, all the lads were there waiting for me and they were curious about how we were gonna handle the situation.

We came to an agreement that Rovers weren't getting away with this, so I contacted one of the Rovers fans that I know personally and arranged a straightener for later on that day. I gathered up as many people as I could and informed them what was happening and they were all on board, so I had to go back up and tell Ross.

I told him that I had arranged for a straightener that was only a few hours away, and I also told him that I found out who stabbed him and that I was going to get him back.

'Now don't do anything,' he said to me.

'I'm getting him back for what he did to you – isn't that what you wanted as well,' I replied.

'I did want it but I don't anymore. I don't want all this trouble over a football match,' he said.

'Well you don't have a say, I'm getting him back for what did to you.'

And with that I left, returning to the lads.

The only thing going through my head was standing all over these scumbags and getting that little prick back for what he did to Ross, and his time was coming soon enough.

As we approached the long road the fight was arranged for in the distance, we saw the Rovers group so we picked up the pace, and then instead of walking we were jogging, then jogging turned to sprinting, then we were both sprinting at each other, until we met and then all hell broke loose. There were bodies flying everywhere. It was great; it was just like what happened earlier that day at Dalymount but now my best mate, Ross wasn't there to enjoy it with me.

And then I see the little prick who put him in the hospital and make my way towards him. Slowly I take the knife that I got off the lads out of my pocket and get even closer. I was just about to make the biggest mistake of my life.

Before I could do it, I heard footsteps running off and Garda sirens in the background. The Garda had just come.

I dropped the knife and ran as fast as I could so they couldn't catch me. I slowed down when I realised they were gone and they weren't following me.

I decided to make my way home. The only thing that was going through my head was that if the Garda didn't come I would have stabbed him, and he could have died, and I would have got caught and brought to court or even put in prison. So the Garda sort of saved me. Then I got a phone call from an unknown number. It was Ross calling from the hospital.

'Did you do anything stupid?' he said to me.

'No, Garda were all over the place, didn't get the chance' I replied.

'You're welcome,' he stated back to me then hung up the phone.

I went blank for a second, then it came to me that Ross had called the Garda and saved me from making a big mistake and doing something very stupid.

I'm glad, he did but I'll still be at the next straightener.

What else are you gonna do on a Saturday?

POLAROID.

Dean Ryan

The sound of my alarm echoed through my house.

'Shit! I'm late again' I muttered as I attempted to lift my head off the pillow. I always hated the fact that it's like sleeping on a bed of nails when I'm trying to sleep at night, but on school mornings when I wake up it magically becomes the most comfortable place on earth. I never was a morning person . . .

I hopped out of bed landing heavily on my feet and it made a loud bang. I was supposed to be quiet in case my mam was still home. She was usually in work before I even woke up for school but I can never tell because her shifts are all over the place.

'Bonney! You're late for school – again!' said my mam.

I just shut my eyes and sighed then replied in a sarcastic tone, saying 'yeah I can see that Mam.'

I quickly got dressed but I couldn't find my school tie. I searched all over my room but it wasn't even with my uniform that I had neatly folded. After a few minutes of searching I just said 'forget it.' I sat back on my bed to tie my shoes and my phone was vibrating like mad beside me, I could feel it off my leg. I was getting lots of texts from my friends asking where I was. I never liked leaving my phone next to any part of me when it was vibrating because my mam is a very paranoid person and has told me all about how I could get radiation cancer from that, it doesn't help that I'm always on my phone. I picked up my phone to see what people were saying.

Emily: 'wer are u hun :D'

Stephanie: 'Bonney please come in today . . . I need to talk'

Kate: 'hey Bon where u at?❤'

Damien: 'everything alri x?'

I had no time to answer anyone because my mam shouted again telling me to hurry up. I grabbed my phone and ran downstairs, leaping off the final step and landing on the side of my right ankle. It was very painful. When I walked into the kitchen my mam shoved my lunch into my arms as she was backed me up to the front door. Before I even got a chance to say anything she said 'I'm not giving you another note today, you're always late'.

I didn't even reply because although my mam is a lovely woman, she can be terribly stubborn at times and she wonders where I get it from. Idiot.

As soon as I got out of the front door I noticed how cold it was. I could even see my breath. It was about half way through the first class of the day and I didn't really want to just walk in and cause a scene, so I did what I usually do and stalled until the second class. I liked my way to school, it was long but I never saw anyone on my way and I liked that. It was also quiet and peaceful. After a while of walking it was ten minutes until the second class started and the school was in my sight. I kept walking but a bit slower this time because I had about five minutes to kill.

I stood in the same spot pretending to be tidying up my uniform when in reality I was just killing time.

It was about three minutes until the second class and I was right outside the school gates. I took my bag off of my back and took out my English copy and tore out a page. I started to write on it until I noticed there was writing on the back already so I ripped out another page.

'Bonney wasn't feeling very well this morning. Please excuse her for being late to school. Jessica Steel.'

As I was putting my copy back into my bag I seen my chewing gum at the bottom of my bag so I grabbed it and put some in my mouth. I took a quick photo and sent it to my best friend Stephanie, who I never got the chance to reply to earlier. I don't want her thinking that I ignored her on purpose.

'Seya in science hun!'

I had written myself a note. The school didn't even know my mam's real handwriting because I've been writing the notes myself ever since I came to this school. I tucked the note into my breast pocket and took my school journal out of my bag and held it under my arm as I walked through the front doors of the school in an attempt to look like a smart good student. I walked into the school office looking confident. The principal was on his way out as I was going in. He was about to say something until I gave him a confident looking smile and held the door open. He had a shocked smile on his face but it worked, he didn't speak to me.

'Hey Bonney . . . late again? What's your excuse this time? Oh let me guess, slept in? Car broke down?' said the office receptionist in a joking tone. I just reached into my pocket and took out the note and handed it to her.

'Oh nope, you weren't well, ahh okay, that's a new one.'

I just laughed and said thank you. She knew me because I was always late. As I was on my way to class the bell started ringing. I always hated that sound, it really does your head in after a while. All of the students poured out of the classrooms. There was one group coming out of class last, all of them were talking about my best friend Stephanie. I couldn't hear exactly what it was but it sounded mean.

I couldn't imagine Stephanie doing anything wrong to someone. She's usually so quiet and she always keeps to herself. While I was standing there thinking, Emily came up behind me and ruggedly shook on my bag in an attempt to scare me. I did get a fright but I played it off as if I didn't. Before I got a chance to say hey—

'Bonney! Did you hear about Steph?'

'No I just heard some girls talki—' Emily just began to speak over me, She did that a lot. 'She got smashed at that rich kid Kyle's party last night and she kissed like everyone there, including Erick the guy with the long hair in 6th year. I don't know his second name.

'What?? That doesn't seem like Stephanie? She's usually—' Emily cut me off again

'Yeah well someone took a video of it and posted it to Facebook. She didn't even know there was a video and came into school. Everyone's talking about it.'

'Have you heard from Stephanie?' I said in a worried tone.

'No, I haven't seen her all day. . . '

Before I got to reply the second bell rang. Emily wasn't in my science class but Stephanie was so I began walking to it. I was in shock at what I just heard. I couldn't believe that something so bad had happened to Stephanie she didn't deserve it.

Stephanie never does stuff like this. This wasn't like her; this wasn't like her at all. When I walked into class I could hear everyone talking about the incident. I noticed Stephanie down the back with her head cradled in her arms in the desk. It was like nobody there even knew she was in the room, they were just talking about her so loudly. It looked like she was crying. I walked over and put my hand on her back and rubbed it.

'Is everything okay Stephanie?'

'Go away,' she replied. It became clear that she was crying.

'It's me Stephanie?' She looked up with stinging red eyes, she looked for so long. I would say it's because they were so bloodshot and full of tears that her sight was blurry. There was mascara all over her eyes. She looked very pale in the face and very run down. I had never seen her like this. I asked what's wrong, even though I already knew; there was an awkward silence so I had to say it a second time. She just shrugged her shoulders. I had never seen her so low. I sighed and sat down beside her.

'Look, all of this will go away, you just need to keep your head high.'

'Everyone knows, Bonney. Everyone. People keep saying mean things to me.'

'Stephanie, I'm here for you. No matter what I always will be.'

She just put her head back down on the table desperately. I put my arm around her and gave her a hug. When I looked back up all I could see were people looking back at me and Stephanie. Before I could say something Ms Cannon walked in.

'Okay class. Today I have a lot of work to do so just sit there and do some other work. Can I trust you to do that quietly?' she said politely. She was a nice teacher but I don't think she was all there, mentally. Her voice made her seem stupid. Even if she was making sense she sounded stupid.

For the rest of that class I just made sure Stephanie knew I was there for her and that everything would be okay, I was interrupted by Ms Cannon many times. After that class Stephanie was in none of the other classes we had together so I got worried and texted her.

I went home before the last class started. I texted her mam asking if she knew where Stephanie was. She didn't reply right away. And usually when I text her mam for other things she replies pretty fast, but not this time. I went onto Facebook and my whole newsfeed was full of the video of Stephanie. I had promised her that I wouldn't watch it but I was so tempted. After a few hours I gave in and turned it on. I couldn't see anything. I could only hear people screaming and calling her a slut. I immediately turned it off, I felt so guilty. I didn't watch the whole video but I did watch the start even though she asked me not to. I felt terrible. I texted Emily all about how I felt about what happened to Stephanie. She was offline for six hours which was unusual for Emily – usually her phone never leaves her hand. About twenty minutes later she saw the message but didn't reply for another five minutes. She called me. The first thing that I noticed was that she was crying.

'Bonney haven't you heard?'

'Heard what, Emily?'

'Stephanie left school and jumped in front of a car. She's dead.' She started sobbing very loudly.

I was in shock. Emily didn't really talk to Stephanie but she had been out with her once or twice with me. She had nothing against her; she knew she was a nice person. All the thoughts were passing through my head. I hung up the phone and then dropped it. My screen cracked. I fell to the floor and began crying, I felt so many things draining from me. I could have helped her. I could have saved her. I should have stayed with her. All these thoughts passing through my mind at once caused me to faint. I awoke with a ringing sound in my ears and the first thing I saw was my phone. That's when I remembered what happened. I started crying again. Everything was just so bad. I picked up my phone and I remembered it was cracked. The crack was in the shape of a butterfly. There I was lying in the floor in my bedroom sobbing. I went onto my phone and I accidentally clicked onto that photo I sent to Stephanie this morning. It was weird the photo was somewhat different this time. It was like a blurry jigsaw puzzle – when I tried to solve it I realised I could put it together. I was frightened, I didn't know what was happening and bit by bit I started to put it back together in my head. It started to come together like the picture of the note I wrote myself once was. Soon I could make out bits of it and I was able to read the sentence. It was weird. Like I was using my mind to do it and nothing else, it took so much focus. Nearing the end I started to feel colder and my sight went a bit blurry. My ears were ringing. At this stage I was terrified. I felt as if a huge weight was being lifted off of my shoulders. I had no idea what was going on.

The feeling of the cold got stronger and my surroundings began to change. Colours were moving around and feelings were changing. I could taste the chewing gum from earlier as well. My clothes changed, I was then back in my uniform just like before, I looked down at it and felt it. It felt real all of the smells seemed real. Every feeling felt real but at the same time it felt like a dream. When I looked back up I was outside school just like before. The weather was even the same. Before I got to think about what was going on I felt something in both of my hands. I looked down and I had the note in one hand and my phone in the other. It's almost like I had travelled back in time. I thought to myself 'this must be a dream! I must still be on the floor unconscious.'

Before I thought too much about it I ran into the school with my journal under my arm just like before. I walked into the office in school this time before I got to it the principal was already leaving. 'I must have taken a bit longer this time.' It all felt so real, this was so weird. The situation in the office was the exact same as it was before. I stepped out and all of the students poured out of the classrooms as the annoying bell rang just like before. Students were still bitching about Stephanie. I got a sudden rush – maybe this happened for a reason. So I could save her. This was all so much to take in. 'Oh yeah this is the part where Emily tried to scare me', I thought and turned around fast and said 'what are you doing, Emily?' I think she got a fright more than I did the first time.

'How did you see me?'

'Magic,' I replied. '

'Ugh whatever, did you hear about Stephanie?'

'Yes. I did,' I could feel the tears building in my eyes; 'I have to go to class Emily.'

Before she could answer I just walked away because I could feel the tears building up. I went to class. Part of me was still waiting to wake up. I walked into science class and there was Stephanie again. I walked down to her.

'Stephanie, is everything alright?' She didn't reply she just continued to cry.

'Step—' she cut me off.

'I messed up, Bonney. Badly.'

'I heard. I'm so sorry that this is happening to you, you deserve none of this.'

'I'm so stupid, Bonney,' she replied as she lifted her head. Her eyes were just like they were before.

This time I noticed a piece of paper in her hand. 'What's that, Stephanie? In your hand . . . '

'It's a note someone threw at me. I couldn't see, my eyes are all blurry.' I took the note from her hand and unfolded it.

'Kill yourself slut' was written on it. I sighed. I said 'Stephanie, do you want to do anything after school today? Maybe you need someone to talk to?'

It took her a while to answer but when she did she said 'sure we could go to my house after school to watch a movie or something?' I could tell by the way she answered that she didn't really want to. I still took the opportunity I couldn't let anything bad happen again. She stayed in school all day this time.

Later on when we got to her house we went to her room to watch the movie. We spent a while taking photos and laughing. I was actually having a great time, which I didn't imagine happening because I was so worried. She got off the bed and reached into her drawer. I was unsure about what she was going to take out. She didn't even say anything. She pulled out a weird grey and blue thing. I had never seen anything like it before. She returned to the bed and held it in the air and it flashed.

'What was that? All I can see is a big grey blob.' I said as I laughed.

'You don't know what this is? Stephanie replied as she also laughed.

Before I could reply out of the grey and blue item came a black slip of paper. Stephanie smiled as she took it out and shook it and blew on it. I was never more confused in my life. When she stopped shaking it she revealed a picture. I was amazed. Even though I hated how I looked in the photo I just smiled just as Stephanie did. It was nice to see her smile.

She told me I could keep the weird camera thing. She stood up and pinned the photo to her wall right on her notice board. Both of us just laughed. We were interrupted by her mam. 'Steph,' she said as she walked in.

'Yeah?' She replied.

'Do either of you want anything?' She said kindly.

Stephanie and I both looked at each other and we could both tell it was a yes. 'Yes please!' We both replied at the same time.

'Ohh it looks like yous read each other's minds.' She walked out of the room.

'We never did watch that movie.' She said.

'Oh yeah,' I replied. I guess time was just flying by. Although my whole reason for being there was to help her, I was really enjoying being with her. I was having a great time, which I didn't think would happen because of my worry. Stephanie hadn't got many movies so we just ended up watching a movie called *Marley and Me*. I had always loved that movie since I was young.

Half way through I said, 'You know what, Stephanie. I have never watched this movie without crying,' we both just laughed.

'You know you can call me Steph right?' I had actually thought about that before. I really liked her full name so I told her that. She just laughed and continued to watch the movie.

By the time the end of the movie came she was crying. I wasn't and I was wondering why because I always used to cry when I watched it. I came to the conclusion that it was because of the whole experience of Stephanie dying – made me tougher I guess. When it came time for me to go home I was scared because I didn't want anything bad to happen. Even though we had a great time and hopefully she didn't feel as alone. When I was leaving the house through the front door her mam asked me if I wanted a lift.

'No thanks, you're fine.' I was trying to be polite.

'It's no bother,' she said as she grabbed her keys and walked towards the door. 'Steph! Are you coming?' She asked.

Stephanie walked to the top of the stairs and said 'No Mom. . . Sorry, Bonney I have homework'.

I had a bad feeling about her being alone. 'I'll just walk if Stephanie isn't coming – I'm too nervous,' I said with a giggle when really I wasn't nervous at all.

'Steph don't make your friend walk alone, come with us.'

Stephanie sighed as she shut her eyes and took the first step down the stairs. She then came the rest of the way when she finished sighing.

'There's a good girl,' her mam said. I really liked her mam, she just seemed very nice and polite all the time. On the way home I had to give so many awkward directions as her mam didn't know where I lived. Finally when we got there Stephanie said 'Bye, Bonney I'll see you tomorrow in school!' Her mam said 'See ya, sweetie' I thanked her and said my goodbyes.

When I got in I noticed how cold it was so I turned on the heating and got changed into my pyjamas. After that I texted Stephanie and put my phone down on the table avoiding the coffee stain in the shape of a ring. It was only after that when I noticed it wasn't cracked anymore. I went into the kitchen to get a drink.

'Bonney? Is that you?' She probably didn't hear me come in she must have been asleep. 'Yeah it's me mam, don't worry.'

She didn't reply to that. She must have just fallen back to sleep. I went back in and checked my phone. Stephanie still hasn't replied. I was worried that she would do something bad. Although she did it before it didn't seem like that was a possible outcome anymore after all the fun we had. It's such a bad thing. It's too bad an outcome I just don't feel like it could actually happen.

I came back in to get my phone then I went upstairs to go to bed. I woke up the next day early for once and got ready. Stephanie still didn't reply to my message; I was very worried. I left the house to get to school before my mam even woke up. Halfway there I got a call from Stephanie's phone. When I seen her name pop up I was so happy. I answered.

'Do you know where Steph is? She snuck out last night I was hoping you knew . . . ' She sounded as if she was just crying.

'No I don't I'm so sorry, I'll do my best to try find her.'

I hung up and started crying a lot, just like before. This was it; she was gone again. Then I remembered how I got back to save her the first time. I stopped crying because I had a bit of hope that I was able to save her, even though I wasn't even sure what was happening was real, I had to try regardless. I threw my bag into a bush where it wouldn't be found as it would only slow me down. I ran as fast as I could in the direction of Stephanie's house. Her house wasn't close, it was a thirty minute walk.

After about ten minutes of running I arrived at her driveway, nearly collapsing with exhaustion. I walked up the driveway and knocked on the door. There was no answer. I put my ear up against the door to try hear any noise in the house, there wasn't a peep. I quickly backed up and looked for any open windows, there were none so I ran around the back. There weren't any open windows out the back either but there was a window near the ground that leads to the basement so I ran and kicked it. It shattered into pieces. There were still sharp bits of glass around the old wooden frame so I did a quick sweep with my shoe to try get rid of any remaining glass there. There was still some left but I hadn't got time to spare so I quickly put my legs through and pulled myself through when I was hanging from the frame I git cut by the glass on my arm. It was bleeding a lot but at the time I didn't really notice because I had worse things to worry about.

I ran up the basement stairs into the hallway where I paused, the entire house was silent. 'Hello? Is anybody home?' I screamed. I paused a second time and heard nothing, standing in the one spot wasn't going to help I needed to keep moving. I ran into the sitting room only to discover Stephanie's mam lying on the floor. I began to feel faint. I almost collapsed. I finally managed to pull myself together. I crouched down next to her and whispered to her.

'Can you hear me?'

There was no response. I was no expert but I felt for a pulse – I remember learning something about it in science. I wasn't sure if I was feeling the wrong spots, but I felt nothing. There wasn't even a heartbeat. I came to the conclusion that she might have had a heart attack. I started crying again and stood up. It was horrible to see her this way. I figured that she must have found out something about Stephanie and had a heart attack. Standing over her body wasn't helping anyone; there was only one way to fix this. I quickly darted up the stairs and barged into Stephanie's room. I walked over to the picture we took when I was in her house last time. I picked it up and began to stare at it. I was shaking, my hands were unable to hold the photo still. I focused really hard on the photo and managed to put the puzzle together. The closer I got to solving it my head began to hurt, more and more. Before I knew it, Stephanie and I were back on her bed and she was holding the weird camera in the air and the flash went off.

'Is everything alright, Bonney?'

'Yeah the flash just gave me a fright that's all.' She smiled.

'Hey do you want to have a sleepover tonight?' I asked

'It's a school night?' She replied.

'Come on, it'll be fun.'

She asked her mam and she said we could once we went to my house early enough to get my uniform. I texted my mam letting her know I would be staying and she was fine with it.

When we went asleep I was worried that she would leave but I fell asleep quite fast. I woke up in a cold sweat worrying about her. She was still fast asleep beside me. It was early so I woke her up and she got ready and we left to go to my house because I still had to get my uniform for school.

When we arrived at my house I told her I would just run upstairs for a quick minute to get ready. My mam was gone to work already. I ran into my room, opened the wardrobe and pulled out my uniform. I went to turn away when I noticed my tie at the bottom of my wardrobe, it must have fallen down. I got ready very fast and ran downstairs. Stephanie was just looking at old photos of me when I walked into her.

'You ready to go?' I said.

'Yeah,' she replied.

When we left my house I started to walk the way I usually walk but Stephanie pointed out that we were last and have to go the short way. I hate the short way, it's so loud and there's so many people and cars.

I didn't like it but she seemed just fine with it. After a while of walking she went really quiet and started to slow down. She looked away from me and then she turned back and started crying.

'What's wrong?' I asked.

'I have to go into school with everyone talking about me again, it's horrible . . . '

She started muttering 'I'm sorry' over and over. I hugged her and I whispered into her ear saying 'Everything would be alright, even if it seems like it won't be right now, it will all get better.'

When she stopped the hug she took a step back towards the road. As soon as I realised what was happening I screamed 'NO!' She walked right out into the middle of the road. I ran right out after her but there was a car coming fast and it swerved out of her way towards me and I had to leap out of the way. The car crashed into another car and they both missed Stephanie, but she ran to the other side of the road into oncoming traffic. I screamed as a truck came closer and closer, it didn't see her. When it got to about three metres away I quickly turned because I couldn't bear to watch her die again. I heard everything happen, first Stephanie got hit and then I heard lots of cars crashing and beeping.

When I looked back around it was complete destruction. Everyone in their cars was injured and dead. I saw one red car with a family all dead apart from the baby. I was just crying, it was all my fault. Then it came to me that no matter what fate had set, Stephanie's death had to happen. I had to let her go. I took my phone out of my pocket and went onto the first ever picture I sent to Stephanie. The one of the note I wrote myself. I focused on it and it took me back. I was so sad that I was letting her die but letting her live just caused so much death.

I was standing there outside school once again. I took a deep breath and a step towards the school. I couldn't bring myself to see Stephanie before she died again. A tear rolled down my face as I whispered 'I'm sorry'.

I turned around and walked home.

A CHANGE OF HEART

Niamh Thornberry

It is not just any other Friday afternoon.

Lincoln is relaxing in his old rocking chair, reliving memories from the past. It is the fifth anniversary of his wife's death, and he thought now of how his wife would join him in the sitting room every Friday morning to read her books; her favourite was *Pride and Prejudice.*

He remembers the way she frowned at him through the lenses of her glasses when he would interrupt her as she read.

A tear rolled down his face as he looked at the small photograph of his wife on their wedding day. She was beautiful; like a daisy in a garden of weeds, she stood out.

He regretted the times he neglected her, he would do anything just to see her one more time. Lincoln was forever turning his sadness into anger and frustration.

His thoughts were interrupted when he heard a loud knock on the door and a voice shouting.

"Sir, sir! I saw the sign outside. Are the puppies still for sale? Please, sir!"

Lincoln grabs his cane and hobbles toward the door. A little boy stares up at him. He is no older than nine and wearing a baseball cap so big it covered his eyes, and a T-shirt reading 'New York Yankees'.

'What is your name, boy?' Lincoln asked.

'Roy, Roy Fischer. I live two blocks away.'

'Go home, boy, there are no puppies for sale here,' Lincoln insisted, raising his voice as he tried to talk over the loud barking coming from his back yard.

Roy hears the barking and proceeds to just walk straight in the house.

'Nice place you got here,' Roy exclaims. 'This big house all to yourself. Where be the misses?'

Lincoln ignores Roy's question and leads him to the backyard.

'These are the puppies – take your pick.'

Roy examines, the cage counting each pup. 'One, two, three, four . . . I'd like him, sir,' Roy says while pointing at the fifth pup. The pup was in the corner of the cage alone away from the other pups.

'You want the runt?' Lincoln sneered. 'He isn't a real puppy, just look at his leg – he can barely run; he is nothing but a nuisance. Go ahead, boy, pick another one.'

Roy glanced down at his feet then quickly back to Lincoln. 'You see, sir, I'm not so perfect myself.' Roy pauses, lifts up his trousers and reveals a brace running from his ankle to the top of his knee. 'I was in an accident about two years ago where it left my leg injured. When I saw that puppy it reminded me how I first felt after the accident, I felt excluded from the other boys at school. I'm sure they laughed at me behind my back and called me useless.'

Lincoln was speechless; he didn't know how to comfort the boy. Roy wiped his eyes and started talking again.

'If you let me have this puppy I can make him feel loved and accepted like I never did,' Roy laughed, 'we could limp everywhere together.'

Lincoln felt ashamed for being so mean to this little boy. Since his wife's death five years ago he hadn't been the same, he became narky and rude towards his neighbours. He now knew something had to change.

If his wife was here she would have invited Roy in, sat him down and made him feel welcome. Why was he acting like this? What has gotten into him?

Lincoln reached into the cage lifted the puppy up and placed them into Roy tiny hands.

'Take care of him, Roy. I believe in you.'

A few weeks later Roy got a letter in the post – it was from Lincoln. It read 'I hope everything is going well with you and your new family member. Please enjoy the game.'

Roy looked puzzled but quickly realised what Lincoln meant by enjoy the game. Along with the letter were two tickets to a Yankees game.

MISTRUST

Christopher Yeates

I was nearing the summit of the Doldenhorn in the valley of Kandersteg, when the storm started to clear up showing the bright blue sky, rolling hills and old fashioned houses of the village of Kandersteg covered in snow.

As the clouds parted above me, I heard a thumping noise and looked up, there was a Bell Boeing V-22 Osprey military grade helicopter hovering in front of me. The pilot looked at me without emotion and then pressed down on a button that shot a missile in my direction. It headed about three yards away to my right. I went running for cover as the missile soared through the air. I heard the missile strike a group of rocks and waited for the inevitable explosion. But it never came. I stepped out from the rocks I used as cover with suspicion and started towards the missile. As I was moving towards the projectile, the helicopter moved away to the right and flew off. When I reached the missile it opened with a hiss and I saw that there were instructions inside for me to get to Zurich airport as soon as I could.

I decided to continue on my original route as I was still on leave. Once I reached the summit of the doldenhorn I made my way back down. It only took me five hours to get down to the base of the mountain. Once I reached the carpark where my car was parked I put all the climbing gear I used in to the boot of my Avions Voisin.

It was one of the first built in 1919 in France by Gabriel Voisin. She's a very rare and beautiful car.

I travelled down the motorway to Zurich after getting a bite to eat on the way out of Kandersteg. When I reached the airport it was late afternoon and I was met by a pair of security guards who led me into a restricted part of the airport. That was where I was greeted by my boss Colonel Gunn, who was the head of the Unexplained Objects Agency (U.O.A.).

When I sat down in front the desk where the colonel's seat is, my partner in crime Kurt Zavala came in and sat beside me.

'Ah, how are you doing, buddy?' I asked 'It's been what, five months since the last time we saw each other?'

'Seven months actually,' replied Kurt. 'During the retrieval of Joan of Arc's helmet in the backside of France.'

'Of course, I still have trouble sleeping due to that.'

'Well then, let's not talk about that anymore,' Kurt said solemnly.

'Yeah, best not to,' I laughed. 'So what have you been up to in the past half year?'

'Travelling the world, trying to catch all the different types of fish that are out there.'

'How's that going for you?' I asked with a smile.

'Not that well,' Kurt replied bluntly, 'they keep on escaping and I also got robbed of all my fishing gear in Brazil.'

'You should be more careful then,' I said trying to keep a straight face.

'It's not funny,' Kurt said trying hard not to shout.

At that moment of time Colonel Gunn came into the room. 'That's enough chitchat boys, we are here to discuss an important matter. We have found a clue to the location of one of the Monks' bases; it is believed to be near Mount Everest.'

It is said that the Monks were an ancient organisation that once collected fabled artefacts believed to have magical powers, such as Excalibur, the Holy Lance, and the Lost Ark.

We were told to go to home and pack our bags for business and get a good night's rest. I decided to travel to one of my houses in Adelboden. When I got there I heated up some food from the freezer and went to bed. I got up at 5am and got some breakfast and had a shower. When I finished packing enough clothes to last me a couple of months, I headed to my study where there was a hidden wall in one of the bookshelves. After flipping a hidden lever I headed into the armoury and started to pack up a couple of guns that I thought would be useful for the mission: a 9 millimetre Beretta NATO model 925B pistol, a 5.56 millimetre, fifty-one-round Sawa automatic rifles and a pair of Colt Combat Commander automatic pistols. After packing a Kevlar body armour piece, I met up with Kurt and we headed to Zurich airport, this time to catch a private jet to Kathmandu, Nepal.

After eleven and half hours in the air we landed in Nepal. We got a company car and drove to a safe house in the city. We packed up some hiking equipment and food supplies and started to ascend Lhotse, a mountain to the south east of Mount Everest. After climbing in the rough terrain of the Himalayan Mountains for six hours we decide to take a break. While Kurt set up a campfire I decided to scout out the surrounding mountainside. Through the powerful set of binoculars I saw someone going up Mount Everest in a wheelchair. We decided to push that bit of information to the back of our minds as it was not relevant to the current mission and we continued on our way. We climbed for another three hours up the side of the mountain through a full force rain storm, with the range of visibility vastly reduced to only five metres ahead of us, and decided to set up camp after the rain died down.

When I got up in the morning I went over to the side of the mountain that had a highly dense forest nineteen metres below where I was standing. I was going to get some more fire wood for the campfire we had set up the previous evening. After a quarter of an hour of wood collecting I had a pile big enough to last us until we broke up camp. When I was trudging through deep mud my boot got stuck in the middle of a giant mud pile. I tried to pull my boot out of the mud but it was as stuck fast. I tried a couple more times and on the last time I pulled it came out, but I went flying backwards and tumbled down the mountain for about ten metres before I was stopped by a blue pine tree. I was covered in tonnes of small cuts and bruises. After such a beating I was out of breath. I tried to call for Kurt but my throat was hoarse and could not shout properly. I kept shouting but eventually I passed out from being exhausted.

When I woke up I started to survey the surrounding area. While I was making sure the area was clear of dangers I noticed an outcrop of rocks that looked strangely unnatural. I then looked at my body to see what the damage was but as if it was a miracle the worst damage that happened to me was a sprained wrist; it did not hurt because of the adrenaline pumping through me. After climbing up the side of the mountain I saw Kurt ten metres in front of me packing up all the equipment and he turned and asked where I had been.

'I went to collect wood and fell, but that's not important right now,' I said excitedly, 'I think I found something that might be worth checking out,' I then told Kurt about the outcrop and he suggested that we go check it out.

We worked our way across to the outcrop and after searching around the area we found out that it was an entrance of some type. When we went in, there was a pedestal with a bowl in the centre of the room. When we went to investigate the pedestal we found out that it was a crude oil lamp full of an oily substance. After getting out my flint and steel I ignited the oily stuff in the pedestal and the whole room lit up with rows of flames lighting everything up. It seemed we were in a temple of some sort.

We were so stunned; it took us a couple of minutes for us to come back to our senses. As we got our senses back in order we started to make our way down a long hallway making sure that we did not activate any of the traps. We searched all the rooms in under an hour, as it seemed the occupants took most items with them. As we stepped into the last room we saw the room only had one press. We were so excited we forgot to check for any traps and when we searched through the press we found a map in the last drawer. We found the journal in the drawer but once I took it out it activated a trap which sent a shock through the walls up to the roof and the ceiling started to collapse and setting of all the other traps we skirted around.

We started to run for the entrance with the whole place falling down behind us. As we were almost towards the exit we heard a rumbling noise behind us. We looked behind us and started to run as fast as our packs allowed us to, as there was a boulder rolling down the hallway towards us, Indiana Jones style. The boulder was almost on top of us as we went through the exit onto grass. The boulder broke through the entrance and started rolling downhill. (Good luck to the next person to get in its path.)

We took an hour's rest to gather our thoughts and to get our breath. We decided to head down the mountain towards civilisation. When we got to the airport in Kathmandu we were rushed through security since we had our weapons on us. We were escorted to a hanger that had a pair of ME 109s in it. As soon as we got our bags packed and seated in the ME 109s we got a call from the Colonel that said we had to get to Dublin as soon as we could. When we were flying over Ukraine a pair of hawker hurricanes swoop down and directed us to land. We said that we would not comply and the pilots started to shoot at us as a result, but we made invasive manoeuvres to get behind them. While they were trained exceptionally well it showed that they were only the new recruits and they did not know how to get away so we shot them out of the skies. As we started towards Dublin again they both went down in flames.

When we touched down we were whisked away from the planes and escorted into town. We walked down a couple of streets and went into what had once been the old Guinness brewery, now the current headquarters of the United Fascist Empire of Ireland. Inside there was an office with a desk that looked as if it had been constructed out of the remains of skeletons; behind the desk was the Fuhrempereor of the U.F.E.O.I., Donal D. Trump. Under the desk was the slugstika, the symbol of the U.F.E.O.I. We were told that we did a great job and that the map showed the next location of a series of clues. We also got a big raise. We were told the next location was somewhere in the middle of the Sahara Desert.

We got the private jet from Dublin airport to Cairo airport. We were allowed to pass through the security without hassle. We were driven to the Cairo embassy and got a four-by-four with extra fuel tanks and extra fuel and supplies.

We left Cairo the next morning at 6am. We travelled for twelve hours before we took a break. After looking at the map we found that we were less than one quarter of the way there. We rested for two hours and decided that we would travel by night to conserve our energy. We continued this way for four days and nights, before we reached the location.

As we reached the location we saw that the whole place was lit up. There was a whole army of tanks and armoured cars with sub-machine guns mounted on the roofs. We decided that it would be safer to walk the rest of the way.

We ran hunchbacked to some sand dunes so we would not get caught. We looked back to make sure we were not followed. When we were satisfied that there was no one there we turned back to look at the area where the lights were. But out of the corner of my eye I saw something move and drew my Beretta and shot where the movement was in one swift movement. As I watched I saw blood pooling out of what I thought was a small sand dune. Suddenly there was movement all around us and before I could fire again I was shot with a needle in my arm. I immediately felt as if I was falling asleep.

As I was coming back to my senses, I felt a soft breeze, which meant I was in a tent of some kind. I realised that I was strapped tightly to a chair. I heard footsteps coming in my direction and suddenly I felt the side of my face sting. Then a voice started to say 'you are now a prisoner'.

'You don't frighten me,' I said. That earned me a punch to the stomach.

'You only talk to answer a question and if you give an answer I don't like, or speak out of turn you will get beaten,' the ominous voice stated 'Do you understand me?'

I did not answer so I was given another punch, this time to the face; I tasted blood and spat it out.

'When I ask a question you will answer it, now do you understand me? ' the voice shouted. .

'Yes,' I said hatefully.

I was interrogated for another four hours or so. By the end of it I was in a sorry state. When the interrogator left I heard it say, 'Don't let him out of your sight, and do not underestimate him or you will have me to deal with'. As soon as the interrogator left I started to format a plan in my head, I also took inventory of the weapons I had left on me. I only had a hunting knife but I can use it with deadly efficiency.

I waited a few minutes to see if there was a pattern of footsteps. When I was sure there was a pattern I then made my move. The first thing I did was cut the ropes holding me to the chair, and then I took out my knife and threw it across the room into the arm of the assailant in front of me and then ran over to him and grabbed him and used him as a human shield against his accomplice. As I moved the other guy was trying to get a shot on me without shooting his friend. As I neared the other guy I yanked the knife out and threw the man into the other one so they would fall over. I then disposed of them quietly.

I snuck to the entrance of the tent and looked outside; I saw what looked like hundreds of tents surrounding one big tent. I went back into the tent I and decided to get one of the guard's uniforms and put it on so I would be inconspicuous. After making sure the guards were tied up I walked towards the middle tent as if I belonged there.

I managed to reach the big tent without being spotted. I hurried inside expecting it to be a command tent. But what I saw was a giant computer lab. I went up to a computer terminal that was in the centre of the room. I saw that they were trying to solve the next clue. I decided to see what type of equipment they had and I found a memory key with 100 petabytes of memory storage (the files took up nearly all of the space on it). I transferred all of the information to the key which I then put safely in my pocket.

After that I went searching through all of the other tents looking for Kurt, but after two hours I still could not find him so I had to presume he was dead. When searching I found the armoury and weapons depot where I got my gear back. I found a couple bundles of C4 on a shelf and put them in strategic places around the camp. After that I went over to where all the vehicles were kept. I slashed the wheels on all except for a jeep, which looked like someone had prepared for a journey. I also took all of the keys just in case they had spare tyres.

I then started towards the exit of the camp and no one noticed me. When I had travelled a safe distance away from the camp I detonated the C4 and the whole place exploded. I then started the journey back to Timbuktu.

After a long tiring trip I finally reached the airport. There was a private airplane waiting on the runway to take me back to Cairo. When I reached Cairo I headed to a safe house by the Nile and on the way I dropped off the memory key to a scientist who would then bring it to the lab to be decoded. I stayed in the safe house for a couple of weeks trying to keep a low profile.

I was told to get to the Cairo docks after two weeks. When I reached the docks I saw a Molch which is a 35-foot long submarine weighing 11 tons and was made by A.G. Weser in Bremen, Germany for the Nazis. I was told by the scientist that the next clue should be somewhere up the Nile, which would be the reason for the Molch to be there. The excavation of the shipwreck containing the clue was uneventful. The clue turned out to be coordinates. The coordinates lead us into the middle of the Pacific Ocean.

I boarded a battle ship that was docked in Cairo and we headed towards the coordinates. The journey took us seventeen days going at full speed of 50 knots (92.6 km/h). By the time we reached the coordinates it was nearing midnight so we decided to sleep it out and dive on the next morning.

The next day I was called up to the crow's nest because the look-out had spotted an enemy fleet coming towards our location. It took them the rest of the day to reach us. At the front of the lead ship there was a figure that looked vaguely similar. When I got binoculars and looked through them I saw that it was someone who I thought was dead for the past month. At that moment I was summoned into the communication room. I was told that I had someone asking for me from one of the ships. When I picked up the receiver I was about to ask who they were when a familiar voice spoke and said, 'So we meet again; but this time we are against each other'.

'Kurt, why are you doing this?' I asked, 'what made you change sides?'

'Why? Because they made me an even better offer than the empire to spy for them, I will let you live if you give over the command of this little project of yours.'

'I would never betray the Empire,' I shouted into the communication device, 'when did you betray us?'

'Well it was just after we went our separate ways, after we were hired by the U.F.E.O.I. now stop trying to delay the inevitable and answer the bloody question already, are you going to give up control or die'

'I choose the third option, of course,' I said.

'What third option is that?' Kurt inquired.

'The one where I kick your ass!' I answered.

'I thought you would come up with something like that, but you have no idea what you just started,' Kurt announced.

After that there was a huge sea battle. We managed a death toll of one compared with their seven deaths. When the other side realised they were fighting a lost battle they all accepted defeat, except for Kurt who shouted that they were all cowards and they will all be killed when they reach the shore.

Then all of a sudden Kurt ran towards the bridge of the ship with what looked like a missile launcher. I realised that he had just shot a missile towards the bridge of my ship. I ran out of the room and narrowly missed the explosion, but I was thrown off my feet over the deck and hit my head against a wall. Through blurred vision I saw Kurt aiming another missile at me when I heard the sea bubbling below the ships and all of a sudden there was a sea serpent that was 100 feet long rising above the ship and went over the other boat before disappearing on the other side. When I looked on the other deck there was no sign of Kurt except for the missile launcher and the bottom of his legs.

I then fainted because of the exhaustion from the past couple of days and due to the loss of blood from numerous wounds.

I woke up in a sterile area with my whole body covered in bandages. Surrounding me were doctors and the Fuhrempereor. The Fuhrempereor ordered all of the doctors to leave. They did so without question. After they left I was told that my mission was a success and we managed to retrieve the Holy Lance. I was also promoted to First consul for life (second in command of the U.F.E.O.I.). I thought that the last of the double agents in the empire were dead. But when we reached shore, the Fuhrempereor suddenly collapsed, I ran over to him and he started to say something but before he could finish he was put under a drug-induced coma. I swore right there and then to find out what happened to him and who was responsible.

AUTHOR BIOS

Sam Callan was born in 1999 in Dublin. He likes to play sport and hang out with his friends. He dislikes school, cleaning and writing about himself.

Adam Corr was born in 1999. He lives in Kilbarrack. Adam likes sleeping, skeletons and sleeping skeletons. Adam's writing style combines both horror and comedy genres. His best friend Coffee Black has gone on to say "Adam Corr is the latest hot writer since Stephen King. I have seen the future of horror, his name is Adam Corr." Adam's favourite colour is purple.

Cian Doyle is sixteen years old and lives in Clarehall. He enjoys going out with friends, watching TV shows such as *Adventure Time* and *Skins* and going on Tumblr. He enjoys music by Beyoncé and Pentatonix. Cian hopes to study science and become a doctor or a lawyer.

Sinéad Farley is sixteen years old. She lives in Coolock with her mam and dad, her two younger brothers, her dog Pixie, her two cats Whiskers and Tiger, her two guinea pigs, Bevo and Oreo and her fish Darragh– AKA the Farley Fam' Farm! Sinéad loves makeup and jumpsuits but leotards are her fave. She had a pigeon named Pidgy who sat on her window sill for a few nights but it flew away and hasn't come back. #FindPidgy

David Farrelly, a male who was born in the year of 2000, lives in Baldoyle, located on the outskirts of Dublin. David has many interests, one of which is Sea Angling, which he does frequently. He has represented his country in international competitions. David also likes swimming, doing stupid things, mountain biking and writing stories about struggles and adventures. He has been described as "The best thing since the yo-yo craze of 2004" by mentor and literary critic, Coffee Black.

Killian Farrelly is a sixteen-year-old from Baldoyle. He is a member of Baldoyle Tae-Kwon-Do Club and is going for his black belt this summer. He is also very interested in competitive fishing and is going to England to represent Ireland this July.

Bronagh Furlong is sixteen years old. Bronagh lives in Donaghmede and likes reading and watching TV shows.

Aaron Gorman is sixteen years old and lives in Bayside with his family. He plays GAA for Naomh Barróg.

Jamie Hannon is sixteen years old. He likes to listen to music, go to the gym and go out with friends. He has lived in Dublin all his life. He hopes to become a personal trainer when he is older.

Paul Herron was born on September 5th, 1999. He greatly enjoys art and music and hopes to one day create and illustrate his own series of comics and perhaps even master a musical instrument. He's got his head in the clouds most of the time and has no idea what the word 'deadline' means, but he has great interest in his work and likes to see projects become reality.

Caoilainn Hogan Boyle is sixteen years old and lives with her mam, dad and her younger brother Matthew. She's always moving house, you never know where she's going to be next. She enjoys playing piano and swimming and is training to be a life guard. Caoilainn is obsessed with animals and wanted to be a vet but she doesn't have the stomach for it. She works in Insomnia coffee shop as a barista and drinks the coffee herself. #Icantgetnosleep

Jasmin Humphrey is sixteen years old and from Dublin. She lives in Baldoyle. She enjoys listening to rock, pop and R&B. She loves skateboarding and photography. Jasmin plans to be a professional skateboarder and photographer.

Jay Kehoe Hanlon is sixteen years old and lives in Kilbarrack. When not listening to Tool or obsessing over *Prison Break*, she is out having a laugh with her mates and taking and editing photographs. She plans to study psychology and hopes to become a successful author.

Stephen Kellett Murray is sixteen years old. He lives in Duleek, Co.Meath. He plays basketball for Swords and has a very creative imagination. Stephen also has two younger sisters who aspire to be like him.

Emma Keogh is sixteen years old and from Kilbarrack. She lives with her mam, and brother. She loves freestyle dancing and competes internationally. She likes walking her dog Bonnie and going out with mates. Emma loves going to Tomangoes, #WhereTheGangGoes, so she can boogie the night away.

Jake Lantry was born in 2000. He lives in Howth and he would like to be a pharmacist. His favourite colour is blue. He likes to eat chocolate and his favourite television show is Game of Thrones.

Shane Lyons was born in Dublin in 2000. He lives in Malahide with his two brothers and one sister. He likes watching TV and going out to town. He dislikes waking up early. Shane is a man of many talents, making amazing stories and being the absolute definition of swag.

Luke Murray is sixteen years of age. He is from Kilbarrack and he enjoys going out with his friends. Luke hates nothing more than waking up early for school but he does love pasta. He wants to move to Australia when he is older.

Dara Ó Cléirigh lives in Clontarf with his two brothers, his mother and father. He believes enjoyment is a social construct and therefore he doesn't feel any. Consequently he has no hobbies and works for nothing but monetary gain. Thinks cats are okay.

Elizabeth Ogundipe was born in Ireland in 2000. She is fifteen years old. She enjoys playing basketball, baking and singing. Her favourite subject is English, she absolutely hates maths. Elizabeth's favourite artist is August Alsina. In the future she would like to study teaching.

Rebecca Ormonde is sixteen years old. She lives in Kilbarrack with her mam, dad and two brothers. She likes singing and playing guitar. Her favourite band is Paramore. Rebecca also likes photography and reading.

Scott Redmond is fifteen and from Coolock. He enjoys playing Gaelic football every weekend for Parnells. He hates school, maths, Monday mornings and cheese. Scott likes going out with his friends.

Dean Ryan was born in 2000 and lives in Baldoyle. He likes sleeping, photography and going out to his mates. He dislikes having to get up early for school.

Niamh Thornberry is sixteen years old and lives in Clarehall. Niamh enjoys reading.

Christopher Yeates was born in Dublin in 2000. He has two sisters, one older, one younger. He likes to read action adventure books and is in the Scouts. He has a dog called Coco. Christopher has recently finished doing the Gaisce at Bronze level.

THANK YOUS

Fighting Words

Katie Bartrand, Sara Bennett, John Butler, Lucienne Brennan, Leo Connell, Evan Costigan, Mark Davidson, Deirdre Davys, Aimée Doyle, Roddy Doyle, Kevin Dwan, Alice Englemore, Emer Flanagan, Jean Hanney, Sharon Hogan, Caroline Heffernan, Jaleesa Hoogstraten, Gerben Letzer, Seán Love, Emmy Lugoye, Ray Lynn, Daragh O'Toole, Clara Phelan, Maritza Pineda, Alina Przybyl, Tess Reichart, Dymphna Reid, Andrew Roberts, Alan Roche, Lindsey Rumberger, Helen Seymour, Sam Tranum and Aoife Walsh.

Pobalscoil Neasáin

Thank you to all the staff and volunteers at Fighting Words for your valuable time and expertise. We would also like to thank Ms Justine Durrant who accompanied us every single Thursday to Fighting Words. Thanks to Mr Pat McKenna, our Principal; Ms Bríd Ní Annracháin, our Deputy Principal; Mr John Coleman, our TY Coordinator; Mr Ger Farragher, our Year Head and all the teachers at PSN for their continued support, especially Ms Geraldine Martin and Ms Claire O'Shea who helped organise our group to take part in this project. Finally thank you to our families.